THE SPACE IN BETWEEN

BRITTAINY C. CHERRY

This is a work of fiction. Names, characters, places, brands, media, and incidents are either the product of the author's imagination or are used fictitiously. The author acknowledges the trademarked status and trademark owners of various products referenced in this work of fiction, which have been used without permission. The publication/use of these trademarks is not authorized, associated with, or sponsored by the trademark owners.

Copyright ©2013 by Brittainy C. Cherry
Edited By: Mickey Reed
Cover Design By: Kevin R. Kimmons
Book interior design by JT Formatting

All rights reserved. All rights reserved. Without limiting the rights under copyright reserved above, no part of this publication may be reproduced, stored in or introduced into a retrieval system, or transmitted, in any form, or by any means (electronic, mechanical, photocopying, recording, or otherwise) without the prior written permission of the above copyright owner of this book.

www.facebook.com/**BrittainyCherryAuthor**

Printed in the United States of America

First Edition: August 2013

Library of Congress Cataloging-in-Publication Data

Cherry, Brittainy C..
    The Space in Between / Brittainy C. Cherry. – 1st ed

    ISBN-13: 978-0615866581
    ISBN-10: 0615866581

    1. The Space in Between—Fiction. 2. Fiction—Romance
    3. Fiction—Contemporary Romance

To Mom.
For seeing me when I felt invisible.

CHAPTER ONE

Andrea

THREE DAYS, FIVE hours, and twenty-two minutes.

Mom kept crying. Her puffy eyes hadn't stopped swelling for a few hours now and she could hardly breathe. I told her it was all right, but she kept hugging me, rubbing my hands in hers. She said that she would never understand why these kinds of things would happen to people, but God was always in control. I felt like that was just something people said. When they couldn't figure out the words, it was always, "In God's hands."

Daddy sat in the corner of the room with his thick-framed glasses brushing against his pepper gray-haired sideburns. He was a calm man by nature. Grams said when he was born there was only a whisper to show he was alive. But when she held him in her arms for the first time, he smiled to her. And he hadn't stopped smiling since. Until today. Today, he sat there in the corner. Looking my way. Not pressuring me to get better. Not pushing me to express anything.

I turned away from Mom as I lay in the hospital bed

and looked outside to the sky. I couldn't grasp what was happening. It was a complex world. How could the sun shine so brightly and look so welcoming in the wake of such an event? The birds sang and danced past the window and the kids laughed down on Jefferson Street as they went to the county's fair. The dogs barked and Ms. Jacobson gossiped. Outside the world of Albany, Wisconsin, was completely normal. Happy. But inside this cold, darkened room, I sat in a hospital bed. My left leg in a sling and my body bruised on the outside, but the internal damage of my soul was the worst.

Mom tried her best to silence her muffled tears by covering her mouth, as if she didn't want me to hear her—to avoid my suffering. But I didn't mind. It was better to hear her than the laughter. She worried for my safety. My calm demeanor scared her the most. But it appeared she was breaking down enough for all of us.

My eyes moved towards the closed seafoam-colored curtain, which blocked the entrance to my hospital room. I looked down and saw two pairs of shoes—an old brown scuffed up pair and high heels (you know, the fancy kind with the red bottoms, that scream, 'We're expensive!'). I knew it was Eric and Michelle, and I watched Dad pull back the curtain to let them in.

They both were silent. Michelle stood tall in a beautifully tight white floral dress featuring a red sweater over it. And there, her boyfriend, my brother, Eric was, wearing his UW-Madison sweatshirt, a pair of slacks, and his scuffed up brown shoes.

I followed after my brother to UW-Madison, where I met some of my best friends. Unlike Eric, I hadn't become a teacher, but I followed with a cool degree in dance. I'm a fantastic dancer.

As my eyes landed on my leg, my heart skipped a beat. I *was* a fantastic dancer.

Say something. I wished they would talk. The staring at me with sad eyes was growing to be too much. So I opened my mouth to speak and was graced with a mouthful of air and emptied words. I tried again, and sounds came out. But the actual words were what slapped me and made my eyes follow after my mom. A never-ending flow of tears poured from me as I smiled to my calm, loving father. "Did someone cancel the rehearsal dinner?"

In three days, five hours, and twenty-two minutes, I would have been walking down the aisle in my white dress inside the beautiful St. Peter's Church. I would have been beaming with a type of joy that can't be expressed in words, but only in a feeling. It would have been a warm feeling of knowing that, once I reached the end of the aisle, Derrick would be there.

I would have been marrying my middle school sweetheart and starting a new chapter. We would move out to New York— him to pursue his singing career and I would be pursuing dance. I would go for my Master's degree if I were lucky, or I would waitress tables (something I have done at Mr. Fred's Diner off Brady Street since I was sixteen). Derrick would probably be discovered before me because he was talented beyond his years, and I would gladly become his trophy wife and the backup dancer in his music videos. Classy!

But I made a mistake.

"It wasn't your fault," Mom said over and over again.

But I knew better.

At the end of the school year, I was always overjoyed when Derrick picked me up. I was saying goodbye to my best friend, Ladasha, who was pretty much the best dancer I'd ever seen. Madison had been the third college she had tried out in the past three years. I don't know why but the first day I met her we clicked. The Caucasian small town girl in me was so amused by the African-American city girl in her. She would make me laugh at the stupidest things in the world, but some days she'd glance at herself in a mirror and burst out crying. I never knew why. I never asked...I just hugged her.

It was tough saying goodbye because she was on her way to New York City. "To make my dreams come true," she smirked. Stating how there was something in her heart calling out to her. So before she could finish her degree, she had to follow the voice. I had no clue what the heck she was talking about, but I hugged her tight and promised to stay in touch.

It was always a treat when I'd see him pulling up to my building in his green pick-up truck. Derrick wouldn't complain once as he helped me load my past year's dorm items into the truck. When it was all loaded up each year, I would make the drive back home. As a 'thank you' for him helping me. It was around four-thirty in the afternoon when we got to the freeway and blasted the newest CD he had recorded.

I hadn't even seen the car's tire explode in front of me before it was too late to hit my brakes. I didn't even remember crying out in pain as my body slammed against the steering wheel. I didn't know the truck had flipped and was slammed from behind with three other cars piling up. I didn't have time to fully grasp what had happened.

But I had tasted it—the salty sweet mix of my blood dripping into my mouth as I sat in the car. It'd taken a moment for me to realize I was upside down. I tasted the coppery sensation that infested my tongue with its disgusting flavors. My eyes were filled with tears mixing with the deep red liquids as I screamed out in angst. My left leg was abusively tucked in between the door and driver's seat.

None of that mattered the moment my eyes shifted to Derrick's seat. His hazelnut eyes shot open and pierced my soul by saying the last word he would ever say to me— or anyone for that matter.

"Andie…"

In three days, I would be pushed down the aisle in a wheelchair, in my black dress, inside the beautiful St. Peter's Church. I would be suffocating from a misery that can't be expressed in words, but only in a feeling. It would be a cold feeling of knowing that, once I reached the end of the aisle, Derrick would be there.

In three days I would be saying goodbye to the only love I have ever known. Three days, five hours, and twenty-two minutes.

But who's counting?

SITTING IN A metal chair that my dad pushed me around in was annoying. My family and I waited outside the church as all of the townspeople gathered around to say they were sorry. I heard some of the gossiping old ladies whisper there might have been alcohol involved. I didn't even have the strength to roll my eyes. Michelle's best friend, Rachel McLean, approached me. Her eyes were heavy with tears as she shook her head back and forth. We were never really close, but she looked as if she were as broken as I was.

"Andrea..." she whispered. I waited for her to get her thought out, but she kept crying, saying she was so sorry, over and over again. My brother came over and walked Rachel away. I was thankful for that. I couldn't watch anyone else fall apart.

Everyone disappeared, traveling in a single-file car line in the direction of the graveyard. I couldn't stop tugging on my black lace dress. My leg itched so much in that damn cast, but I didn't complain. Mom didn't complain either when she dressed me. It was a new chore for her, but she never let it appear that way. I was thankful for that, too.

I stared at the church. My wedding church. Mom looked at me with the gentlest eyes and bent down so she was closer, seeing how I was so low. "Andrea, we should get going. It's been a long day. And if you don't want to stop by the graveyard, we should still stop by Derrick's parent's house..."

I could feel Daddy's hand on my shoulder. I wasn't sure how long it had been there, but I wasn't in a hurry to have it removed. Eric was there too with Michelle, who looked awful. She never really felt comfortable in uneasy situations. Who could blame her? The smile always plastered upon her was erased that day. As I looked around, I realized everyone's smiles were gone.

Eric didn't know what to say to me. What could he say? There were no words that could make any of this better. Stupid tears kept falling. There were so many times I didn't even know I was crying. Eric bent down and wiped my eyes.

"It's all right, Andie."

"Don't call me that," I whispered as I smiled brightly towards them all, "Listen. Really. You can all stop looking at me as if I'm broken. I'm not. People die." I couldn't stop giggling.

"Grammy Tammy died and you guys didn't throw a fit. So why should we be freaked out now that my twenty-two year old fiancé is being buried into a deep hole in the ground as we speak? You know what's shitty?" I watched as my mother's eyes widened. I never cursed in front of my parents, and I could tell it was a surprise to her ears. Especially in front of the church. "Sorry, Mom...you know what's crappy? Derrick didn't even like cemeteries. He hated them. He wanted to donate his organs and be cremated."

The way everyone remained silent as they watched the first of my many breakdowns was pretty amusing. I continued. "And I mean, how did you all not know that? He wrote a song about it. *'Windy Sunday'*. I'm sure you didn't listen to it though. But he talked about how cemeteries were a waste of perfectly good space and how he wanted to float away into the winds. Why didn't anyone say, 'Hey, Andrea, do you know how Derrick wanted to be handled after you killed him?' Why didn't anyone ask me, Daddy?"

I looked at my dad, whose eyes were filling with emotion. "Why didn't anyone ask? Because I wasn't his wife? Because I had no say in how to bury my dead fiancé's body?"

I couldn't speak anymore. I sobbed into my brother's arms. I was surrounded by love, but I'd never felt so alone.

I SAT IN my old bedroom and listened to Mom and Daddy send away the guests who'd showed up to look at me with their pity eyes. I hadn't cried since the funeral, and that was a few weeks ago. Mom thought I should see a therapist or something. She said I wasn't dealing with my feelings in the right way. Who knew there was a wrong way to feel?

The engagement ring on my left hand remained in place, glimmering from the light shining through the window. I shut the curtains. The ring didn't deserve to shimmer in such a perfect way anymore; the meaning behind it was now void. While I was in my college dorm, I practiced my wedding vows in the mirror, wanting to perfect them. What a waste of time. I moved the ring up and down my finger as I stared at the white, zipped-up bag hanging on the top of my closet door. My wedding dress was inside it. I couldn't confront it yet. I was almost certain I could never deal with that.

Daddy stood in the doorway, his soft eyes smiling

towards me. "What you thinking about?"

I shrugged my shoulders. The answer was so obvious that I was surprised he asked. "Derrick."

He walked to my window, pulling open the curtains. *Dangit, Dad.* As we looked out the window, we saw more people walking up to our house with those stupid gloomy faces they had grown accustomed to delivering my way. The problem with living in a small town was that it was a small town. One stoplight in the middle of 'downtown' by the bakery. A themed Christmas party every year. Fred's Diner. A small town, filled with small-minded people. And the accident was the biggest story since Peter Ericks stole the school's history books because he said they were filled with the devil's teachings. That was in 1993.

Daddy opened the window and the breeze came, lightly kissing my cheeks. A wave of guilt washed over me. I felt a heavy weight on my soul for making it hard for my family to be happy. I could tell they knew I was still a mess, but they wanted to give me time to get better on my own.

My eyes shifted to the ground, unable to connect with Dad's. "Don't you miss your crafts, Dad?" He was a jack-of-all-trades. From building lawnmowers to homemade water pumps, Daddy did it all. He loved to get his hands into something new each week. But since the accident he had been catering to me nonstop. He would say, "Don't worry about such things," but I did anyway.

"My friend Ladasha moved out to New York City." I paused, fearful of his reaction. "I was thinking after I get the cast off I might go join her."

"Andrea…" He started to disagree with my idea, but I

didn't give him much of a chance.

"Everyone sees me, Daddy. They look at me and remind me that I am broken. They make me want to break down into tears just by glancing my way. They whisper— Dad... you gotta let me go. Ladasha already said she could get me a job and everything if I needed her to. I mean, I was going to move to New York anyway. Might as well now."

He sighed and removed his glasses, rubbing between his eyes. He looked over to me and plopped down on my mattress. "Your mother's going to have a heart attack."

I smirked. The first smile I had in a long time. "Yeah well, that's not way out of her norm, now is it?"

CHAPTER TWO

COOPER

"I'M PREGNANT," SHE said. I looked to my wife, and she had a look of terror in her eyes. Iris was beautiful. Slim, olive skin, soft honey brown hair running down her shoulders, brown eyes that could make love with anyone. And she was telling me she was pregnant. I was almost certain I knew why her eyes looked so scared right that moment.

Iris covered her mouth with water filling her eye sockets. I'd never seen her like this before; she must have been terrified this pregnancy would end like the others. I guess she was already tapping into her hormones as she walked over to me and touched my hand. She felt like ice. "Cooper...say something."

Say something? No. I couldn't. I wouldn't. My mind was busy doing mathematics. I raised an eyebrow. "How far along are you?"

"Five weeks."

Five weeks. My heart started pounding against my chest, wanting to leap out. I shoved her hands away from me; her touch alone made me a different man. No. This didn't make sense. None of this made any fucking sense. How the hell could she be five weeks pregnant if we hadn't had sex in five months? Tears started pouring from her eyes as I witnessed my wife cry in front of me for the first time ever. I couldn't even trust her tears to have meaning because they were falling from a web of lies. My fingers were becoming tight, and the only way I could control them was by forcing my hands into fists. "Who?"

"Cooper..." She cried.

"Dammit Iris, who the hell is he?"

"It doesn't matter."

"It does."

She wiped her pathetic eyes and sobbed into her hands. Her body was shaking uncontrollably, almost to the point where I thought she would pass out. I glanced to her stomach. I wanted to throw up. She opened her mouth, and at first, nothing was heard. She swallowed a deep breath of air and released it through those damn lips that were once upon a time attached to mine.

"Speak up!" I ordered her, and when she did, I went quiet.

Tom Reed.

The name didn't take long to settle into my head. I knew who he was. Iris and I had just wrapped up filming *his* wedding on our reality show, *The Davidson's Weddings*, a few weeks prior. Five weeks ago to be exact. I had just finished editing wedding photos of him and the new Mrs. Reed. And during that time he had somehow managed to get *my* wife pregnant.

"Wh—what? Did y'all fuck before or after he cut his

wedding cake? Iris, was it before or after his first dance? Did the camera crew catch you? Good God." I was pacing now, running my hands over my face, feeling the sweat drip from my forehead. Pacing back and forth in a home I was no longer a part of. My southern roots were slipping out of my dialect the angrier I became. My fingernails digging deeper into the palms of my hands. I couldn't believe she would do this to me. To us!

"Cooper, I still love you," she promised. She reached for me and I couldn't help but let out a harsh laugh. The laughter was cut short. I felt drippings running down my clinched fist. Sweat? No. My knuckles were bleeding. Why were my knuckles bleeding? My eyes shifted to the shattered photo hanging on the wall in front of me. There was broken glass covering the carpet and I stepped back, confused. Did I do that? Shit... The DNA in the blood coating the photograph was sure to be a perfect match to my own.

Iris was standing in the corner across the room, panicked. I'd scared her. The fucking pain that started to shoot through my hand shook me a bit. I scared myself. I lost grip on everything around me. The room started to spin. My eyes blurred over. My mind started mocking me, screaming inside my head, 'Tom Reed, Tom Reed, Tom Reed.' *Over and over again.*

"SHUT UP!" I shouted, wrapping my hands around my head, covering my ears, and blocking out all sounds. I wasn't sure if I was speaking to my wife or the fucking Tom Reed chant on repeat inside me. I needed to leave; I needed to walk out the front door before my anger took me to a level I wasn't sure I could control.

Did she really say that? Did she say she still loved me? Son of a bitch.

I needed a divorce.

WHISKEY WAS THE only liquid lingering in my body by this point. My hands stayed clenched around the glass in front of me as I brought it to my lips and drank down my brown toxin. Did I need another drink? I squeezed my eyes shut and looked around. People appeared to have two heads, and some had three. I glanced to my hand where my wedding band was and slid it off, tossing it into my wallet.

Yup. I needed another drink.

"Maybe you've had enough." The bartender came over and took the glass away. I'd been coming to this bar for awhile now—drinking and forgetting. Well, trying to forget. I hated how she was always with me in a way. I hated how she wasn't physically around, but had the ability to reside in my head. When I closed my eyes, I saw her face. When I licked my lips, I tasted her mouth. It pissed me the hell off.

I met Iris after I'd agreed to shoot a famous couple's engagement photos. I never did anything involving weddings; I was more into edgy, raw, human-connections type of photography, the true grit of emotions. But the couple had been damn helpful when my career was starting out, tweeting my name to their followers online, telling their other famous people to look out for me. So when they asked, I had no right to turn them down. They showed up to the shoot with this stunning woman next to them, their wedding planner.

We started the shoot at five in the morning. By five in the evening I was addicted to Iris. Two weeks later we had our first date. Three months later we were engaged. Within less than a year of knowing one another, we were married. Instant love, people called it. It wasn't long before we were offered a television series to handle luxury weddings.

If I could go back in time, I never would have agreed to do the engagement photo shoot. I needed another drink. The dude behind the counter hesitated.

"Fuck you. Get me another."

The look in the bartender's eyes pissed me off. He felt sorry for me. Fuck him. I could go find my whiskey elsewhere.

"Cooper..." He leaned forward, eyes on me. He had four heads now. I shook myself and tried to focus on the ass who wouldn't get me another drink. He continued to murmur some bullshit I didn't want to hear. "Paparazzi—don't go—water." Blah blah blah. My cell phone went off and I saw Iris's name plastered on it. What a stupid name. *Drop!* Into the stupid glass of water went my stupid phone with my stupid wife's name on it.

I stood up, allowing myself a few moments to find my footing. Digging into my wallet, I tossed the ass a few bills and stumbled to the exit. It was dark outside, but the streets were bright. My hand flew up to shield my eyes from the lights. Or flashes, I should say. Dammit. The ass was trying to tell me that the paparazzi were here looking for a story.

They must have heard about my pregnant, cheating, whore of a wife.

"Don't you have someone else to be following? Get the camera out of my face." I pushed my way through them, pissed off. I was a fucking reality television star, not damn Brad Pitt. *Leave me alone.* I blamed Iris for this. I blamed Iris for everything. They kept following me, searching for something to sell. I staggered back and forth, trying to keep my balance, but it was tough when everywhere I turned, there was a fucker pushing me the other way.

Fine.

I'd fly.

It appeared my flying skills were lacking. My feet landed on top of a parked taxi as I tried to hurry across the street to get to my hotel room. My new home. Losing my balance, my ass landed against the hard, metal hood. Standing back up, with a pain shooting through my back, I huffed and puffed.

"Are y'all happy!? Did you get your fucking pictures!?" I hollered at the men holding the cameras. So many lights. I took off my shoe and threw it at one of them. They laughed, as if they were somewhat enjoying my breakdown. More lights joined in the party, this time red and blue flashes.

My fingers wrapped around the back of my neck, trying to get a grip on the craziness occurring. I tried to focus in on the officers approaching me. It looked like there were sixteen of them, but there were really only four. Damn alcohol.

"Sir, we need you to get down," one of the cops

shouted. I laughed—shocked that he was looking at me as if I caused this problem.

"Why don't you do something about these stalkers!? They won't leave me alone!" I could have really used another drink. The real world was still too real for me.

"Sir! Get. Down. Now!"

I was sick of it all. Sick of this lifestyle. Sick of the cameras. Sick of the fame. And fucking sick of my wife for doing this to me. I looked at the cops and chuckled at their serious demeanors. One had his hand on his cuffs and another with his hand on his gun. What was he going to do? Shoot me?

"I'm a guy trying to get to my hotel, and I'm the bad person here? I mean, seriously?! Do you not know who I am?!" I jumped off the taxi, into the street, where a large group had arrived with cell phones in their hands, videotaping me as if I were the damn circus.

I staggered near the cops and pounded my hands against my chest. Trying to explain the situation. Someone screamed I looked crazed. What? Screw them. I'd had a bad fucking day.

"This is getting out of control. Look, do you know who I am?" I was annoyed now—with everyone. The paparazzi. The random folks. The damn cop with his hand on his gun.

"Do you know who I am!?! Stop with the flashes!" I screamed as I barged at the paparazzi, ready to rip the cameras from their hands. Instead, I was stopped. My body began twitching, my hands shaking involuntary. Every muscle in my body became rigid, and I dropped to my knees.

I was wrong. The cop's hand wasn't on his gun.

It was on his taser.

MY PALMS WERE sweating as I continuously rubbed them against one another. My eyes rested on the clock's ticking sounds. The sounds were mocking me. Time moved so fucking slowly and I couldn't take much more. The air was hard to breathe; I'd been in this place for far too long and was longing for my escape. Rubbing my lips together, I looked to the ground and started to count the floor tiles. That would past the damn time.

"Cooper, what are you thinking?" the old doctor with the clipboard asked me. The nametag hanging on his white coat read Doctor Downey. His thin-framed glasses fell slightly down his nose and his brown-eyes studied my face. I shrugged my shoulders and looked around. We were surrounded by other people, sitting in a circle, having our daily 'group therapy' session.

There were three types of people in this hell. People number one—the people who were actually crazy. Like 'I see dead people and talk to fucking cows' type of crazy. People number two—the people who worked there, who looked even more insane than the crazies. Yet the only way to tell if they were mentally insane or employees of the messed up system was to glimpse at their shoes to see if they still had their shoestrings. The crazies didn't get strings in this place. I looked at Dr. D's shoes to make sure the shoestrings were there. Sometimes it was hard to tell.

And there were people number three. They were the people who were surrounded by others who continually attacked a person and fucking battered them to a point where there was a snap. People number three snapped and needed a break—a vacation to the land of crazy just to avoid the truly insane individuals who were walking outside in the real world.

I sat back in my metal chair and glanced down to my shoes. I wasn't an employee. I didn't talk to cows. So I guessed I was a three. I looked toward Dr. D and asked him to repeat his question.

"What are you thinking, Cooper?" he asked. I laughed loudly and shrugged my shoulders. I rested my hand on my hairy face and chuckled even louder. I hadn't been allowed to shave since I arrived and it felt strange to feel prickly hairs growing in. A daily reminder of my time spent here. You know what I was thinking? I was thinking my wife was a cheating, pregnant whore.

But I looked at Dr. D, knowing if I stated my true thoughts he'd think I needed to be in the mental health clinic longer than I wanted to be. I rubbed below my bottom lip and shrugged, "Nothing."

He studied me for awhile. I almost thought he could see right through me. I stared back, my green eyes giving his browns quite the battle. He pushed his thin-framed glasses up his nose and nodded, turning to Claire—the born-again virgin who was addicted to cocaine. "What about you, Claire? What are you thinking?"

The older dude seated next to me smiled and whispered, "You'll be okay." He didn't look insane, but his missing shoestrings told me otherwise. "You just have to go through what you're going through to get to what you're getting to."

I eyed the older dude to look for clear signs that he was crazy. Some of the people in here twitched, some of them screamed, and others broke everything they could get their damn hands on. But this guy...he had calm blue eyes and a full grayed beard which somehow made me want to get to know him. He had friendly eyes. If I had to be in this place for a few more weeks, I would need an ally. I turned to him and allowed him to be my new 'friend'. "Thanks, man. What's your name?"

"Most people around here call me J.C. But you can call me by my real name, Jesus Christ."

The blank stare on my face had to be priceless; I looked for a sign of sarcasm from him, but it was nowhere to be found. Slowly turning around in my seat, I remained stunned. Jesus Christ, where the hell was I?

CHAPTER THREE

Andrea

WHEN I ARRIVED to New York, I was so glad to have Ladasha come running in my direction, wrapping her arms around me. I nudged her in the arm, grinning. "You don't know how happy I am to see you."

"Ditto. Look at you! I can't even tell you were in a cast!" It felt good to have that dang thing off my leg. Every time I looked at it, it was a daily reminder of Derrick, so having it gone was a plus. Now if only I could get my memories to disappear. Ladasha bit the bottom of her lip and narrowed her eyes. "Listen, so you'll be staying with me and Kate at our apartment. I hope you are okay with a couch as a bedroom..." Her begging eyes appeared, hoping it would be all right, but she had nothing to worry about. I couldn't care less.

I was out of the small town and in the city that never sleeps. The city people went to lose and find themselves. I was so ready to leave old Andrea in Wisconsin and rediscover myself, leaving all the tears and pain in the past. It had been five months since the accident, but sitting in my bedroom at my parents' house made it feel like yesterday. And I was so sick of yesterdays.

Ladasha snuggled her head into my shoulder, holding onto me tightly. I really hit the jackpot in the friendship department with this one. Ladasha was a beautiful human, inside and out. Her wardrobe demonstrated exactly who she was. It was sexy with a twist of flirtation attached to it. She always wore cropped, flowing tops that would showcase her flat stomach and belly button piercing. Her jeans were so tight they would appear to be her own skin if one didn't notice the back pockets. Many other girls who would try to wear the risky outfits Ladasha sported would be tagged as a slut, but not her. Ladasha made the outfits somehow become classy—they were a part of her personality. She had beautiful caramel skin and legs that could spin for days. She was a floater, both on the stage and in life, and her outfits always reminded the world of that.

"Oh...and I forgot to tell you about the job..." My best friend's smile read 'forgive me' and 'try to understand' as she proceeded to tell me she was now officially a stripper. "I mean, you wouldn't be a stripper, of course! You would be a shot girl!" Her wide-toothed grin tried to make her new employment seem a bit better, but I wasn't buying it.

"Ladasha! Stripping?! Are you kidding me?!" I cried. Everything I knew about strippers involved drugs, sex, and Channing Tatum. Okay, well, two out of three weren't terrible, but still.

"It's a form of dance..." she said.

"It's a step away from prostitution," I echoed into the air.

"I made three hundred dollars last night." Well, I

couldn't argue the numbers.

The first night in the apartment was the toughest for me. I stood in front of the bathroom mirror with tears running down my face. I missed him so much it hurt to breathe. Ladasha didn't ask me to talk about it. She just hugged me. She had met Derrick a few times throughout the school year and knew we were meant to be together forever. She just hadn't known how short forever was.

I headed to the couch and pulled out my MP3 player, put the headphones in my ears, and listened to Derrick sing as I cried myself to sleep.

The days went on but the memories didn't grow fainter. I walked into the strip club, wearing pretty much my underwear with the *Up and Under* logo pasted on my ass. The men were pigs, of course. Whenever I walked around with a tray of shots and one would reach for me, I felt the urge to slap him hard across the chin. They smelled like rum and filth, and they wanted nothing more than to touch a pair of boobs. And I was making it *pretty* easy for them to stare at mine.

Returning home, I went back to my regular routine of tears. I felt so ashamed of myself that missing Derrick didn't fade away.

Kate, the other roommate, didn't hold any pity for me like Ladasha did. "Is she going to be crying all the damn time? It's effing annoying!" she hissed with her thick Brooklyn accent. She wasn't one to hide her feelings and voiced them any chance she could get. "I'm serious, Ladasha. I cannot take it anymore. Do something. I'm going to Ricky's for the night."

She barged out of the apartment, taking with her the

attitude. Ladasha rolled her eyes and joined me on the couch. As she sniffed the air, her eyes filled with questions of what she smelled. She set sight on the men's cologne bottle on the coffee table. Picking up my pillow, she inhaled it, taking in the tangy scent. It was Derrick's favorite. I felt so pathetic. But Ladasha smiled and tossed her legs on top of me.

"If you ever want to talk..." she offered. I declined.

DERRICK WRAPPED HIS arms around my waist and swung me side to side in my dorm room.

"Babe, stop, I have a class to get to." I loved when he would visit during the week, but he made it extremely difficult to make it to class on time. Or, well, to make it to class at all.

His kisses behind my ear made my strides to attend lecture vanish. "I love you, Andie," he whispered, his lips gently tugging on my earlobe.

"I know."

He placed his hand on my chin and pulled me in closer to him, staring me down with his beautiful brown eyes. His long eyelashes blinked and he looked saddened a bit. "What's wrong?"

"Nothing. Everything's right when I'm with you." He took my hands and placed them across his chest, holding me tight. "You're the reason this beats. You're the reason I

don't feel alone in this damn world. When I feel invisible, you see me."

"Derrick..." I whispered, placing my hand on the side of his face.

"Will you marry me, Andie?"

A chuckle escaped my lips, we always joked about marriage, and I knew it would happen, just not now, five minutes before my class. I pulled away and picked up my books.

"I'll see you after class, babe." I kissed his cheek and he smirked, sliding his hands into his pockets. Opening my dorm door, I heard him call after me.

"Andie Evans, catch." I turned around as he tossed me a box. My eyes filled with tears, studying the small box lying within my hands. Derrick swayed back and forth, "Open it."

My fingers lifted the lid and the tears began to flood my cheeks. "D..." I looked to him and he was now down on one knee. "Ask me again." I softly said, walking over to him.

He took my hand and kissed my palm, "I want you. I need you. I love you. Will you marry me, Andie?"

WHEN NOVEMBER CAME, the earth's breaths were getting pretty chilly. I stared out of the bathroom window and looked at the first snowfall happening before my eyes.

Whenever Mom or Daddy would call, I would tell them I was doing great. Working at a nice restaurant down the way and looking to get back into dancing. Which was pretty true. After Kate got fed up with my annoyance and moved out of the apartment, Ladasha and I needed more cash for rent. So she offered me a chance to get on stage.

"Come on, you're a fantastic dancer!!!" she cheered. I shook my head. I would be lying if I didn't watch the girls onstage and see that it really was an art form. The way they moved their bodies and took perfect upside down spins around the pole made me almost want to dance again.

"Just think about it. I'll have Roger give you a practice run someday soon. Maybe a few lap dances for some dudes. Come on, what could it hurt? Listen, I gotta get to work. There's some Chinese food in the fridge. Eat something, skinny. I'll see you later." My best friend rushed out of the room, leaving me there alone once again, with my thoughts.

I hated being called skinny. Mainly because I *was* skinny now. It wasn't that I was a hippo or anything before; I was 5'8" and weighed 130 lbs. Too big to be a ballet dancer, but just right for contemporary dance. After the accident I lost a good fifteen pounds. Most girls would be thrilled, but I didn't like it about me; heck, there wasn't much I enjoyed about myself lately.

I rolled my eyes and stood up to go dye my hair in the bathroom. A change was needed, even if it were only a physical one.

I promise to love you without reservation. Comfort you in times of distress. Encourage you to achieve all of your goals.

"Stop it..." I hissed as I stood in front of the bathroom mirror. My reflection was mocking me. Reminding me of who I used to be, the person I had left behind in Wisconsin. Every stupid freckle on my face reminded me of who I was, giving me a new desire to never pass by a mirror.

Laugh with you and cry with you. Grow with you in mind and spirit.

I closed my eyes and took a deep breath. *Stop it...stop it...* My hands formed fists and slammed against the sink counter. I was losing it again. My mind was traveling to places I wished to forget. My brain was dishing out old memories which had once made me smile, yet they were now tainted with sorrow and regret.

Always be open and honest with you and cherish you...

"STOP!" I screamed into the mirror as my eyes flung opened. I stared at the now tear-filled blue eyes. I could run from the rest of my past with such ease, but each time I looked in the mirror was a constant reminder of who I used to be. What I used to be. Slowly I was becoming disgusted with my inability to move forward with life; I just kept living the same nightmare over and over again.

Reaching for the pair of scissors on the counter, I pulled my long, gold-soaked locks of hair into my hand and stared at myself once more in the mirror. *Please...*

...For as long as we both shall live. For as long as we both shall live. For as long...

I started cutting my shoulder-length hair. One strand at a time. Two strands. Five. Seventeen. Chopping. Tearing away at each layer more aggressively. Tears hitting the floor at the same speed as the golden strands. I closed my eyes as I chopped the final parts. Opening my eyes, I let out the breath I'd been holding for quite awhile.

Picking up the box of black hair dye, I looked at the new Meg Ryan, *You Got Mail* haircut I was sporting. The clock on the bathroom wall ticked loudly behind me, reminding me that time was still moving forward as I stood still. I looked at the clock, which said it was a little before midnight, and the streets of New York City were still alive. The sounds of sirens blaring made my skin crawl, and I watched the wicked window inviting the winds into the apartment, blowing the curtains with the crisp, autumn freshness.

I let out a sigh and began to overdose my hair with the dark ink, which ran down my face. I watched as the clock struck midnight.

CHAPTER FOUR

COOPER

I STOOD OUTSIDE our New York Apartment and waited for her to answer the door. I would be lying if I said my heart didn't skip a beat when I saw her. She looked amazing. Fuckin' A, she was gorgeous. She smiled brightly and invited me in. "No, I just wanted to drop this off. You got my mail?" I handed Iris my key to the apartment and watched her disappear to retrieve my mail.

When Iris returned to the porch, she handed me my letters and sighed. "Come on, Cooper. Let's talk. When did you get out?" I didn't listen and turned to walk away. She was pretty much begging for my attention, "Seriously? That's all I get?"

Turning back to her, I studied her stomach; she had to be about five months pregnant and she was starting to show. "Yeah, Iris. That's all you get."

I could feel my mind going back to the night I found out she was pregnant. It was hard to focus on the moment before me and I was about to lose it when I saw her and her stomach standing in front of me. I reached into my coat pocket and squeezed the stress ball I'd become accustomed to carrying around with me. Fuck. I shouldn't have come here.

"It's just, when you called I thought you were coming home..." she whispered. She had a bit of hope in her eyes, hope that I would give her the hug she was desperately in need of, hope that I would forgive her, and hope that I would come home.

What home? I thought to myself. I hadn't had a home in quite some time and didn't want Iris to get the wrong idea. "I said I was coming to drop off the key and pick up my mail. That's all."

Her hand reached out and grabbed my wrist. I raised an eyebrow, "You don't want to do that, Iris." She let go instantly. Looking down the street, I saw a few people with cameras snapping away at me. First, I was shocked. That was until I looked up to see Iris and realized how gorgeous she was. Even more beautiful than normal. High heels on to answer the door and not a hair out of place. "You called the paparazzi?" I questioned.

She glanced in their direction and back to me, whispering between her teeth. "If you come inside, we can talk. They'll get their pictures and we can figure out where to go from here. You've been all over the tabloids since your..." She cleared her throat. "Since your *vacation*."

"Unbelievable." Stunned. I was fucking stunned by the actions of my twisted wife. "I'm done, Iris."

I turned, choosing to walk in the opposite direction of the paparazzi, leaving a desperate woman standing there. The last thing I heard was her voice hollering down the street, towards me I assumed. "Okay! Love you."

THE SPACE IN BETWEEN

How did we get so messed up? I swore there was a time when we were happy, but that was a long fucking time ago.

IRIS WALKED INTO the living room wearing a tank top and panties. I smirked as I sat editing pictures from a photo shoot over in Paris. "Let's go to bed." She offered. I kept working; I had to get the edits to the magazine by the end of the week. She walked over to me, sliding between the desk and I. Wrapping her legs around my body, she rubbed her face against me. "Bed. Please?"

"I'm almost done..." I explained as I tried to peek around her sexy body pressed against mine.

Her hands rose to the air and her eyes lit up. I stopped peeking around her and allowed myself to take in the beauty of my wife. My hands lifted her tank top off and I rested my head against her stunning body, delivering her a few kisses.

"Bed?" I offered and she laughed lightly.

As I lifted her up, she snuggled her head into my shoulder and kissed my neck. "I'm pregnant." My walking came to a halt, and she looked me in the eyes. "We're pregnant." She didn't cry, but she was happy. I could see it in her face, and she could probably see the joy in mine. We had tried so fucking hard for so long and we were officially pregnant.

I covered her lips with mine as we continued onto the bedroom to celebrate our new beginnings.

I COULDN'T HELP but roll my eyes behind my sunglasses as I strolled down the streets of Manhattan with Kyle, my manager and best friend. He was rambling off nonstop about something or other, but I wasn't really in the mindset of listening to him. As we walked past a newsstand I cringed, seeing my and Iris's photo plastered on the cover. Most of the time, the headlines were extra insane. Total bullshit. But this time, some read 'divorce,' 'mental health clinic,' and 'cheating scandal.' They were spot on. Then again, whenever some famous couple had a fight, it was a divorce and cheating scandal with a sprinkle of crazy. So Kyle informed me to lay low and ignore it all.

It was tough to ignore it as the paparazzi scooted down the streets of New York with us, hardly giving us enough room to breathe. I was tired of all of this shit. Pulling my baseball cap lower, I cussed under my breath and continued walking.

"I told you not to go see her," Kyle scolded me. I informed him of the mail exchange between Iris and me, and let's just say he was less than pleased. "I mean, seriously. If this is going to blow over, we gotta communicate. You understand?"

My silence was enough to make him realize I was out

of it. He softened his tone, patted me on the back, saying we should grab a bite to eat. The paparazzi's questions were echoing in my ears. "Hey, Cooper! Over here! Where's Iris?" "Coop! My man! Can we get an exclusive?" "Where have you been? We heard you took a trip to a mental health clinic after your breakdown at the bar a few months ago. Are you crazy? Tom Reed?"

When I heard Tom's name I snapped my head up, rage running through me. Turning towards the cameras my eyebrow cocked up. *Tom Reed. Tom Reed.* None of the paparazzi's lips were moving. They weren't asking about Tom Reed at all. My fucked up mind was just dishing out some more reminders of my messed up life.

The paparazzi drew in closer. My body tightened up. I was caged in by the wild animals chasing me. They wouldn't let up. And that feeling I'd felt when Iris told me she was pregnant started creeping back into me. This was after all, her fault. She was the reason why they wouldn't leave me the hell alone. She was the reason...

"Unclench your fists," Kyle whispered harshly. I didn't even know they were clenched. Relaxing my fingers, the fist format faded. Kyle smiled brightly for the cameras as he poked me in the side and delivered me a confirming grin. I took the order, smiled towards the cameras, and waved.

I was so happy when we sat inside the restaurant. One thing they weren't allowed to do was follow me inside.

"My cousin is having a Christmas party. I got the invite when I picked up my mail from Iris." I cringed when I said that. Even hearing her name from my lips made me sick.

"You have a cousin?" Kyle asked. I rolled my eyes and thought back to the proper invitation I had received. It was very fancy, the words written in beautiful cursive. The perfect shades of reds and silvers. A perfectly tied bow at the top.

"They asked me to be the photographer."

Kyle laughed so hard he almost spit out his food, but he managed to choke it down. "Fat chance. What, do they think they can use your services whenever the hell they want? Get real."

It was true people had a tendency to try to use me once I made it big, but I didn't see my cousin's family as those types of people. Within the past five years, my uncle Wayne had created a brilliant 'As Seen On TV' item that sold like wildfire and sent him to the outskirts of the small town he'd raised his family in.

Uncle Wayne made twist-on caps for beer and soda cans that kept one's drink safely covered during outings to sporting events, parks, picnics, or whatever the hell people did outside. Needed to be outside? Uncle Wayne had a cap for that. They came in different colors. Some kept items chilled, some had inserts for straws, and let me be the first to say I had no clue why the hell people would buy them.

But my uncle had somehow hit it big, and he wasn't afraid to live large. Therefore, they could have any experienced photographer at their holiday party, and the fact that they wanted me was kind of a compliment. But I hadn't really spoken to them since the accident with my parents...

Kyle swiped a few fries from my plate. "I see you got your shoestrings back." He laughed unnecessarily loud at his stupid joke. I chose to ignore the comment. He continued asking questions about my last few months spent in a mental clinic to 'regroup.' "Come on. Tell me what it was like there. Was it like that one movie with Jack Nicholson? *One Flew Over The Cuckoo's Nest?*"

"Fuck you, ass. It turned out to be a nice place. There were actually a lot of nice people there. I met Jesus."

He choked on the water trying to go down his throat. I got a laugh out of that. "Excuse me. What?"

I looked at him as if he were crazed. "You know, Jesus? Jesus Christ? Really down to earth guy. Deep, too." I pulled out the stress ball in my pocket and showed it to Kyle. "He actually gave me this to help me deal with my issues."

Kyle was becoming uncomfortable as I watched him shift around in his chair. It wasn't surprising—anything that wasn't money or sex made Kyle uncomfortable. "We should really talk about the next steps for you. How to rebuild your image after this small mishap."

I agreed 100%. I emailed him earlier with a road map of what I wanted to do. He hadn't mentioned anything about it, so I figured I should bring it up. "What do you think of my idea?"

"I think it's fucking ridiculous. That's what you get for being around other crazies for so long." After spending time in the clinic, Kyle assumed my new idea was the wacky medicines wearing off. "So as I said before, we should talk about the next steps."

I informed him I didn't want to talk about *his* next steps for me, but he didn't care. "Cooper, you are at the top of your career! This little slip up isn't stopping people from wanting to work with you! BIG people! Our type of people! You make millions each year, and there's no reason for that to change."

I didn't care about the damn money. There was a time when I'd taken photographs out of pure love for it. Kyle should have known that—he had known me since we were kids. "It's not about the money. That's not why I do it. Well, that's why I did it before with Iris, but that's not why I want to do it now."

Kyle smirked. "Did Jesus tell you to say that?"

I couldn't get him to understand where I was coming from, but I was determined to try. "Shut up, I do it for…" I gestured to the front window. "Look." We stared out the window and watched the life experience from the restaurant. There was a couple running, holding hands to get into a taxi. There was a man hollering at someone, probably a poor intern, on his cell phone. Three extremely attractive girls in high end fashion walked by, laughing with each other. An overwhelming level of excitement filled my gut as I realized that now Kyle would be able to understand what I was trying to get at.

"See? Everyone has a story. The couple holding the taxi, the angry man on the phone, the happy fashion girls. The guy…" I stared out the window with a glimpse of disgust as I looked at a guy by the stop sign. "The guy licking the stop sign. Emotion. All kinds. Not just the happy 'wedding day' kind. That's what I want to capture on film. Real life. It's not all cake and first dances."

Kyle nodded. "Iris really fucked you up."

"Why can't I want to do something different?"

"Because different makes you the guy raping the stop

sign. Listen, I get it. You and Iris were a duo team. Husband and wife. Iris, a top notch wedding planner. You, a top notch photographer. Your own show. So what?" Kyle picked up his phone and started scrolling through his emails, once again only half-paying attention.

"You're not listening, Ky."

He wasn't.

Kyle kept staring at his cell phone and shook his head. He went to text someone. "It's my fuckin' job to listen to you, Coop. And okay, you ended up in the funny farm for a few weeks. Big deal. What famous person hasn't taken a va-ca to the world of crazy? Look. The magazines are going mad. Neither you nor Iris is doing any interviews, and if you get out there first, POW! It will be spun in your favor. You know she's cooking up some nasty story. She always was a media whore."

"Are you deaf?"

Kyle put down his phone and looked to me. His demeanor grew serious, something that didn't happen often. "I know you've been through a lot this year. And I heard about the kid..."

"Don't."

"Coop, I'm sorry. I know how long y'all had been trying, and for her to pull that kind of shit..."

I shifted my eyes to my plate and went about eating my food. I didn't want to think about Iris or anything dealing with her.

Kyle's phone went off as he received a text message. After he viewed it, he shifted from serious to extremely giddy. He turned back to me and I could tell by the smirk in his eyes that he was about to say something stupid. "Guess what you're doing tonight?" I patiently waited to hear my crazy manager's plans. Kyle moved around with excitement as if it was Christmas morning. "You're going to a strip club!" My friend sat at the table, trying to force feed his 'brilliant' idea to me. It wasn't working. "Don't you see? This is what you need. A good lap dance, and maybe a nice one-night stand if you're lucky."

I wasn't as interested. "Of course, and some nice herpes on the side."

Kyle sat back in his seat; he appeared fucking shocked by my statement. Really? Was it *that* shocking that I didn't want herpes?

"You're so judgmental it's sick. It really is, Cooper. Jasmine is a very pleasant girl."

"So let me get this straight. You want me to have sex with a prostitute that you've slept with? No thanks."

"Stop it, stop it." Kyle was outraged. Growing extremely protective of this Jasmine chick, he snapped at me. "She's not a prostitute, jerk. She's a stripper, and I don't appreciate how you are talking about her. My God. When did you become so disrespectful? It's disgusting. Besides, it's her friend who you are meeting up with."

"You're serious? I thought you wanted me to lay low?" My fingers ran across my eyebrows, trying to figure out if he were serious or not.

"Look, Coop. Think of this as a renewing of your life. I'll get you through the back entrance. No one will ever know. Jasmine just texted me the girl's number. You got your new phone? Type it in. I'll tell you what. If it works, you do one of the many magazine interviews that are coming in. You deal with your issues with Iris. You at least consider the other television offers I have been getting. And you do what you do best, and make us a shitload of money."

"And if it doesn't work?" I questioned.

Kyle lowered his eyebrows and rubbed his fingers across the bridge of his nose. "If it doesn't work, we'll look into your 'indie photographer' mumbo jumbo."

"Really?" That sparked my interest enough.

"Really. Jesus would agree. Listen, just don't get all... weird. Okay? Like, don't tell anyone about this 'I met Jesus and he changed my life in a psych ward' type crap. Get a lap dance. Maybe have a little sex. Just try to act like the guy you were before you found out your wife..." Kyle's sentence faded off and I was quick to chime in.

"Found out my wife was a cheating, pregnant whore?"

Kyle nodded as he picked up his bread roll and took a bite out of it. "Exactly."

CHAPTER FIVE

Andrea

PROMISES. PROMISES TO love one another. To pick up the milk on the way home. To not raise your children like your parents raised you. To follow each other's dreams. Promises to fight at least once a month over some mediocre crap—and follow it up with some killer make-up sex. To be with one another forever and always. Til death do us part. *Til death do us part...*

Screw promises.

I just got a promotion.

It smelled like crap in this place—a miniature dressing room with too much hairspray, too many perfumes, and an overload of glitter. I stood in front of the full-length mirror that had a feathery boa lying across it and studied my body. I was wearing nothing more than a safari hat, a black trench coat, and five-inch-high stiletto heels. I hadn't even noticed I was digging my fake nails into the palms of my hands until Ladasha came over and placed her hands on my shoulders.

"You don't have to do this, Andrea," she said. I

guessed she could see the fear in my eyes. I shook my head. Our rent was falling behind and she had already stretched herself thin to make me comfortable in New York City. Plus, I was the one who ran off our other roommate with my issues. I wasn't going to let Ladasha down again.

"Don't worry, Shot Girl. I got you a good one tonight." Jasmine grinned as she sat at her cramped makeup table. She was the best dancer in this whole place, and our boss, Roger, made sure to always give her the closing number on stage. Jasmine made more money in a week than some people working in Hollywood, but she also had a side job that helped up her profit. Her thick Brooklyn accent and hoarse voice filled the air as she applied more mascara onto her outrageously fake lashes. "If you're lucky, you'll get him to take you to his place afterwards. You'll be eatin' off that money for the whole month."

My stomach bubbled up as I shot a dirty look her way. "I don't sleep with guys." The thought alone made me think of Derrick, and instant guilt hit me.

Jasmine stood up from her seat and chuckled as she walked to me with her jet black hair falling down to her waist. "Wasn't it just yesterday you didn't even strip, Shot Girl? What you waiting for? You waiting for God to pay your bills? I don't know about you but I'm gonna get mine right now, and I suggest you do the same."

With that, she left me standing there, filled with an overwhelming feeling of vomit trying to escape from my gut. Ladasha rolled her eyes and told me not to listen to Jasmine, but how could I not? She was right— just yesterday I wasn't a stripper.

I looked at myself and watched my bottom lip quiver.

Ladasha tried to convince me there was another way to get the money for rent and I shouldn't worry about such things. But I wasn't ready to back down. I could do it. I just needed her to give me a few of her comforting words to ease the freak out that was about to be released into the world.

Ladasha could tell how seriously I was in need of a pep talk so she delivered her best one. *"Pretty Woman,"* she said.

"What?"

"Pretty Woman. Name the rules. Before she was stupid and went and fell in love and got rich and shit." She was serious. Most of Ladasha's best pep talks were based off movies. She was addicted to all movies, and it would be a shock if she didn't know what was playing in the nearest theater.

I nodded as I thought over the rules of *Pretty Woman*. "No personal information. No kissing on the lips. No second meet up."

"Unless it's Richard Gere," Ladasha tossed in.

"It's not Richard Gere."

"Listen. Just go in there and be your super sexy self. Shake your booty. Collect the cash. If it's a freak, have Frank handle him. And leave. Easy!"

Right. Easy. Pretty Woman *rules*. I thanked my friend and left the dressing room. Walking through the strip club, I ignored the howls from the hungry perverts coming my way. I felt like a piece of meat about to be tossed into the ring with a pack of lions. As I approached the VIP rooms that had Frank, the security guard, standing in front of the door, I let out a halfway smile.

"You doing a VIP room, Andrea?" he questioned. I informed him it was a test drive; he nodded and opened the door. "You got fifteen minutes. After that, I grab you out." I closed my eyes and did a quick prayer to God that it wasn't a creep. *Please, God. Don't send me a motherfreakin' creep.*

I stepped into the room in my shiny heels and Frank closed the door behind me. When I opened my eyes and stared at the man sitting across from me, I gasped. He was beautiful. He wore a button-down black long-sleeved shirt with charcoal slacks. Even with the clothing, I realized how perfectly made his body was. He quickly rose to his feet and started speaking.

"Hi," he said as he reached his hand out to me for a handshake. I stood there, confused. Did strippers normally shake hands with their 'client'? How did I know? I was only a stripper-in-training after all.

"Right." He pulled his arm back and placed both hands in his slacks. Involuntarily, my eyes watched his hips start to rock back and forth. "So, yeah. I don't normally do this, but…yeah." He murmured to himself and cussed under his breath. "My manager thought it would be a good idea. A new start, a fresh take…"

Did he not recognize me? He looked so different from the last time I saw him in person. Sure, I was only thirteen, but his dimples hadn't changed. His crooked smile still remained the same.

Cooper Davidson had been sculpted by the gods. His tan, smooth skin, his low-buzzed blond hair, and his green intense eyes were like the ones of fairy tales. His lips were able to create a grin that made every woman melt and every straight man jealous. And to top it off, the gods had given him a voice box with a southern drawl that made all of the girls of my hometown crazy when he would come visit his cousin during the summers.

"You don't remember me?" I whispered as I stepped closer to him. Sure, my hair was going through a strange gothic-black, short-cut phase, which was much different than my usual blond, long waves. But still. I was still me. What was I thinking? Of course he wouldn't remember me...

Cooper stared at me and raised an eyebrow, his mind tracking through his past. My eyes followed his mouth, watching him bite his bottom lip and step closer. He stared into my blue eyes with such curiosity floating around in his greens. I saw it happen—the moment he remembered who I was. And then I remembered who I was. I was officially a stripper in training. A wave of embarrassment washed over my face. My eyes shifted to the ground. I didn't feel worthy to look his way. I was so ashamed of the path I had traveled in the past months.

Cooper took a finger, lifted my chin up, and grinned widely. "Andie Evans."

I cringed a bit, but I smiled. "Andrea. I go by Andrea now."

He nodded. "Of course. Holy shit. How the hell are you?!" He pulled me into a tight hug and held me close. It felt good to be held. It had been so long since...

I pulled away and released a sad grin. A short gasp fell from my lips at the touch of his soft fingers brushing away tears that started falling from my eyes. My heart landed in my throat, filled with nerves and worry. The idea of my mom and dad finding out about my job was terrifying, yet Cooper quickly eased my fears. "I'll never say a word. I promise. Holy crap. Andrea Evans as I live and breathe. It's been, what? Ten years?" We were both in a state of shock. He took a seat and I sat across from him, removing my stupid safari hat.

"Ten years. You went to become a famous photographer and I went to become..." I laughed at myself. The red velvet walls in the room with the dimmed sex lighting told him exactly what I'd become.

"You look beautiful." He praised me. He hadn't changed a bit; he was as charmingly sweet as he'd been when he delivered me my first kiss on the cheek at the age of seven. "Last time I saw you, you were falling in love with a guy that wasn't me." He smirked.

I nodded my head. "Derrick Stevens."

"Ah! That's the jerk's name! How is Derrick Stevens doing nowadays? Fat? Unemployed? Gay?" He laughed in a joking manner.

I shook my head, resting my hands in my lap. "Dead."

Cooper's eyes widened in horror as Frank knocked on the door and opened it to inform us that our nice 'lap dance' was over. I looked to Frank and then over to Cooper. He was frozen with a distressed look. I sighed, knowing I couldn't leave him like that. I didn't know why, but something inside of me felt like he deserved my attention. Something wanted me to stay in the room. I couldn't put my finger on it, but it was an urge that I didn't want to walk away from. Even if my mind hoped to run for the hills, my body was content with its whereabouts.

I turned to the security guard and gave him my fakest

grin and a wink. "We're gonna need a little bit more time, Frank."

Frank closed the strip club VIP door and my eyes stayed on Cooper. The poor guy looked as if he killed Derrick himself. I almost laughed, but knew it would be inappropriate. Only a girl who was emotionally damaged to the core would laugh at such a situation.

"I'm sorry, what's funny?" Cooper's eyes filled with concern. I arched an eyebrow and touched my fingertips to my mouth. It was curved into a grin where uncontrollable giggles were escaping. I shook myself and stopped laughing. Nothing was funny. It wasn't long until the silence grew haunting and Cooper replaced the dead air with questions.

"When? What happened? Do you want to talk about it?"

Six months ago. A car accident. No, never.

I nudged him in the knee, needing a change in subject. "So what have you been up to?"

His lips parted as if he wanted to speak but they shut fast. He was handsome, but the twitch in his eyebrow showed me he was also in need of repair on the inside. An overwhelming need to know more washed over me. Could it be that someone was as messed up emotionally as me? Did he have a story, too? I wanted to know. No, I *needed* to know. I needed to not feel so alone for a moment in my life. My eyes pleaded for him to continue his thoughts. He cleared his throat and bit the tip of his thumb.

"I left my wife."

I watched as his face deepened into a shade of red. It was a somewhat new hurt inside of him, I could tell. His beautiful eyes told a story of sorrows and regrets—something I understood. It was my turn to ask the questions. "When? What happened? Do you want to talk about it?"

Five months ago. Tom Reed. No, never.

I glanced down to my hand resting against his leg; it must have landed there when I tried to give him some comfort after hearing that he was going through a divorce. I moved it away fast, feeling as if I had somehow cheated on my nonexistent relationship.

Frank pounded on the door to the VIP room and reopened it. "Andrea. Times up! Seriously!" He was probably getting heat from Roger. I could tell because Frank would never raise his voice to anyone unless his boss was raising his voice to him. Cooper stood up, pulled out his wallet, and handed Frank a stack of bills. The guard looked down and counted the bills quickly with his eyes before slowly closing the door.

"So you moved to New York?" he asked me, reclaiming his seat. I nodded and explained how I needed to get away from the small town. He understood, remembering what a gossiping place I grew up in. There was a silence filling the room. For the longest time it felt as if we were staring at each other and a part of me was strangely all right with that idea.

"You wanna get out of here?" Cooper asked.

I laughed, nodding. He must have been able to see the need for escapism in my eyes. I sure as heck saw it in his. "Absolutely."

MY HANDS SHOOK as I placed the key into the door and turned the knob. Cooper stood behind me, patiently waiting. I know he noticed, but he didn't mention the small limp I had in my leg. It wasn't as bad as before, but it was still something someone couldn't miss. As we walked into the small, crammed apartment I welcomed him to my home.

"It's nice."

"It's not." I laughed. I walked to the kitchen and opened the fridge, "You want a drink? A beer?"

"No thanks. I'm not a big drinker nowadays." I looked into the fridge and realized there weren't any beers anyways. Ladasha must have taken the last one, which was fine—she was the one who bought them. Closing the refrigerator door, I looked down, realized I was still wearing my trench coat, and remembered that underneath it I was only sporting a leopard print bra and thong. Horrified, I turned, on a mission to go change. Before I could make my way to my bedroom, Cooper's hand had somehow found mine.

My body tingled at his touch, and I cussed for allowing myself to feel anything of the sort. His southern accent was somewhat hidden from his life in New York, but I heard it creep out as he spoke to me. "I'm sorry about Derrick. My gosh, Andrea. I couldn't imagine. I'm so sorry."

I looked down at our hands and my heart picked up its speed. I couldn't stop thinking about what was going to happen next. What was going to happen next?! He pulled me closer to him. *So close* I could feel his breath against my cheek...*So close* I could have sworn our lips were touching. I allowed my eyes to shut as he lifted my chin. With every exhale he took, I inhaled his breaths. Time kept moving, but we stood still. Allowing our breaths to be all that were heard, all that were felt.

"I'm broken, Cooper," I whispered. If he were to let go of my hands, I was certain I would shatter into a million pieces. His touch was the only thing holding me together.

"Me too." He inched my face closer to his, but he didn't kiss me. No, his lips lingered around my face as I slightly parted my mouth more. When I lifted my eyes, they met with his. The intense green eyes I was losing myself in made a small sigh escape me. He studied every part of my face. He ran a finger across my upper lip and then traced the bottom. Over and over again. Starting from the left and *slowly* moving to the right. I placed my hands against his chest, not wanting to tumble from his simple gesture. Yes...It was simple, but powerful, that small touch.

He stroked my short hair behind my ears and kissed my forehead. Gentle and loving caresses to my face made me long for his taste, yet I knew he wouldn't make the first move, out of mere respect. I pulled his lips closer to mine and nodded, granting him permission.

What was I doing? What was I *feeling*? All I knew was that whenever he touched me, I didn't feel alone.

He sheltered my mouth with his, which was enough to make my body grow weak. Yet he was there to catch me. One of his hands traveled to my lower back, his fingers massaging me. As his tongue began to explore mine, a light moan escaped from my lips. All my life I had only kissed one man, but I knew I could secretly get used to kissing the handsome soul in front of me. And that thought alone terrified me.

He led me to the couch, thrusting his body on top of mine. His mouth began to travel down to my neck, kissing me with nice pecks and sucking me gently with each new location. My toes curled into the couch cushion and I couldn't stop from arching my back as I longed for more. He placed his hand on my bare leg and began to travel under the trench coat up to my thigh. Everything inside of me heated up more and more at his touch. I lost all connections to the real world. It was just the two of us. Sampling each other. Discovering each other.

"Coop..." I whispered. With immediate care, his eyes shot to mine and he stopped his actions. A level of guilt filled his eyes, which made him even more attractive. I shook my head, pulled his face closer to mine, and murmured, "Bed." His guilt vanished with the taste of my lips. He lifted me up and carried me down the hall as I wrapped my legs around him and rested upon his strong body.

I needed Cooper that night and I could tell he needed me just as much. It was our escape from reality. Time didn't exist when I was with him that night. There were no yesterdays and no tomorrows. There was no thought involved, just passion. One kiss after another. One embrace made everything else seem meaningless just for a few moments. My mind was emptied. The feeling of overthinking every little detail of life vanished. The replaying of the accident wasn't happening within my head during those moments. Yes, we both were in need of some space between our all too messed up realities. Real life was too tough to face, and right now Cooper was forgetting about his drama in the world and I was forgetting about Derrick.

Derrick.

My eyes slowly opened to find Cooper kissing my nose. We'd finished our escape from reality. Our bodies spread out on my bed, clothes scattered across the floor, and my eyes shifted away from the handsome man lying next to me. And I remembered.

Derrick. I felt dirty. The same dirtiness washed over Cooper's face as we sat up in the bed. The night's autumn breeze was chillier than most nights as it flew past my open window. I quickly stood to shut it. All the heat that had run through my body a few minutes ago was long gone, and I was freezing.

Bending down, I wrapped a sheet around my body and handed Cooper his shirt. I couldn't even hold in my smile as I watched him stand from the bed. He had the most perfect butt I'd ever seen. I couldn't find the strength to look away as he slid his boxers on—he was gorgeous. I was torn. My heart was crying out as the pains of my previous actions were now creeping into my mind, yet at the same time I wanted round two of Cooper Davidson.

"I can't believe we just did that," he stated as he continued to get dressed. I couldn't believe it either.

I had a feeling Cooper wasn't one to partake in random flings. And it wasn't extremely random what we'd done— we *knew* each other after all. We'd grown up together. Well, kind of.

"I don't know if you felt it...I mean it just felt like..." He paused and shook his head as he continued to button his long-sleeved shirt. My softened expression probably showed him I'd felt it too. It felt like an escape. A way out for a moment in time. But the moment passed, and time had a way of never standing still.

He looked at me in my sheet and studied my curves. I aggressively pulled the sheet tighter to my body and watched as his eyes shifted away from me. He clearly could tell how uncomfortable I was.

"Let me take you out to dinner," he suggested.

"No."

He turned to face me and delivered a smile which made every inch of my skin tingle once again. How did he do that? "Why not?"

"It's against the rules."

"What rules?"

The rules I had already pretty much destroyed. The *Pretty Woman* rules. No personal information. That kind of went out of the window when I walked into the VIP room and saw him standing before me.

No kissing on the lips.

Crap.

And no second meet ups. I could hold up to that one. I felt pretty silly thinking about the rules, but Ladasha had taught me them, and it was my duty to follow through with at least one of the rules. And going out to dinner with gorgeous Cooper Davidson was not allowed.

"Come on, tell me. What rules?" He was interested as he raised one of his eyebrows. Everything he did was sexy. The sweat dripping down his forehead? Sexy. The way he bit the tip of his thumb? Sexy. The way he growled in my ear while nibbling it? *Sweet mother of everything righteous*...He could call me names, ignore my existence, tell me to piss off, and it would still make my body want him to claim me all over again. But, he would never do those things. He was too much of a southern gentleman.

I blushed at the thoughts filling my head, and lowered my voice to answer his question. "The *Pretty Woman* rules."

He drifted over to me, sporting his perfectly perfect dimples. "You do know how that movie ends, right?" Cooper turned away from me and slipped into his pants. I couldn't help but let a small grin slip from my lips. I realized the expression of pleasure plastered on my face and shook it off as Cooper kept talking. "I just...I don't want to be one of those guys. I want to take you out to—"

"YOU BITCH!" was heard from the living room. Ladasha was home. "How the hell did you get Roger to let you get a damn promotion without even staying the whole freakin' night?! And how the hell did you get someone to pay six hundred dollars for a damn lap dance?!" she hollered.

My eyes widened, looking to Cooper. "Six hundred dollars?!" I paused. Well, he got what he paid for.

"I picked up a pizza on the way back, dude. Seriously though. Teach me your..." Ladasha barged into my bedroom before I had a chance to tell Cooper to somehow turn invisible. The piece of Brooklyn style pizza in my roommate's hand froze in mid-air as Ladasha saw me wrapped in a sheet. Her eyes landed on Cooper and she finished her sentence. "...secrets..."

Her eyes bugged out when she realized there was a man standing in my bedroom. "What did I miss?" she questioned as the cheese on her slice of pizza slid to the floor.

"I should probably get going," Cooper said, and I agreed before he even finished his thought. We wedged our way past Ladasha, who was fast to follow behind us. Cooper turned to me once we reached the front door, smiling. "I would really like to see you again though, Andrea. I've never done this before." He paused and his cheeks turned rosy with embarrassment. "Well, I've done this, just not like *this*. Ya know?"

He was cute, trying to find the right words. But I couldn't help but feel a knot in my stomach growing larger and larger. "Coop," I whispered, trying to make him understand. But his green eyes lit up at the sound of my voice. He rested his hand on his chin and studied me.

"Andie," he whispered back. I didn't correct him. To tell you the truth it sounded kind of nice. I opened the front door and allowed him to kiss me on the forehead before he exited. "I'll call you."

"Don't," I begged.

He grinned and strolled down the hallway. I could still see his dimples in my head as he walked away. I stepped into the hallway and looked in his direction. "No really, Cooper. Don't."

Tossing his hand up in the air, he waved goodbye to me. I sighed. That goodbye wave was sexy, too. And that would probably be a problem. I stepped back into my apartment, closed the door, and slipped down to the ground. Ladasha walked over and slid down to join me.

"Was there an extremely sexy man in our apartment?"

"Yep."

"And you...had sexy time with him?" she questioned.

"Yep."

A level of silence filled the room. We sat there, both a bit stunned. Finally Ladasha found the ideal words to say. "Take that, Richard Gere!" she hollered and stood up to do a victorious dance. It involved a lot of awkward air humping and invisible ass slapping. I couldn't help but chuckle at my overreacting friend. As I glanced at her, my smile faded when I realized what I'd done. Ladasha also figured out what I'd done and her smile evaporated.

"Andrea..." Her voice was soft, filled with concern; I shook my head and stared forward.

I'd just had sex with Cooper Davidson.

Crap.

I WAS DIRTY. Turning on the shower, I stepped inside as the water began to hit my skin in random spurts. Picking up the soap, I started rubbing my ghost-white skin, scrubbing harder and harder, trying to erase the past few hours from my memory.

I promise to love you without reservation. Comfort you in times of distress. Encourage you to achieve all of your goals.

No...

I scrubbed more intensely, watching my skin turn red, trying to make the guilt that had somehow sunk into my soul disappear. My tears began to mix with the water droplets. There was no way to tell the liquid streams apart from one another. I let my body fall to the tub and sat there. I sobbed into my hands, allowing the water crystals to slap me with the reality I was now facing.

MICHELLE WAS FORCEFULLY *dragging a kid over with her as she came to visit Eric and me. The kid looked a few years older than me, maybe nine or ten.*

"You guys! This is my cousin Cooper. He's spending the summer here because his dad is crazy." Michelle sang, bouncing up and down. He had a camera hanging around his neck and shifted his feet on the ground, not looking up at us.

"What's with the camera?" I asked, watching as his eyes rose up to meet mine. My tummy started swirling around as I watched his lips curve into a nice grin and his dimples appeared.

"My mama gave it to me, before I left. What's your name?"

"Andie Evans. This is my brother Eric." Cooper didn't look over to acknowledge Eric, he just kept smiling at me, making me feel a bit weird. "Why are ya looking at me like that?"

His cheeks reddened and he went back to looking to the ground, kicking around dirt. "Just never seen anything like you before, that's all." His eyebrows frowned as he slapped his face. "I meant that in a good way. It came out wrong."

Michelle rolled her eyes and began walking near Eric. "Come on you guys, let's go to the park. Last one there buys everyone ice cream!" Eric and she went running off down the street.

Cooper cleared his throat and held up his camera in my direction. "Can I take your picture?"

I ran my fingers through my hair, and prepped myself for my first ever photo shoot. Placing my hands on my hips, I turned to Cooper, begging him to only capture my good side.

His hand ran over his face and his green eyes smiled my way. "Don't worry. I don't think I can miss it."

CHAPTER SIX

COOPER

I SAT IN Kyle's office watching him grin ear to ear at me like a proud papa. "Hell yeah! See! What did I tell you? A one-night stand has a way of changing a dude's perspective on an issue. Now we can move on, and I got a few papers for you to sign. Which magazine do you want to reach out to first? Star? Us Weekly? I can get the cover on People." Kyle went searching on his computer, with his pleased grin still framing his face.

I had to admit, I couldn't stop smiling either. "Listen, Ky."

He snorted and nodded his head as he kept at his computer. "Oh I'm listenin'. Tell me all about it. Was she good? Did she use the feathers? Jasmine uses the feathers."

"No. Listen, Kyle. I mean really listen." I slammed my hands on his keyboard, which made him whine like a puppy dog in pain. He fell back in his chair and tossed his hands up in defeat.

"Okay. What?"

Clasping my hands together, I leaned in closer to him.

"I like her. I like her a lot."

The sudden shift of character in Kyle's eyes was drastic; he knew where this was going, "Shut up."

"She's different, Kyle." My heart started pounding as I thought of the night before. Andrea was mysterious and different from anything I had ever felt with Iris. There were parts of her that were the same Andrea I knew when I was younger, but there was so much more depth to her nowadays that I found so fucking attractive. "And the way she kissed me..." Her lips... Andrea Evans's lips could make any man daydream of kissing her for the rest of their lives.

"One. Night. Stand. That's it, Cooper. One night! None of this instant love bullshit again. You know where instant love put you last time? In the damn psych ward!" Kyle hollered at me, but I wasn't interested in his opinion.

"She's beautiful. Not the type of beautiful most people see. But a sad type of beautiful, the type of beauty that changes people. And..." I chuckled, thinking of how insane what I was going to say next sounded. "You're going to think I'm crazy."

"I already do. Tell me anyway."

"But Jesus...in the mental health clinic... he told me I would meet someone. And a few weeks after I got out of the clinic, POOF! I'll be damned, there she was. And I have *you* to thank for that! If it weren't for you sending me to that club, it wouldn't have happened."

Kyle sat there, stunned for quite a bit of time. "Get the hell out of my office. And take your damn pills!"

As my cell phone went off from a text message, my eyes widened when I saw the name 'Andie' displayed. She finally got back to me after the few text messages she seemed determined to ignore. I stood up and nodded, walking near the door. "I'm going to see her."

A firecracker was lit under Kyle's seat, sending him skyrocketing from his chair. "What! No. Noooo. She's a stripper, Coop. You can't actually be *seen* with her!"

"I'll see you later, Ky."

I glanced back into Kyle's office in time to see him tossing his paperwork into the air and kicking the side of his desk.

He was so dramatic sometimes.

SHE LOOKED PERFECT. She was wearing a pair of sweatpants and a sweatshirt, and somehow she managed to look fucking great. Her eyes were hidden behind dark sunglasses, and I instantly stood up from the table at the café when she walked in. She quickly raised her hand to stop me from greeting her. She took the seat across from me and I lowered myself back down.

What was there to be said? I figured I should take a stab at it.

"Andie last night was—"

"Call me Andrea, Cooper. And last night was a mistake." She removed her sunglasses and roughly rubbed her hands across her tired face.

Sitting back in my chair, I looked at her, taking note of

the puffiness of her eyes. I had a small feeling I was the cause of her suffering. I didn't know what to do or how to make it better. I laid my hand across the table to give her comfort, but she refused it. I felt like such an ass. She'd opened up to me last night, and I took advantage of her.

"I'm sorry," was all I could think to say.

Lowering her head she shrugged. "It's not your fault. But if you could do me a big favor and pretend this never happened? Please? I'm not the same girl I was back then when you knew me."

"And I'm not that same guy, Andrea." The fact was that I didn't want her to be that same girl that I knew. I was so deeply engrossed with the broken creature before me and I wanted to capture her out-of-order smile in my mind forever. A beautiful mess she was. She was everything my soon-to-be-ex wife wasn't. And I wanted to know more. I asked her to give me a chance.

She wouldn't. She explained once again how she had already broken one too many rules.

"Please. Cooper, trust me. You're better off. Don't text me anymore. Don't show up at the club. Don't reach out to me. I'm sorry about all that is going on in your life, but that's not my problem. And to be honest, my issues aren't yours."

Andrea stood up from the table, placed her sunglasses back on, and walked out of the café. I wanted to follow after her, but hell, what right did I have to do such a thing?

CHAPTER SEVEN

Andrea

UGH. I FELT terrible for how harsh I'd had to be with Cooper, yet I knew if I hadn't been he would still show up. And I'd needed to make it clear to him that I wasn't interested in getting to know him, or anyone else for that matter, anytime soon. I stood outside of the café and literally counted the beats of my heart. One hundred and twenty beats per minute. I turned back to look through the glass window at Cooper and pounded my fist against my waist.

"We need rules," I insisted as I barged back into the café and sat across from him.

"*Pretty Woman* rules?"

I smirked at his sarcastic tone and took off my sunglasses. "I'm serious, Cooper. Listen, I'm messed up. I really am. And you're…" I stopped, not wanting to offend him. He sipped at his coffee and kept his eyes on me.

"You're going through some stuff, too."

"This is true."

"But for the first time in a long time… last night… for a

small bit of a moment, I didn't feel like constantly dying." I rubbed my eyes, and cussed under my breath, realizing there was eyeliner on my fingers, which meant it was smeared all across my face. Without hesitation, Coop took a napkin and wiped the hot mess that had attacked me and turned me into raccoon eyes. A rush of heat ran through my body from his touch, a feeling I would beat myself up for later on.

He sat the napkin down and held up his index finger on his left hand. "Andrea. Over here is Chaos. Which we both know pretty well. And over here..." The right hand index finger flew up. "Over here is Order. I'm gonna assume both of us are pretty damn far from Order, yet we've already hit rock bottom Chaos. So how about we just explore the space in between the two?"

The space in between. The place where we wouldn't have to talk about the past or worry about the future. The place where we didn't get personal or talk about our dreams and fears. The place where any level of affection and tenderness was simply a way to forget about past hurts. A type of drug that drowned out the rest of the world. I could do the space in between.

"We can have a code word so we don't have to call or text each other asking for..."

"Sex?" He smiled as he raised an eyebrow. I could feel my cheeks redden as I nodded.

His eyes shifted towards the table next to us, where a woman was holding her drink. "Soda pop."

"Soda pop?"

As he lowered his voice, his eyes narrowed and zoned in on me. "Soda pop has a way of always being wet and with the right amount of pressure... with the right amount of constant shaking, it will suddenly..."

"—Explode..." I softly sighed. He was being overtly sexual. He sat back in his chair and sipped at his coffee. Crap, now I knew my whole face was the color of a freaking tomato. Back to the topic at hand and not how I was suddenly in need of a Coca-Cola.

"And when one wants out?" I asked.

"One walks away. It's that simple. No strings. No commitment. No sitting by the telephone waiting for a call. If person A finds Order in their life first, then person B must respect that and move on." He leaned across the table closer to me and his sexy southern sounds made my insides twist. "We need another safe word. If it gets too serious."

"Panda," I said.

With one eyebrow raised, he questioned my word choice. "Panda?"

"It's my favorite animal." I leaned closer to him as he moved a piece of my hair from my face.

"That sounds personal."

Crap. He is right. Before I could respond, his lips were traveling over mine and I let him explore my palate awhile before pulling back. Somehow overnight I had grown quite addicted to his kisses. Perhaps it was his kisses alone that dragged me back into the café. He picked up a toothpick from the table as he stood up and placed it between his lips.

"Panda works for me." He winked at me and walked out of the café leaving me sitting there, biting my bottom lip. I wanted to chase after him, push him up against a wall, and slide my tongue against his neck. I wanted to moan his name softly as his hands traveled to my butt and lightly squeezed it. I wanted him to lift me up. I wanted to wrap myself around him as I whispered the words soda pop into his ear over and over again.

But I figured I should play it cool. I didn't want to seem needy. I'd wait for him to text me. There was no way I'd text him.

Crap, crap, crap. Panda, panda, panda.

CHAPTER EIGHT

COOPER

THEY WERE PLAYING reruns of our reality show that night. I couldn't help but watch. How did my life get like this? Shutting off the television, I sat in the dark hotel room and stared at my hand that had driven through a portrait a few months ago. The fucked up truth was I appeared a lot more like my father than I ever wanted to. That thought was messing with my brain. Reaching into my wallet, I pulled out my wedding band and ran it through my fingers. I kept thinking about what Jesus had told me in the clinic about Iris. "What your wife did had nothing to do with you." But was that true?

I wondered if I had been there for Iris after the two miscarriages, instead of at the bar drinking, how different things might have been.

My mom was an artist. Growing up in a house with an artist and an alcoholic, was quite interesting. I remember one night my father wanted her to stop painting her 'fucking pieces of shit' and cook him dinner. It was three in the morning, which was when mom said she found her inspiration. Looking back, I realized she was really up at three a.m. to make sure the asshole came home from the bars and didn't end up in a ditch somewhere. I'd sat and watched him yell at her, spit at her, and belittle her from the top of the stairs.

"You stupid bitch. Stop wasting our money on this garbage." He yanked her from the canvas and started saying things that could fuck up anyone's mind. He threw her painting and raised his hand as if he were going to slap her across the face.

My stomach twisted as I watched my mom cry and beg him to stop drinking. When I saw that hand of his hovering over her, I leaped up and screamed, shoving him away from her. The taste of the blood dripping from my upper lip was a surprise to me when he shoved me across the living room floor. The way my father's eyes shifted to a person I'd never known terrified the living hell out of me. "Stop it!" I heard Mom cry as she raced over to me and stroked my hair. "Are you all right, Cooper?" Tears were streaming down my face and I shook my head. That night and many other drunken nights, were forever captured in my brain. A memory photograph book I wished would vanish.

That was the first summer I went to stay in Wisconsin. My mom had packed me up and sent me on an airplane by myself. Ever since she'd met my asshole of a dad her connections to her family faded. He moved her away from everything she knew and kept her to himself in his home state of South Carolina. Mom didn't think much of it—she was in love. But on the day she called my uncle for help, he was more than willing to allow me to spend the summers at their home. Before she sent me off the first year, she handed me a Polaroid camera—that camera changed my life.

My father was the alcoholic, yet it appeared my mother was the one with the illness. Dad was her sculpture and she was trying to shape him into something he wasn't. I wondered, if she would have gotten on the plane with me, how different things might have been.

I slid the wedding band back into my wallet; I wasn't ready to part with it yet. Shit. I was going to let her be the first to text, but sitting in the dark hotel room with nothing left but memories was too much. I was in need of some forgetting.

Fuckin' A.

Soda pop.

CHAPTER NINE

Andrea

HE LIGHTLY STROKED the side of my face with his hand, my arms and legs intertwined with his. His body heat against mine made it easy for me to not want to move from that hotel bed ever again. This time it was different. He kissed me harder, deeper. His arms forcefully flipped me over as his mouth covered every inch of my body. He was trying to forget a lot that evening. I didn't mind. It made it easier for me to forget, too.

"I should get going..." My mind started racing trying to figure out how I would exactly get home. Ladasha and I had just paid rent, and I only had a few dollar bills left after the taxi ride over here. I didn't know it would cost that dang much and now I was completely...

Oh my... .One moan and my worries about money disappeared. Cooper started to touch me in ways that made everything better. The way he massaged every single inch of my body with only his thumbs made me want to scream his name for the rest of my life. His hands traveled to my stomach, sending shivers throughout me.

"Coop…" I whimpered as I closed my eyes. I heard a muffled growl on my neck as he continued to kiss me lower and lower…Down, down, down…

My back was ready to arch at his command as he climbed on top of me. My hips thrust towards him, begging for more attention. I didn't want to stop him. I ran my fingertips across his back, pulling him closer to my body. His lips glazed over mine as he lifted my thighs.

His sweet whispers turned me on more and more each time. "I want you so bad," he hissed as his tongue explored my breasts. My lips parted in time for him to slide his tongue inside. He lifted my hands and held them tightly against the mattress.

My quiet moans grew louder as the two of us grew closer to one another. His eyes locked with mine for a moment's time before we both shut them and let our heat fuel our connection. The world became a blur. There was nothing wrong on this earth within that moment and time. For the feeling of seclusion alone, I could see myself never leaving Cooper's side.

For the next two rounds of Cooper Davidson that occurred after the passionate kiss, I forgot all about my money worries. And I forgot about all my demons that were trying to eat at me each and every day. Soon all that was heard was our light breaths of exhaustion.

Best freaking soda pop of my life.

But it was time to go home. Before he could try to get me to stay a few rounds longer, I stood up and started to step back into my clothing.

"Let's get breakfast tomorrow," he proposed. I rolled my eyes to the ceiling and continued to get dressed. "Come on, you need to eat."

"Not with you." I laughed.

"Come on, doesn't that sound good?" He stood up and wrapped his arms around me, nibbling on my ear as my eyes closed. That *felt* good. "Eggs, bacon, muffins…Come on, Andie."

My mind filled with the image of Derrick calling my name for the last time ever. I had shivers running through me—unnerving memories taking over my brain. My eyes opened and a wave of coldness washed over me as I whispered, "Panda." Cooper stepped back, unsure how he had offended me. I smiled and shrugged my shoulders as I put on my jacket. "It's nothing personal."

"It's definitely personal." He could see the hurt in my eyes, but I ignored his expression and walked towards the door. Crap. How was I getting home? All I knew was I couldn't stay here any longer. Not with the way my emotions were lighting up. I stepped into the hallway and started walking down towards the elevator, but froze when my arm was grabbed.

"Here, take a taxi home," Cooper said, handing me cash. I felt ashamed and shook my head.

"You don't have to pay for what we did."

Cooper narrowed his eyes and looked at me as if I were crazy. "I'm not. I'm paying to get you home safe." He wrapped my head in his hands and kissed my forehead. I tried to hold the tears back. But I didn't take his money; it felt way too soon to be taking anything from him.

I pushed it back to him and smiled. "Thank you, but I'm good." My voice cracked as I said it and continued walking. A guy held the elevator for me and I got the feeling I would be taking that elevator ride and walk of shame quite often.

A SIGH OF relief filled my body as I stepped out of the hotel building and saw a taxi waiting a little ways down the street. Walking over to it, I had to tap on the window. It appeared the driver had snoozed off, and he was startled when he opened his eyes to see me.

"Hey, sorry. Are you running? I could use a ride."

He sat up in his seat and smiled a warm grin to me. He was an older man, probably in his fifties or sixties. He nodded at me and told me to hop in. Sliding into the back of the taxi, I gave him directions and allowed my body to sink into the hard cushions as I closed my eyes.

"What's wrong?"

I opened my eyes to find the driver speaking to me. What was he talking about? He was looking at me through his rearview mirror, eyes filled with worry. He motioned to my eyes which had tears falling. Crap. I quickly wiped them and gazed at his identification at the front of the car. His name was Joe, and he was a complete stranger, asking me what was wrong. Did I really look that broken?

"I'm sorry, didn't mean to pry. It's just... You're such a young girl. No need to look so sad."

He had no clue. I gave him a short smile, informing him that I was fine. It turned out I was a liar.

"I've been there before, too. A dark place. You wonder how things are ever going to be all right, ya know? But they will be. You gotta trust in the process. No one can be sad forever. Not even you."

I wished I could believe that. But sitting in the taxi, I was growing sick, watching the amount of money add up on the clock. When Joe pulled up to my apartment building, I sighed. I was five dollars short. I would have to run upstairs to borrow some cash from Ladasha.

I stepped out and went to hand him the money, telling him I would be right back with the rest. He pushed the cash back to me. "Keep it. Take care of yourself, all right? And if you ever need a ride, give your ol' buddy Joe a call. I know how easy it is to get lost in the Big Apple, and I'm pretty good at helping people find their way home." He handed me his card, delivered me a warm grin, and pulled off.

After that night, Joe became my official driver for my nightly flings with Cooper. He never charged me, which was sweet, but he also never judged me, which was even sweeter. He spoke to me about his wife, how much he loved her, how much she cared for him. He spoke of their struggles and how they worked through the issues no matter what. They had been married for almost forty years, and he prayed for forty more.

I wondered sometimes if I would ever get married.

DERRICK STOOD ON stage in front of the microphone, looking handsome as ever. When he performed he became the song, transforming into the lyrics, fully committing to the words. I just turned twenty-one, so I was filled with excitement to see him perform for the first time in a bar. He was so amazing up there. Such a natural.

A few of his friends filed in and surrounded me, looking as proud as I was to see him up there. His best friend Steve slugged me in the arm and before I could smack him, he pulled me into a hug.

"Welcome back home, soon to be Mrs. Stevens." Steve said as he sat down next to me.

"Thanks. Good to be back, as always." My eyes looked up to Derrick who was grinning in my direction and I turned to Steve, "Does he ever talk about how he misses me?"

Steve picked up his beer and rolled his eyes. "Don't do that Andie. I'm not your messenger boy." I fed Steve my best puppy dog eyes and whimpered. "He wrote you a new song."

My eyes widened with excitement. I loved when he wrote songs about me. I bit my bottom lip and looked up to my baby. "He loves me, huh?"

Steve cleared his throat and nodded, chugging his drink. "The best way he knows how."

Derrick finished his song and spoke into his mic. "A big thanks to everyone coming out tonight for your love and support. Now I'm gonna take a small break and go have a drink with my future wife."

He slid in next to me and kissed my neck. "You did amazing." I beamed with pride.

"I'm so happy you're here. I called you earlier, but it went to voicemail. Figured you weren't going to make it." He smiled and picked up my cell phone.

"Of course I was going to make it, don't be dumb." I warned him. Kissing my nose, he went searching through my phone. "What are you doing?" I wondered out loud.

He held up his finger to me and began speaking into my cell phone. "Hey! You have reached the voicemail of the soon-to-be Mrs. Andie Stevens. She cannot get to the phone right now, but leave her a message and she'll call you back! Bye!"

I smirked at his corniness and grabbed my cell phone back from him.

Mrs. Stevens. I could get used to that.

I SAT ON the couch, looking at all the missed calls on my cell phone from my mom. Seven. It had been awhile since I'd spoken with her, but I couldn't listen to her sob on the telephone anymore. I looked at the number of voicemails on my phone, which was exactly seven, too. Rolling my eyes I prepared to listen to my mom beg me to come home.

"Hi, Anders, it's your mother. I was just calling to see how you are doing. I haven't heard from you in a while. I wanted to see if you were able to make it to Thanksgiving. I know you said you were busy with your jobs...but...we would really love to have you. We've never had a

Thanksgiving without you..."

I placed the collar of my shirt into my mouth and bit down on it, as if to hold back my tears. "It's already sad enough that Derrick's family won't be joining us. His mom is pretty lost. But to not have you at the table..." Her sniffles were heard. *Geez Mom...*

"We all miss you. Whenever I say I want to call you at work your dad refuses to let me. Says it's not that kind of job. Daddy says he loves you and is keeping you in his prayers. I love you, too. Call me when you can. And honey, you should really change your voicemail."

I closed my cell phone and glanced at the coffee table in front of me. Ladasha always left her cell phone out for me to use for one reason and one reason only. As I lifted it, a level of shame washed over me. I began to dial my cell phone and listened to my voicemail. The moment I heard Derrick's voice speak to me through the telephone, my heart skipped a few beats.

"Hey! You have reached the voicemail of the soon-to-be Mrs. Andie Stevens. She cannot get to the phone right now, but leave her a message and she'll call you back! Bye!"

I ended the call, bit my bottom lip, and dialed again. This went on as long as I could allow it to until I picked up my cell and texted for a beverage of sorts.

CHAPTER TEN

COOPER

IT'S AS IF I was slowly breaking through with Andrea. Each night we met, the closer we grew. Each night we met, the softer her eyes became. Each night we met, our bodies stayed intertwined for longer periods before she or I ventured home. We never spoke about the past, and we never spoke of the future. Hell, that was good enough for me. It turned out you could learn the most about a person by lying next to them each night, listening to their breaths, watching what made them grow nervous or happy or angry.

I would be a liar if I said I wasn't slowly falling for Andrea, but I couldn't let her know. Because I was pretty damn certain she would run the other way. I would be slow with my actions, slow with my approaches, and give her the time she needed to find Order. To find me.

Yet today Kyle found the need to drop a huge damn bomb on me when I showed up to his office. I couldn't believe what he was telling me. Iris had lost her mind if she thought she could blackmail me into meeting with her. "I'm not doing it," I promised. I wasn't going to play her nasty games as she tried to get me back.

"She's been talking to the press about your dad," he said, staring directly at me. He wasn't focused on one hundred other things like always, which meant it was serious.

"He wasn't my dad."

"Cooper, you know what I mean. Listen, Iris has clearly lost her fucking mind and is talking about selling the stories. And I mean *all* of the stories."

"She's bullshitting. She wouldn't do that." She had to be. She wasn't evil; she was just a pregnant, cheating whore.

"Do you really want to take that chance?" Kyle pounded his fists against one another, his brows lowered. "Hold off on the divorce papers. Talk to her. Find out what it is she is after exactly. She wants a few pictures of you two together, happy in front of the paparazzi."

"That's crazy."

"That's Iris. Just do it, Coop. And one day this will all blow over." I wanted to believe him, but the stress filling his eyes told me he didn't even believe it. He'd been saying that for weeks now. And nothing had blown over. If anything, it was getting more complicated.

"ALL PACKED?" MOM asked, strolling over to me. I was heading off to Wisconsin to spend my third summer at my

cousins and I was finishing off an important project to take with me.

"What's this?" she questioned, picking up the book I crafted.

"Nothin'," I said, trying to grab it back from her. "Mom, come on, stop."

Her eyes started to tear up as I gagged at her overreaction to the book. "Who is she?"

"A friend." I wanted her to be more though, and I was hoping the book would help her notice me more. It was filled with pictures I had taken of Andrea and me over the past two summers. She was the most beautiful girl I'd ever known and I was prepared to ask her to be mine once my plane touched down in Wisconsin that evening.

My eyes shifted to my mom and I noticed a fresh batch of bruises on her wrists. "Mom, what happened?"

She smiled and shook her head, ignoring my question. "She'll love it, honey."

My heart broke whenever I saw my Mom hurt. My voice cracked as I tossed a marker across the floor. "I don't see why you stay with him...He's an asshole!"

"Cooper Michael! Watch your tongue!" She scolded me. She wrapped her hands around my face and kissed the top of my head. "You may want to add a little more ribbon."

On the plane ride, I sat next to the window, murmuring to myself, trying to create the perfect words to ask Andrea to be mine. The old man sitting next to me smiled and nudged my shoulder.

"Let me hear it, son," he said, and his wife looked over to me and grinned, nodding in agreement.

I was wary at first, but could use someone's help. I cleared my throat and sat up straight. "Andrea. I know we have only known each other for two summers. But if you think about it, we have only experienced about ten summers in our lifetime, so two summers together is actually a lot. And, I think you're pretty. Like pretty, pretty. So I mean, if you would like to date me, I would like to date you. And if we held hands, I promise I would never let go."

The old lady looked over to me and placed her hands on top of mine and grinned. "Perfect."

Perfect. I was ready, I would call her my girlfriend and I would kiss her cheek if she wanted me to. My heart was in my throat as I headed over to Andrea's house with Michelle. Michelle was yapping away as always, but I couldn't pay attention. I held the book close to my chest, excited for what Andrea would say.

It didn't matter. None of it mattered because by the time I reached her house, I saw another boy making her laugh. Hugging her. Holding her hand. I looked to my cousin and asked who he was.

"Derrick Stevens. He moved here in December."

December. He'd claimed her during the winter all because I was stupid and waited until the summertime.

CHAPTER ELEVEN

Andrea

LADASHA WALKED INTO the apartment to find me laid out on the couch and jumped on my legs with her jacket still on. She smelled the air and looked alarmed. "It doesn't smell like Derrick today." It didn't. I didn't spray his cologne into the air—I forgot. I guess I was too busy thinking about...

...*Coop*...

There was something about that guy that made me feel as if someday, I could be happy again. Then I would look to my engagement ring and hate myself a little bit more.

She didn't question the smell any longer. Her face was grinning ear to ear as she looked at me. "I tracked down my mom," she said effortlessly. I shot up from my laying position and stared at her, shocked. Ladasha never spoke of her mom, and as far as I knew she didn't have a mom.

"What?"

"That's why I came to New York," She explained, "To find my mom. My grandma said she was over this way and after long nights of finding people who knew her, I found her."

Why was she not freaking out about this? How was she so calm? There was so much I wanted to know, so many questions. I couldn't understand how any person could walk away from Ladasha and not look back. She was too special.

"She was strung out. Drunk, high, God knows what else." Ladasha's smiley face faded as she thought on what she'd witnessed. "She didn't know me. She didn't know my name. She didn't know my age. But she knew my face and I knew hers."

Ladasha's long eyelashes blinked as the tears formed and were prepared to fall. "And a knot formed in my gut because I am her. That's who I am going to be in a few years."

"That's not true," I hissed at her. It wasn't. Ladasha was a strong woman. She was a friend. She was a sister to me. And she was nothing like her mother.

"Isn't it? Look at me. I'm a fucking stripper, Andrea! With no family. No one. There's not a lot I got going for me."

"You got me," I said. I wiped her falling tears and reminded her she wasn't alone. As long as my heart would beat, she would never be alone.

"Meow."

I narrowed my eyes and looked at my friend, confused. "Excuse me?"

"Oh...that wasn't me." Ladasha opened her jacket and revealed a beautiful orange and brown cat resting against her chest. "I found her at my mom's. She looked hungry and there was no food over there. So I brought her home with me." She paused and looked at me with worried eyes. "That's all right isn't it? I didn't want her to go hungry..."

I laughed, took the cat into my hands, and listened to her purr. Ladasha was considerate. She was loving. She was talented, smart, and compassionate. She was nothing like her mother. I asked the name of the cat, and she grinned.

"Freckles."

Welcome home, Freckles.

I glanced at the time on my cell phone next to me and looked to Ladasha. "So I thought you were working tonight?"

"Roger gave me the night off. Turns out the ass kinda has feelings."

Placing Freckles on the ground, I cleared my throat. "Oh that's nice." I checked the time again and bit my bottom lip.

"Why are you acting weird?"

"What? Me? I'm not acting weird. So do you have any plans tonight?" I quickly asked, and she looked at me as if I had three heads.

There was a knock on the door and Ladasha narrowed her eyes on me. She turned towards the door and back to me. "You're not wearing Derrick's cologne." She whispered as she continued to sit on my legs.

"I know, I forgot—"

"No." She cut me off quickly and sniffed the air around me. There was another knock on the door, but Ladasha didn't care. "You're actually wearing perfume."

I laughed and shook my head.

"No. You are. And...you are not wearing Derrick's

sweats. You're wearing a dress. A red dress." *Knock Knock.* I should be answering the door but Ladasha was still holding my legs down against the couch.

"It's no big deal," I said as I tried to get up. *Jesus Christ, Ladasha is strong.*

"You're wearing your sexy panties, aren't you?" She mocked me as my cheeks turned as red as my dress. She shot up, went over to the door, and opened it. My heart skipped a beat when I saw Cooper standing there, camera around his neck. Ladasha's eyes landed on him and the camera before lightly shoving his shoulder. "What kind of weird shit are you two into?"

I covered my face with a pillow as I erupted into laughter. I watched as Cooper turned even redder than me and tried to explain how he took his camera everywhere. Which was true! Ladasha just wasn't buying it.

"I don't think we've actually met each other. I only witnessed you leaving my best friend in a sheet." Ladasha grinned with her tongue in her cheek. Cooper looked like a young guy who just met his girl's parents for the first time. I wanted him so bad when he was sexy and aggressive, but the timid, shy guy was just as yummy.

"I'm Cooper." He shook her hand and Ladasha held his grip for a moment, staring into his eyes.

"I know you, don't I?"

He grew a bit uncomfortable and I watched as his body stiffened. "I don't think so..."

"You're from that reality show! *The Davidson's Weddings,*" she exclaimed as Cooper nodded like his biggest secret had been revealed.

Ladasha let go of his hand, walked into the kitchen,

and grabbed a couple beers. She proceeded to toss one to me and tossed one to Cooper, who sat his down on the counter. "I hate reality shows. It takes away from the real actors. I mean, why would I watch some reality bullshit when I could watch Joseph Gordon-Levitt or Ryan Gosling for two hours? Reality television is ruining real talent." She opened her can of beer and sipped at it. She shifted her eyes to Cooper. "I mean, no offense."

"None taken. I completely agree with you." Cooper's nervousness began to subside as he got a feel for the type of loud personality Ladasha held inside of her small frame. I stood up from the couch and looked over to him, still standing by the door. I mouthed an apology to him for the sudden change of plans, and he smiled and winked at me.

"You look amazing," he said as he approached me and displayed his dimples.

"What? This? I just tossed it on."

Ladasha grunted loudly at the idea of me just tossing on a dress, and I shot her a stern look, which silenced her giggles.

"So what about your wife? Are you two not together?" Ladasha asked. She walked over and made herself comfortable in the chair. I had a feeling this was going to be a long night. Cooper sat on the couch and I sat next to him. Ladasha's question was pretty personal, and I could feel my heart start beating faster.

"Panda?" I whispered his way.

He grinned and shrugged. "It doesn't count if she asks." He turned to Ladasha and answered the best way he knew how. "It's complicated."

"Complicated? Like Nicholas Sparks complicated?"

she questioned. My gosh. Dasha was on tonight. Question after question.

"I can't say. I've never read his books or seen his movies," he confessed. Was I surprised a twenty-five-year-old male hadn't taken to reading Nicholas Sparks novels or watching his movies? Not really. But Ladasha was shocked. Her mouth dropped to the floor and she shot up, disappearing into her room.

While she was gone, I turned to him and he pulled me into the curve of his body. I fit perfectly and it felt good to be near him. "I'm so, so sorry. I thought she would be at work, and she had a really hard day so I can't really ask her to leave, and I totally understand if you want to call Panda and hit it out of here and—" I rambled on and on until my words were silenced with his kiss.

"I don't mind."

Oh my gosh...I was so glad he didn't mind. Ladasha reentered with a collection of movies in her hands. I quickly removed myself from Cooper's hold and smiled as my best friend wiggled her way to sit right in between Cooper and me.

"Okay. We can start easy with it. We'll start with *A Walk to Remember*. Then lead into *The Notebook*."

A double feature night was happening with the three of us. Cooper wrapped his arm across the back of the couch and chills ran through me as he lightly caressed my arm without Ladasha noticing. His eyes were glued to the television. And I couldn't be certain, but I was pretty sure he was tearing up during a couple of scenes.

Halfway during *The Notebook*, Freckles entered the room and walked across the television set. Cooper shrieked as if he had seen a ghost. "Holy shit! You have a cat!?" he shouted with his green eyes widened.

"We got her today. Isn't she sweet?" Ladasha grinned as she picked up our new housemate.

"I—I'm not really a cat person," he stuttered.

"You're afraid of cats?" I asked. He cleared his throat and said no. Ladasha brought Freckles near him and Cooper dramatically went flying over the back of the couch. "Holy crap," I giggled. "You're afraid of cats."

Cooper frowned. "I had a bad experience once. Remember my cousin Michelle's cat? Oscar?"

"Yeah."

"Remember when it went missing one summer night?"

Yeah. I remembered. Eric, Michelle, and I spent weeks hanging up flyers in search of that cat.

"Yeah. I kind of took my uncle's car and drove him to a different city after he attacked me in the kitchen."

I cracked up laughing. "Bullcrap." The look on Cooper's face was priceless; he appeared as if Freckles was a lion ready to kill him. He lifted his shirt and to show Ladasha and me the marks from his fight with Oscar the feline.

I narrowed my eyes to zoom in on the marks Cooper was certain were there, but I didn't see anything. He glanced at his side and pointed. "Come on, I know you see that!" Higher his shirt went.

Ladasha raised an eyebrow as she looked at Cooper's abs and murmured, "Meow."

Cooper let out a small chuckle and lowered his shirt as he mumbled to himself. "It must be the lighting in this room."

Right. The 'lighting' is to blame for his invisible scars. How come I didn't think of that?

Ladasha's eyes met with mine and she gave in to a fake yawn with Freckles in her arms, "I'm so tired. I hope you two don't mind me dipping out on the movie..." She winked at me and walked into her room. "It was nice meeting you, Cooper."

"You too, Ladasha." He grinned.

Door slammed. Ladasha was gone.

"Afraid of cats?" I smirked as Cooper came over to me and sat on the coffee table directly across from me. Whenever he came near me, I could feel my insides become twisted. He made me so nervous in the best possible ways.

"You don't understand. Oscar liked you. You were pretty."

"*Were* pretty? Past tense?"

He leaned in and took my hands into his. He kissed my palms. "You know what I mean."

I shook my head and stood up. "I'm going to go take a shower and head to bed. Sorry this night fell apart." Walking to the bathroom, I could feel his eyes glued to my body. I knew he thought I was more than pretty.

When I peeked back at him, I could see him running his hands over his face. "All right well, I'll talk to you later." He walked to the front door and opened it, but quickly closed it once he heard me whisper.

"Join me."

THE HOT STEAM filled the room, fogging up the bathroom mirror and windows. "Cooper…" I moaned as he pinned me against the wall and ran his fingers across my back. I watched as the water hit against our wet bodies and delivered us with more passion than we had yet discovered. He lifted my lips to his and slid his tongue into my mouth, allowing his to cover mine.

"Coop, please…" I begged as he lifted my right leg up and lightly massaged my upper thigh. My moans were growing louder and he lightly whispered how much he longed for me, making me hotter and hotter.

The water dripped down his nose as I kissed his chin and whimpered for more. As he reached to run his fingers through my hair, his arm accidently hit the soap shelf and sent it to the ground, making a huge crashing sound. I burst out laughing. He joined in on my laughter, and Ladasha started banging against her bedroom wall, which was on the other side of the bathroom wall of course.

"Keep it down, freaks!"

I couldn't stop laughing. It was clear soda pop wasn't in the program for tonight's events, so it was best the two of us let that idea go.

The water kept showering down over us as we sat down in the tub. Cooper's body behind mine felt so right. We didn't speak. We just lay there with our eyes closed. Cooper kissed my shoulders, sending a coolness down my back. I was slipping in and out of sleep as he whispered to me. I nodded, stood up, and stepped out of the shower as he followed my suit, shutting off the faucet.

His beautiful eyes studied my body as I held my arms up in the air. He picked up my towel and wrapped it around my body. Enclosing his arms around me, I led him to my bedroom. We lay there in the darkness next to one another for what seemed like forever. "I should go," he whispered into my ear as I was almost asleep.

"It's late. Stay," I sighed. His soft kiss to my lower ear and his arms wrapping around me told me what his choice was.

"I was wondering what it would be like, too."

"What's that?" I asked, looking into his beautiful eyes. I chose to only blink whenever he did, just so I wouldn't miss those eyes staring into mine.

"Moving on." He kissed the tip of my nose and closed his eyes. For the first time in a long time, I wasn't sad anymore. I didn't have this ever growing numbness to my soul. I wasn't emptied inside.

I could feel again.

CHAPTER TWELVE

COOPER

SHE WAS SLEEPING when I woke up next to her. I didn't want to move. Dammit, she was so stunning. Her arms were wrapped around a pillow and her beautiful body covered with a sheet. Her bare shoulders peeked out at the top of the sheet, and I couldn't help but allow my lips to travel to them, giving her soft kisses. I watched her legs wrap together and for awhile I just stared at her body rising and falling. Her breaths were even, calm and steady. Hell, she even slept perfectly. If we never left this spot, if she never rolled over to greet me, if our lips never found way to each other again, I would be all right with that. This moment, right here... This was enough.

I remembered her, from when we were younger. She probably didn't remember me as well. My nine-year-old self actually believed he loved her at one point.

I was a smart kid.

My mind wandered back to my conversation with Kyle; I knew I had to meet with Iris in a little while, but I hadn't found the strength to move my eyes away from

Andrea.

I lightly kissed her nose and watched her wiggle it as she opened her eyes. "Good morning," I said.

A small grin rested on her face as she closed her eyes. "I've been thinking. Eggs and bacon sound good."

She wanted breakfast. With me. The walls she was so determined to keep up were crumbling, and I felt for the first time, Andrea Evans was finally letting me in. And I was about to crush that smile on her face.

"I can't. Not today."

Her eyes reopened, and this time her blues were somewhat embarrassed. Fuck me, I was a terrible person. "No. I was just kidding anyway. Remember? The space in between. Nothing more, nothing less." She sat up in the bed and pulled the comforter closer to her body. My heart cringed as I watched her toughen up.

"It's not that. I want to get breakfast...I just need to handle some—" My phone started ringing, so I glanced at it and quickly answered.

"Hello?"

"Hi, Cooper?" The elderly voice on the phone was familiar to me; it was Ms. Wells from my hometown in South Carolina.

"Ms. Wells, is everything all right?" I turned away from Andrea as I listened, but I knew her eyes were glued to me.

"Oh, everything's fine. I wanted to update you on your mom. It's been awhile since I called. She has had a few rough nights this past month, but she seemed to settle down a bit this week."

"Is she okay?"

"She's fine. I gotta tell you though, she's been asking for you."

I felt like such a shitty son that I hadn't found the time to visit my mom. I glanced at Andrea, who looked concerned. The thought about how I didn't want to push her away after she was slowly opening up to me filled my mind. My conversation with Iris could wait, but Andrea couldn't. Maybe if I introduced a small bit of my past to her, she would open even more.

I went back to speaking with Ms. Wells, knowing Andrea was listening to my every word. "Thank you for calling, Ms. Wells. I'll be there as soon as I can."

Hanging up the phone, I ran my hands over my face. This sudden plan of mine could really blow up in my face, but I had to take a risk. Andrea sat up from the bed with worry in her eyes. "What is it?"

"My mom. She's not doing so well." I lied. I lied through my teeth and promised myself I would make up for the lie later on. "She's in South Carolina, and if anything happens to her...I gotta get going." I knew what I was going to say next sounded insane, but I had to ask. "Will you come with me? I just...I don't want to do this alone. I would ask someone else but..." I laughed. "There is no one else."

Her brows lowered. *Please say yes.* She was in deep thought and she finally spoke.

"Give me a few minutes to pack," she whispered.

While Andrea packed, I stepped into the hallway and called Kyle to let him know what was up. First, he yelled at me about rescheduling my meeting with Iris. I told him I was going to see my mom. He felt extremely guilty and sent good vibes. He loved my mom like he was her kid. Growing up, my mom made sure to look after him as much as she looked over me. He would always deny it, but I knew he would go visit her when I was on a long photo shoot or filming the reality show, to make sure she wasn't alone, and I'd thanked him for that. He'd just grumbled, calling me crazy, and delivered me his smart ass smirk which told me all I needed to know.

I wished the meeting with Iris could go without happening, but alas, Kyle went on to plan a new meet-up time. "You ready?" Andrea asked me as she glanced outside her front door into the hallway. I hung up my phone and smiled.

"Yeah. Let's go."

CHAPTER THIRTEEN

Andrea

I DIDN'T KNOW what I was doing. How did I end up sitting next to Cooper on an airplane to another state? If there was ever a moment to scream the word panda, now would be that time. I knew Roger was going to flip with me missing work, but it seemed Cooper's wallet would keep Roger quiet as long as needed.

He looked extremely drained as he stared out of the window. I could tell his mind was racing, probably thinking of the worst possible outcome. I knew the look because I had been there all too often.

"What is she like?" I asked. I placed his hand in mine and held on to him tight, letting him know he wasn't alone.

Cooper turned to me and I watched as his eyes softened from his troubled look. "She's funny. And artistic. Clever. She bought me this camera." Cooper looked at the camera around his neck and quickly snapped a photo of me. My lips curved into a smile as he continued. "She also bought me my first camera. She's the reason I got involved with photography. I remember when she gave it to me, she said..." He paused. He was getting lost in his mind again, but this time with warm memories. I patiently waited for him to share with me.

"She said that an okay photographer could capture a surrounding. A good photographer could capture an expression. And a great photographer—a great photographer could change someone's destiny for the best. And she leaned in and kissed my forehead and said 'Son, what are you waiting for? Go save some lives. You are destined to be great.'"

"She was right."

He shook his head in disagreement. "I photograph weddings and had a reality television show. I sold out my greatness for money."

"If you could do anything, what would you photograph?"

"Children." I saw a spark in his eyes as he said this. "I want to work on this one project where I photograph children's expressions next to the elderly. You would be shocked by how much emotions don't change throughout life. Happiness is the same in the eyes of a one-year-old and a one-hundred-year-old. It's a beautiful thing." I could hear it in his voice—his passion. It was like he wasn't even speaking to me—he was feeling what he loved.

He went on to tell me how interested he was in human beings as a whole. How complex we were as a species, how much darkness and light lies in each of us. "So if I could showcase any of my work to the public, it would be that. I would showcase us." He paused and wiggled his nose. "Well not 'us,' you and me, but you know. 'Us' as a universal whole." He rested his head against his seat and tucked a piece of hair that had fallen before my eyes behind my ear. "Although I would love to photograph us, too."

"I think it's brilliant. You should do it. And for the record, just because you went through a period of time where things were rocky doesn't mean you still aren't destined for greatness."

His crooked smile appeared as he nudged my shoulder. "Ditto." He lifted the armrest separating us and stared at me. I knew what he was wondering, and it made me smile because I could tell without him even asking.

"A studio. I wanted to open a dance studio."

"Wanted to?"

I grinned as he ran his fingers through my short hair. "I want to open a studio. My mom says it's unrealistic and I should really think about going back to school for a more career-focused major. That's just Mom though. She worries. Daddy says I inspire him to dream big. He's my biggest fan." I chuckled to myself, thinking about how heavy-footed Daddy was. "He even took dancing classes for my..." I stopped. *My wedding.*

Cooper could tell what I was going to say and he rubbed the back of my neck. His eyes told me that he was fully invested in our conversation. He listened without judgment of any kind. I wiggled in my seat, feeling a bit uncomfortable with how relaxed I was becoming around Cooper. But I couldn't help it. He made it so easy to not be...sad.

"I would love to see you dance."

"I would love to see your photography. Do you really believe what your mom said about a great photographer? That they could change someone's destiny?" I asked.

"Definitely."

I laughed a little. "Maybe you should take my photo." I yawned and thought of the lack of sleep from the night before. Cooper lightly tugged me closer. I effortlessly curved into his body and rested my head on his shoulder. "Maybe we should change the rules a bit," I suggested. I bit my bottom lip, unsure of what he would say. All I knew was I liked learning more about who he was. And I liked having someone I could speak to who wasn't from my small town who knew everything about Derrick and me.

"What are you thinking?"

As he studied my face, I studied his. His perfectly chiseled jaw line made me melt every time I looked his way. "Maybe we should be friends." It was as if I could feel his grin as he kissed the top of my head.

"I would love to be your friend, Andrea Evans." He paused and I watched him travel into the depths of his mind, stroking his fingers up and down my arm. "You know what else my mom said when she first gave me my camera?" He asked. I waited for his reply and listened closely as he continued, "She told me the first picture I should take should be of something beautiful and I should allow it to change me."

"What did you take a picture of?"

His eyes shifted to the window. He stared out into the clouds and his voice softened, "You."

CHAPTER FOURTEEN

COOPER

I COULD FEEL my heart pounding as we walked into the nursing home. Andrea had no idea about my mom's condition. She held on to my arm the whole time. I walked over to the front desk and received a warm smile from the old woman sitting, reading a magazine. The old woman was Ms. Wells. Her warm grin welcomed me and her small arms wrapped me in a hug. I bit the tip of my thumb, looking down the hallway in the direction of my mom's room. "How is she?"

"We had a rough morning. But after her meds this afternoon, so far so good." Her hand rested on my arm. "How are you, dear?"

I gave her a halfway smile and she nodded in understanding. At least it was nice to know Mom wasn't at her worse. "What year?"

Ms. Wells escaped into her mind. Searching for the exact detail I was requesting. She ran her hands through her silver hair and I saw her eyes sparkle as she retrieved the information. "2009. It must have been a happy time for her.

She hasn't stopped grinning."

Shit. I glanced back to Andrea. She was standing there trying to connect the dots of what was happening. Hell, if I were her I wouldn't know what to think. Digging into my jeans pocket, I pulled out my wallet, grabbed my wedding band, and slid it onto my finger. The light in Andrea's eyes slowly faded as she gave me a sad grin.

"You can wait out here if you want," I told her. I didn't want to drag her too far into the craziness that was my family. I just wanted her to see me in a different light than the bedroom. It wasn't until that moment when I started to regret my decision to invite her.

"I would like to come, if that's all right."

Dammit. She's perfect.

We walked over to my mom's room and I could feel the heaviness of the situation growing on my shoulders. I was praying. Praying she was all right. Praying she would know what was happening. Praying she was my mom today.

As Andrea and I walked into mom's room, I saw her sitting at a table, working intensely at something. I held up my hand to Andrea as a signal for her to wait by the doorway. I didn't want Mom to have too much of a commotion with me entering with another person.

She heard my shoes squeak as I walked inside. I sighed out loud when she turned to look at me and didn't appear frightened—she looked...Excited.

"Cooper!"

There was nothing sweeter than hearing my name from my mom's lips. She knew me today. She was quick to stand up and rushed over to me, wrapping her arms around me. I held on to her for quite awhile. Maybe Ms. Wells was wrong. Maybe somehow Mom's mind had traveled back to present day. Maybe she wasn't trapped in the sick time capsule that kept her wandering down a dark path of memory lane.

But quickly my grin faded.

"I thought you weren't coming back from the honeymoon until next week, honey."

Shit. It was 2009. And I'd just married Iris.

Her eyes shifted to the doorway and landed on Andrea. "Well, what are you doing out there, Iris? Come on in! Let me get you two some coffee! I can't wait to hear all about it!"

"No, Mom, we don't need coffee. We had some on the way." I walked over to Andrea and spoke softly. "I'm so sorry..."

She shook her head and smiled. "What's her name?"

"Grace."

Andrea approached her and pulled her into a hug. "It's so great to see you, Grace."

I laughed. I was amazed by how okay Andrea was with all of this. She was going out of her way to make the situation seem somewhat normal. The weather here was in the 70s. It was pretty damn nice to walk outside without coats. But what was nicer was seeing Andrea in a tank top and tight jeans. No makeup. It wasn't needed. She seemed so simple. So perfect. She never worked as hard as Iris did with her appearance, which made it so easy to fall for her natural beauty.

"Honey, what did I say about that? Don't call me Grace! Call me Mom! Come on, now. Sit, sit." Mom ushered her into the room and sat us down on her bed. She took the chair across from us. It was so strange. We were sitting in a nursing home, yet in my mom's mind we were sitting in her living room. How could that be? I wished I could take a drive through her brain to see what was happening.

"So how was Thailand?" she questioned.

Andrea looked at me and nudged my arm. "You tell her, babe."

I went into explaining the beauties of Thailand. The wonderful elephants we rode. The beautiful buildings, the museums, the amazing stone structures. The pandas at the Chiang Mai Zoo were pretty astonishing, but the fact that the word panda was now forever engraved in my heart as a connection to Andrea made it even more remarkable. It was her favorite animal, and there was not a doubt in my mind that the woman I wished I could have taken to Thailand was sitting next to me.

I found myself falling for her each moment our eyes locked. Each time she caressed my hand. I knew I wanted to fix Andrea, to help her move on. But the truth of the matter was that she was somehow fixing me.

Mom was happy. I hadn't seen her happy in such a long time. Whenever I asked Iris to come visit with me, she said she felt uncomfortable with nursing homes. And she hated lying to my mom about the time period. She thought it was unhealthy the way I played along with her illness. But I didn't think of Mom as being ill. I thought of her as being lost. And if I were lost, I would hope to have someone around me who was willing to help me find my way home.

Her eyes shifted to Andrea's ring finger and she gasped. "Where's your ring!?"

Shit. There wasn't a ring. At least there wasn't until Andrea reached into her purse, pulled out her engagement ring from Derrick, and slid it onto her finger. Holy crap. She was as fucked up as I was, and I found it pretty damn sexy. I knew it was messed up.

The three of us talked for hours, discussing stories of the past and welcoming Andrea into my history. "You know, I bought him his first camera." Mom smiled like she was the proudest woman on this planet. It felt good to see her feeling well.

"Yeah, he told me. He said you inspired him to be great." Andrea leaned near my mom, her expression filled with care and compassion. "He also said you're the greatest artist he knows."

"Yeah, well you know. Cooper's a liar like that." She winked at Andrea as we all laughed. I couldn't think of the last time I was able to actually sit down and have what felt like a real conversation with my mom. Sure, she thought the year was 2009, but it was turning out to be the best year of my life. Who said you couldn't rewrite history?

"YOU WERE BRILLIANT!" I exclaimed as Andrea and I walked out of the nursing home. "I haven't seen her like that in... forever. Thank you, Andrea." We walked over to the rental car we picked up from the airport, and before opening the door for her. I stared at her. She leaned her back up against the car and her soft lips curved into an easy smile. I stood close to her and repeatedly kissed her forehead. "Thank you."

"Thank you for allowing me in." Her eyes shifted to the ground, and I could tell there was something on her mind.

"What is it?"

"Can I ask what happened to her? Or you can still call panda on this situation."

My foot began to tap the concrete beneath us as I started to relive the accident. It was right after I'd moved my mom away from my dad. I was out of state doing a photo shoot spread for a magazine and I received a frantic call from my mom.

My father had showed up and forced her to take a ride with him in his piece-of-shit pick-up truck. I was sure his breath was drenched in its normal whiskey cologne. At some point on the line, I could hear my mom screaming. She seemed absolutely terrified and she dropped the phone in the car. "I should have been there."

"You didn't know. There was no way you knew."

"Yeah but, didn't I? I should have moved her out of the state. Away from him." I continued to tell her how the truck got wrapped around a pole and my mom slipped in and out of coma. My father died on impact. And when she finally woke up, she thought it was 1992. She thought I was her brother, Travis, and she was so deeply in love with my father and hurt that he wasn't there.

"The doctors thought her mind would start to

unscramble itself over time, but after the first year, there was little hope."

"Is that why you don't drink?"

No. I didn't drink because it landed me in the mental hospital. But I didn't want her to know that. "Part of the reason."

"I'm so sorry, Cooper."

Her blue eyes grew very blue, something that happened when she became emotional about a topic. The idea of a car accident still had to tug at her bruised heart. This trip wasn't about making her sadder, so I needed to let her know it was okay. "Today was a good day. Let's hold on to that."

She wrapped her arms around my back, and pulled me closer to her. We stood there for a moment, taking in what we had witnessed with my mom. The nurses glowed with how we left Mom in a better state than she had been in awhile. I planned to return tomorrow. But right now, all I wanted to do was hold on to Andrea.

She pulled my lips to hers, lightly kissed me, and nibbled on my bottom lip. "I'm hungry."

I raised an eyebrow and felt a sudden twitch in my jeans. "A soda pop hungry?"

She tossed her head back and laughed as she rolled her eyes. "I'm hungry, Cooper. Food hunger." She climbed into the car and I closed the door for her. Wandering over to the driver's seat to get in, I couldn't help but smirk at her reaction to my question. Hell, you gotta try.

CHAPTER FIFTEEN

Andrea

IT FELT GOOD to laugh. I sat across from Cooper in the Italian restaurant and I was famished. For the first time in a long time, I felt like I could eat everything around me. The conversation with Coop was so easy; he made me feel comfortable, and he never came on too strong. I glanced at the rings still on both our fingers from earlier with Grace. Holding my hand up to him, he slid off the engagement ring, and I did the same for him.

"So my cousin is dating your brother."

"Yup. Since middle school."

"And they are throwing the big Christmas party."

"Yup." My mom had been calling me nonstop since I missed Thanksgiving, and now she was getting heavy on my case because I wouldn't be home for Christmas. I wasn't ready to return. I felt I was slowly moving to Order, but I knew the moment I stepped back into Derrick's and my hometown, I would slide back down to Chaos. It was the curse of the small town.

For the past few years, Eric and Michelle had thrown

big Christmas parties at Michelle's family's mansion. Every year there was a theme to the party. Each year, I would be in charge of the group dance that happened at the beginning. Not this year. This year, Rachel was in charge of it. The whole town would come to drink, laugh, and gossip. That was all too much for me. The bruise was still too painful. So I made up lies. I told my mom if I weren't working, I would lose my 'jobs.' I told her I had auditions for dance schools in the next few weeks. I told her I was pulling my life together. I told her anything and everything to try to get her to back off a bit.

Of course she didn't care. She just wanted me home. So she kept badgering me, asking me—no, begging me—to come home at least for the holiday. That was when the ignoring of her calls happened.

"Are you going?" His eyes stayed on me. At times it was hard to look at his handsome self. I watched as he wiped the sweat falling from his forehead with a napkin, thinking about how I would love for him to make me sweat. But I remained focused on the conversation at hand.

"No. I'm not." He looked surprised, I shrugged my shoulders. "Are you?"

"Nah. I haven't seen or spoken to them in years. And it's pretty short notice for me..." That was good. It would have been awkward for both of us to attend the party. After the connection we had discovered, I could see going back to Albany, Wisconsin, as a terrible idea. The whispering, gossiping ladies of the town would have a field day with us, making up nasty lies to keep their minds busy for a few hours each day.

Out of the corner of my eyes, I saw a young girl,

probably ten or so, arguing with her father as they gestured towards Cooper. "I think you have a fan."

Cooper saw the uneasy father, smiled, and waved the two over. Excitedly, the daughter came bouncing over to the table, pulling her dad's arm. The girl gasped with joy. "I don't know who you are!"

I couldn't help but raise an eyebrow. If she didn't know who Cooper was, why was she so excited to see him? The girl's dad rolled his eyes and joined in. "So sorry. My daughter saw you from our table. Her mom and she are huge fans of your show."

Cooper turned his charm on high, and I melted inside as I listened to his soft southern tones directed at the girl. He made the interaction feel completely comfortable. A gift of his, I supposed—making anyone feel comfortable.

"Is that so? You like my show?"

"I don't know who you are," the girl repeated.

Her father sighed. I could tell he was exhausted from a long father-daughter day. Daddy used to have the same look when I was a kid. "It's opposite day. She knows who you are. Right, April?"

Her lovely smile brightened the room as she nodded. "You are not going to take my wedding photos when I'm old enough to not like boys."

"Of course not. Well, don't have your daddy and mama call me when you're not getting married."

"Who aren't you?"

Cooper's eyes shifted to me for a brief moment before turning back to the southern belle. "This is not my date."

I could feel my cheeks redden. I was—er, well, *wasn't*—his date.

THE SPACE IN BETWEEN

The father grabbed his daughter's arm and started to pull her away. "Okay, I think that's enough. Time to leave them alone."

Cooper smiled. "Happy Opposite Day, April." The two walked away, and I sat there speechless. He was so smooth with the way he handled situations. He grabbed my hand from across the table and kissed it. "It's opposite day."

"That's what I hear."

AFTER DINNER, WE pulled up to Cooper's house he kept in South Carolina. It was beautiful—a perfect, southern, large piece of property. It was gated off from the outside world, and had green grass and wildflowers gracing the front yard. As we pulled into the drive-way, I noticed some detailed cars sitting there.

I had a strong feeling Cooper was a lot richer than I had known. Yet, it seemed that it didn't go to his head. He was nothing more than a kind-hearted guy who happened to have a heavy checkbook in his pockets.

"It's so stunning here." I looked at the white house with the large porch and yellow shutters on the windows. I felt as if I'd walked into a movie. Ladasha would have loved it; it looked like a place that belonged in a Nicholas Sparks movie. Cooper stepped out of the car and wrapped his arm around my waist as I dissolved into the curves of his body.

"Yeah, I forgot how much I loved this place. Iris and I only stayed here awhile before she decided she wanted to move to New York. But this..." His eyes sparkled as he looked around and opened the door to the house. "This is home."

We spent the rest of the night in his bedroom, discovering more gems about each other. The only things we didn't speak about were Iris and Derrick. Those two were off limits.

Cooper had played baseball when he was a kid. His middle name was Michael. He once did the cover for a magazine involving tigers, which was terrible for his fear of cats. He got in a fist fight with a guy who was cussing out a bartender who made a mistake in a restaurant. He wasn't religious, but he believed in Jesus.

Little known facts about Cooper Davidson.

He was lying down on the mattress, staring at the ceiling. I watched his chest rise and fall each time he inhaled and exhaled. "I mean, think about it though..." He said, lifting one of his arms and resting his head in the palm of his hand. "What if there was something or someone bigger than all of this? Bigger than us? And what if he appeared to us in our darkest moments? Just as a person to give us a little extra push? I mean, what were the odds? Me walking into the strip club in New York City that night to meet you. Andrea...this *has* to mean something."

Maybe he was right. Maybe there was some kind of higher power that pushed Cooper and I together that night. Who knew? I didn't believe in much after the accident. I doubted everything and everyone. But if there was something out there...Something bigger, like a grand order to this crazy world, then I promised myself that I would thank the higher power if I ever got the opportunity. I would thank them for sending me Cooper so I wouldn't feel so alone.

His eyes met mine and he grinned, falling back onto the mattress. "You think I'm crazy."

Shaking my head, I scooted closer to him, and brushed my fingers across his chest. "No. I think you're passionate about your beliefs. And I think I like it. I like how you get lost in your thoughts sometimes."

The right side of his lips curved into a halfway smile. He placed his hands on my sides and lifted me up, so I was now straddling him. "Yeah? What else do you like about me?"

I grinned, knowing that the list was growing daily. My fingers traced his lips, feeling him sigh against my touch. "I like your lips. But not just because they deliver kisses in the gentlest way, but because when they move, they are sincere with their words. I believe whatever comes out of them."

I moved my fingers across his cheek. "I like your dimples, because they only appear when you are happy. And I like that you're happy when you're around me." His smile grew wider and his dimples grew deeper, making my heart skip.

My hands wrapped around his head and I lowered my lips to his forehead, resting them there. "I like your mind. How it works, how it cares." Next my eyes locked with his, our lips almost touching, as I continued speaking. "I like your eyes, and how they focus on whoever's around you. And you don't just notice them, but you *see* them. Many people look, but they don't see."

And lastly, I lifted myself up, and placed my hands on his chest. I tried to hold back the tears as I cleared my throat, realizing what I liked most about him. "And most importantly, I like your heart. I *really* like your heart. Because when you walked into that strip club, you didn't judge me. And when your mom was lost, you didn't scold her. And when that little girl said it was opposite's day, you didn't demolish her beliefs. Each time you just smiled with those dimples, saw us with those eyes, and comforted us with those lips."

The playful energy grew extremely serious as the two of us just sat there. I smiled his way and he smirked back to me. Shoving him lightly, I climbed off of him, and turned away. I poked fun at him, trying to take away from the seriousness of it all. "Come on, this is clearly the point when you tell me what you like about me."

I felt him sit up and position himself behind me. When he started to give me a back massage, I pretty much died. He had the hands of Gods and knew exactly how to work them. *His hands...I liked those, too.* I was his the moment he touched me. My eyes closed and I allowed my body to relax into him massaging my lower back.

"What time is it?"

Opening one of my eyes, I glanced to the nightstand and looked at the alarm clock.

"11:58." My eyes shut again, too comfortable to remain open.

"It's still opposite day."

"For two more minutes."

I could feel his breath on the back of my neck as he whispered to me. "I don't like how you smell like honey and cotton candy. I dislike your blue eyes that I don't get lost in. I *really* dislike the seventeen freckles on your face. You know the eight on your forehead, six on your cheeks, and three on the tip of your nose? *Sooo ugly.*" I felt every word he said run through me as he continued speaking.

"I haven't thought about you every day since we met that one night." He kissed my ear over and over again—my favorite kisses. I felt the butterflies flying into my stomach. I was growing more and more nervous with each word. I wasn't sure how much more I could take, but he kept going. "In your eyes I don't see the missing pieces I've been searching for. And I know this isn't crazy... but I think I hate you, Andie."

The wind was knocked out of me. I opened my eyes. No…It was all too fast. It was only a few hours ago we'd decided we would actually be friends. Friends with benefits of course, but just friends. And now he was telling me that he loved—*err, hated*—me.

And the first thing that came to my mind was Derrick. How could I do this to him? It was only a few months ago he'd passed away. And I was sitting in a bedroom with another man.

CHAPTER SIXTEEN

COOPER

WHAT THE FUCK was I thinking? *Son of a bitch. Please stop crying.* Andrea's eyes were flooding with tears. She turned her back to me and kept saying it was all right. That she was fine.

"Clearly you're not, Andrea." *I'm sorry.* I couldn't believe I put my foot in my mouth in such a stupid-ass way. "I didn't mean it!" I swore. Yes, I did mean it. I loved her. I couldn't help it. How could anyone not love such a woman? Broken pieces and all. But if telling her I loved her meant she would shatter even more, then I would take it back. I would laugh it off. I would want her to doubt there was any truth to the matter.

She turned and wiped her eyes. Laughing, she shrugged her shoulders. "I'm all right. It's my fault. I shouldn't have gotten so personal with stating the likes earlier. I'm sorry, it's just…"

She paused and shifted her feet on the ground. I wished I could wrap my arms around her and protect her from the demons that were attacking her fragile thoughts, but I knew right now wouldn't be the time or place. I gave her the time she needed to arrange her thoughts.

"It's just—it's all crap, you know? That "Til death do us part.' That 'love forever and always' garbage. I mean, I know Derrick and I weren't officially married, but we believed in the vows the first day we met. And here's the thing…The person who dies from the car crash, he gets to leave. That's the end of it for them. But there's the other person still left behind in this damn place. The person still attached to those bullshit vows. And you're stuck. And you can't move."

She was overwhelmed. Her poor eyes were bloodshot and her small body shook with sadness. What was I doing? It was only a little over six months ago when she went through the worst tragedy any person could experience. The words she spoke were cutting me because I never truly stopped to see how she was still in mourning.

"And out of nowhere, it seems you start to forget the little things about him. His smells are gone from the pillows. His laugh is hard to imagine. And you feel guilty that you're forgetting, so you try hard to hold on to something that's not even there anymore. And you feel ashamed…"

Her eyes met mine and her legs trembled as she bit her bottom lip—a trait she had when she was nervous. "And you feel ashamed because you *like* so many things about someone else. And you feel as if you're cheating on your loved one."

"Andrea…Derrick would want you to be happy."

"I don't deserve to be happy."

"Why not?"

Her tears ran down her cheeks and she shook her head back and forth. She was fighting the biggest battle with her inner self. "Because I killed him."

I could tell it was that one thought which had been haunting her since the accident. I could tell she had never said those words before, but she thought them daily. And I could tell she meant it from the bottom of her heart. "No, you didn't."

She nodded franticly, everything about her being falling apart. "Yes I did. I did. I should have watched the road better. I should have focused. If it weren't for me, he would be alive."

I stepped close to her and she stepped back, shaking her head. I cringed a bit, watching her clam up. "Andrea..."

"I don't deserve to be..." She cried, rubbing her hands across her face.

"Don't say it." I warned her. She didn't think she deserved to live...She believed she should have died. That thought alone made me die a little. She shifted her eyes to the ground, shaking her head back and forth, gasping for air as her lungs went into overdrive. She was having a panic attack, and I was scared shitless that she was going to pass out any second now.

"Andrea, look at me. *Now*." I demanded. When her eyes met mine, I made sure not to lose her. "I need you to do something for me." Her head tilted to the side, wondering what I would request. Her tiny body was still a wreck from shaking.

I lowered my voice and held my arm out to her. "I need you to let me hold you, okay? Can you do that for me? I need to wrap my arms around you, and have you cry into me. Forget everything that has happened between us. Forget everything else in the world. Right now I just need to be the wall you lean up against to keep you from falling tonight."

A small breath escaped my lips as her fingers intertwined with mine. Relief filled me, watching her move closer to me. I couldn't give her space anymore. My arms wrapped around her small frame and I held on. She cried into me as she proceeded to break down even more. "Slow down your breaths, Andrea...*Slow*." The tears started to form in my eyes and I blinked them away before she would notice. Knowing that she was hurting in such a major way broke everything inside of me. I never felt so helpless in my life.

I held on to her for a long time after that. I didn't care how long we had to stand there; I was prepared to hold her for the rest of my life if she needed me to.

"I CAN SLEEP on the couch," she offered. I shook my head; she needed rest.

"No, of course not. You stay here. I'll grab one of the guest rooms."

"Are you sure?"

"Andrea." I smirked and nudged her to the bed. It was nice to see she had calmed down a bit. "If you need anything, I'll be two rooms down."

"I'll be all right."

I stood in the doorway, eyes on her. There was nothing I wanted to do more than protect her from any harm. But that night I did all I could. I shut off the light and walked out of the room. "Coop." At the sound of my name I was standing in the doorway, turning her light on once more. I waited for her to continue speaking as she rubbed her fingers over her tired eyes. "I'll be better tomorrow," she promised.

Leaning against the door frame, I shook my head. "No you won't. But that's okay... I'll wait."

She sighed, shifting around the bed sheets. "For how long?"

I could tell she thought she had run me off, but I wasn't going anywhere. "I'm here, Andrea. I'm here. And I'm not going to rush you. And I'm not even asking anything of you. But I'm here whenever you need me to be. How long will I wait? Take forever and multiple it by infinity. And then I'll wait some more."

Seeing her small smile appear made me grin. I nodded, told her to try to get some rest, and disappeared down the hallway to try to find a few hours of rest for myself.

CHAPTER SEVENTEEN

Andrea

MY SENSES WERE awakening to the smell of coffee lingering under my nose. The morning sun was dancing through the blinds and touching my cheeks. I rolled over in the bed, taking in the delicious aroma. My eyes stayed closed for awhile; they were so heavy—so tired.

I ran my hands through my hair, sat up in my bed, and looked at my surroundings. On the nightstand next to me was a tray with eggs, bacon, and a bagel. In a small vase were a few beautiful flowers. Pinks, yellows, whites. I assumed Cooper picked them from the front of the house. A sigh fell from me; even after last night he still picked me flowers.

As I picked up the cup of coffee, I breathed in the strong flavors before I sipped. *He even added cream and sugar.* The perfect amount. The coffee was still steaming hot, so it couldn't have been that long ago since Cooper delivered it.

I gobbled a piece of bacon down, and that's when I noticed a note sitting on the tray, under the vase.

ANDREA MAE,

My lips curved as I saw him call me by my middle name—one of the little known facts I'd shared with him the night prior.

> I hope you slept well. I left to go visit my mom for a few hours. I made breakfast (don't worry, I ran to the market for fresh food. You're not eating old food from the fridge). Enjoy! If you need or want to go anywhere, the keys to any of the cars are in the garage against the wall. Call me if you need anything
>
> -COOP

Part of me was sad I'd missed him, but then again I didn't want to face him after my breakdown last night. I didn't know what had happened; perhaps it was the wine or maybe the unconventional confession of love. Possibly it was both. All I knew was that I was pretty freaking embarrassed.

What would I do while I waited for Cooper?

DANCE.

I stretched on the tennis court in his backyard. The sun was covered by thin clouds, and would reintroduce itself to me every time the clouds traveled on to their next location. Placing my iPhone on the ground, I turned on my favorite music station. The tweeting birds added their own soundtrack to the moment, making it that much more special.

My heart was still aching for Derrick each day. But Cooper made the aching less intense. Cooper made me feel like I was floating. He made me feel alive. And since he wasn't here right now, I would turn to the next thing that made me feel good no matter what. Dance.

Rumi once said, "Dance, when you're broken open. Dance, if you've torn the bandage off. Dance in the middle of fighting. Dance in your blood. Dance when you're perfectly free."

I wasn't free from Derrick's hold on my soul yet. But I would dance anyway. The music started to blare from my small speakers and I moved across the tennis court. It was my stage and I, the dancer. I would spin, I would leap, and I would feel. Feel the excitement of losing myself in the dance. It was my drug and I was ready to overdose on it. I would twirl until the world appeared dizzy. I would bend my body and make love to the movement. My breath would be in total control. I was the instructor and my legs were the students. They would move when I commanded them to. They would fly when I needed them to.

I danced for hours. I danced as the sun grew tired. And then I danced some more.

I thought I heard the click of his camera before it happened—I didn't stop moving. I kept going. As I spun I could see him inching closer, snapping away at me. I posed for him. I leaped. I explored the space.

I let go.

I let go because I was sure he would catch me.

His sexy smile was hidden behind the camera, but I knew it was there. I finally brought myself to a halt. My legs were exhausted, so I allowed them to lie down on the tennis court. I lay down on my back as the sweat dripped down my face. It'd been so long since I allowed myself to stop and remember something I loved to do.

He lay down next to me, shoulder to shoulder. Turning to him, I felt the butterflies return. "How's your mom?"

"She had another good day. I think you helped make her better yesterday."

I bit my lower lip. He made me feel the best kind of nerves. "I think you're making me better."

Instant comfort. I glanced down at our hands; he held mine and we both lay silent with our heads turned up to the sky. I was surprised at how he wasn't extremely freaked out by me. Why didn't he go running after last night?

"Thanks for breakfast."

"Anytime."

I smiled. Because I knew he meant that.

CHAPTER EIGHTEEN

COOPER

THE SUN WAS shining brightly, but the winter breeze made coats necessary. I sat across from Iris outside the coffee shop, wishing I could be anywhere but there. We were wearing sunglasses, smiling at each other as the paparazzi stood back and took our photos. The trip to South Carolina had come to an end, and instead of sitting across from Andrea, I was stuck with my wife.

Iris was about six months pregnant, sporting heels that looked to be cutting off all blood flow to her feet. How could she be so damn stupid?

Through a grin I whispered, "You're a bitch." And she grinned and took my hand into hers.

"When are you coming home?" she softly asked. I wanted to pull my hand away and walk off, never to see her again, but what she had on me was big.

"Why were you talking about revealing information about Ken?" Turning to my father's past to get back to me was as low as one could get. I asked her what I had done that was so dirty that she would turn to these crazy measures.

"You left me." Her tone was so sincere and filled with sorrow that I almost felt sorry for the woman sitting in front of me. *Almost.* She saw the paparazzi and knew we wouldn't be able to hold the real conversation we needed to have, so she offered walking to our apartment—her apartment—so we could figure out where to go from here.

As we walked, Iris made sure to have me wrap my arms around her waist. Andrea was floating through my mind. I secretly wished she were the one my arms were wrapped around. I wished she were the one taking me home.

Right as we stepped into the apartment, I released my hold on her and started to holler. "What the hell are you trying to do to me, Iris?!"

"You left me, Cooper. You walked away and didn't look back. What was I suppose to do? You wouldn't talk to me." She cried as she took off her high heels and her jacket. "Tom doesn't want anything to do with the child. He's expecting his own with his wife…"

Tom Reed. The man who got my wife pregnant was ready to deny his own child to keep a lie going on for his wife. What a piece of shit. But there was one main issue I had to know. "What does that have to do with me?"

I wasn't the one who cheated. I wasn't the one who got knocked up by Tom. I wasn't the one who took our vows and threw them into a closet at the rehearsal dinner of our last episode of *The Davidson's Weddings.*

Iris walked over to me and placed her hands in mine. She led my hands to her stomach, making me raise an eyebrow. "We can raise her together."

Her. It was a girl. I would be lying if I said for a split moment I didn't consider it. That poor baby girl had walked into a crazy life, and it wasn't her fault. She deserved a dad. Not a father who would deny her existence for the rest of his life. She deserved a mom. Not a mother who wanted to lie about who her real father was. She deserved to have someone treat her like a princess. She deserved to *be* a princess. She deserved a dad.

But that wasn't me.

"You've lost your mind." I pushed her hands away from me and shook my head in disappointment. She was desperate. I could see it in her face.

"I'll give you a month. If you don't come back to me, I will expose everything. Your stay in the mental hospital. You breaking glass frames in your house. You leaving your pregnant wife. You leaving your mom to film a reality show…"

"Go to hell!" I hissed. She'd crossed the line. She had no right to bring my mom into this topic.

"I'm already there, Cooper!" she cried into the air.

"You cheated on me, Iris! *You* cheated. Not me!" What was wrong with this creature I used to love? I didn't know the person standing before me, and she was fucking making me sick.

Iris disappeared into the kitchen and returned with an envelope. She handed it to me. "Well, that's not what these photos say." She crossed her arms and rested them on her growing belly, "Those are just copies. I have more."

I opened the envelope and ran my hand over my mouth, sighing. *Shit.* I scanned the pictures and looked back to Iris. "You had me followed?"

"Hell yes I had you followed, Cooper. Who is she?"

Unbelievable. I stared at the different photos of Andrea and me in my hands and I didn't know what to think. It was all there, from the moment we first walked out of the strip club, to our café meeting, to the hotel hallway when I tried to give her taxi money. Even photos of us going to the airport.

"I can't believe you right now."

"Me?! I can't believe you stooped so low to go for prostitutes!" she yelled as my hand formed a fist and slammed against the wall; the veins were popping out of my neck. How dare she.

"Dammit, she's not a prostitute!"

Iris's brown eyes softened from her anger. As if she had any right to be angry with me. She let out a small chuckle and a giggling fit happened. "Don't tell me you like her. Holy crap, you like a prostitute."

The blood was boiling inside me and I knew I had to leave before I did or said something I would regret. The memories of the last time I stood in this apartment were floating back to my mind. It was cursed. This fucking place had to be cursed.

"I'll give you until New Years. To come back to me. Or I go to the tabloids," Iris said before I left.

"Get one thing straight, Iris. I am *never* coming back to you. Never." I couldn't breathe. I didn't know what to do. As I walked out, the paparazzi were still there, hammering me with questions about the rumors between Iris and me. The child's gender. The next season of the show. I tried my best to ignore them as I slid on my sunglasses and walked faster. It was all too much to ignore when a small girl, around the age of six, was walking with her mom and was pushed by one of the paparazzi.

"Jesus! Come on! Y'all are knocking over kids!" I hissed as I helped the girl up.

The man who made her tumble over gave me a devilish grin and said, "What are you talking about, Cooper? You kicked her over, not us. Have you been drinking? You should be more careful."

I wanted to kick his ass. I wanted to wrap my hands around his neck, shake him, and scream at him to wake the hell up. To get a real fucking job instead of finding a way to be a stalker and get paid for it. They were sick creatures who made a living off of destroying lives, just to sell a photo.

But I couldn't. I walked off and tried to figure out what the hell to do about Iris and Andrea.

I WALKED AROUND Central Park with my camera, taking photos. Shit, it was cold. I pulled my winter coat tighter and wrapped my scarf around my mouth to shield off the chill. I always felt at ease when I was doing what I loved. What I really loved. Unlike the garbage reality shows I had somehow gotten sucked into doing with Iris. She said it would make us grow closer. I told her couples who did reality shows were doomed to fail. She disagreed.

I was right.

I was avoiding Andrea. She had texted me a few times earlier that week calling for Soda Pop, but I couldn't. I didn't want to be seen with her in the city with the paparazzi covering my every move. It was to protect her. I should have told her about the photos. But if I did, I would lose her for sure. I had to work this through my head, figure out the best way to handle it without pushing her away.

The sunlight had faded for the night. I made my way to a bench and let out a heavy sigh. I needed more time to figure things out. More time to find a way to keep Andrea's name out of the tabloids. The first moment I'd seen her, I'd promised her I wouldn't say a word about her stripping, and now Iris was threatening to tell the whole wide world she was a damn prostitute.

My phone went off as I read the newest text message that slapped me with guilt.

Did I do something wrong?

I stared at all of the former text messages before this one, and they only read 'soda pop' between her and me.

She'd never written anything more than that, so to read those words stung me. *Did she do something wrong?* No. But I couldn't tell her. Not yet.

CHAPTER NINETEEN

Andrea

FREAKING A, I missed him. Why hadn't he called or texted? It'd been weeks since we last talked. Did he find Order before me? I felt so stupid for even thinking on the matter. Maybe I'd scared him off with my breakdown about Derrick. I wouldn't have been surprised. If I were him, I would have run too. I wish there was an un-send button for text messages, but there it was—my needy text sitting in his inbox.

Focus on something else. I needed a distraction. Dance.

It had been a few weeks since I had my first dance on the stage. The first night was terrible, the second night was embarrassing, and the sixth night was a bit better. Roger must have been pleased with my performances, because he was getting closer and closer to offering me the closing number. "We'll see," he would say whenever I'd ask. I wanted a shot at it. Jasmine told me there wasn't a chance in hell she would give up her spot, but everyone knew I was better than her. My degree in dance was really paying off. Thank you, college education.

When I walked onto the stage each night, it was as if I were in a trance. I tried not to think about it too much because it was all too depressing. So I danced. I moved my body. And I blocked out my thoughts. In a way it was somewhat a form of art. And moving my body in a way to create art was all right, in some twisted way.

The crowd that night seemed extra intense. There were loud rackets of noise traveling from the club to the dressing rooms. Bachelor parties, probably. I hated bachelor parties the most because the stupid bachelors always forgot that they were getting married in the freaking morning. So much disrespectful grabbing. I stopped applying my makeup when Ladasha walked over to me and leaped onto my makeup table.

"I've been thinking. Maybe I'll go back to school."

"You should."

Ladasha smiled, nodding with confidence. "I should. I always wanted to be a lawyer. Or a doctor. Or hell, a fuckin' English teacher. If it's the number two you spell it T-W-O. If it's like, 'I'm gonna have sex with him and him, too" it's T-O-O. That's my type of English lesson. I might even be the first black female president. Wouldn't that be political gold? The president's an ex-stripper." She grabbed her breasts and smiled widely. "Vote for Ladasha! I'll watch a few political movies for tips. It can't be that hard, right?"

She was slipping into her dark thoughts. I could tell when it happened because she always tried so hard to cover her sadness with goofiness. I knew better. Ladasha laughed lightly as she went back to applying her makeup, but I saw the slight glimpse of disappointment slip through her eyes.

"You can do it," I assured her. Ladasha could do anything if she didn't find the need to always run after awhile. I was really hoping she wasn't feeling the need to run any time soon.

Just then, two other strippers, Maria and Shelly, walked into the room and took their seats, doing what they do best—gossiping. Maria shook her head in disbelief. "Can you believe that?"

"Hell yeah I can believe it," Shelly chuckled, picking up a pink, glittery wig to go with her pink, tacky thong.

"What happened?" Ladasha asked.

"Jasmine got caught doing an escort job. Cops picked her up." Shelly paused for a brief moment to roll her eyes, and then continued to speak. "She's so stupid. That's why I don't mess with that shit. I may take my clothes off, but I ain't licking, kissing, or sucking nothing."

Maria nodded in agreement, pulling on her fishnet stockings, which would be 'viciously' ripped off in about twenty minutes. "Now her kid's in the system. That kid ain't got a chance at a life with a prostitute mom and a locked-up dad."

Ladasha quickly turned to defend the poor kid's life. "You don't know what the kid can make of himself. Give him a chance." Her whole being shifted and she was to the point where humor wouldn't fix her emotions.

"The only chance that kid got at a life is selling crack on the corner to the other messed up brats."

Ladasha's eyes couldn't hide the self-pity pouring out. I quickly reached across to her and squeezed her hand, delivering a shot of comfort. Locking eyes with her, I sent her a simple nod, reminding her that she wasn't alone. It was the same reminder she gave me when I first showed up to New York—no words, just a look of understanding. Her halfway smile and one-shoulder shrug was all I got before she went back to her makeup. Turning to the other girls, I asked the next question on my mind. "So who's doing the closing number tonight?" Jasmine always got the closing number. She and Roger had a 'close' employer/employee relationship. I called her a slut, Ladasha called her a businesswoman.

Shelly smiled through her mirror in my direction. "You're gonna want to add a lil more blush tonight, Wisconsin."

Suddenly, Roger came barging into the dressing room, causing some of the girls to squeak in horror and throw things in his direction. He rolled his eyes, uninterested. "I aint gonna see nothin' that everyone else in the club hasn't already seen." His eyes shifted to me. I hated when he looked at me. Roger was a creep, but then again, I was a stripper. I guess I kind of had it coming. I watched him chewing on the end of his short cigar, puffing rings of smoke into the air. His hairy face matched his hairy chest that was semi-hidden under his one-size-too-small black tank top. Too bad it wasn't completely hidden. Disgusting.

"Andrea, you got a person in a VIP room requesting you." He turned to leave as I shot up from my seat.

"Wait! Is it true I have the finale tonight?"

"If you keep bringing in people who pay hundreds for fifteen minutes with you in the VIP rooms, you can have anything you damn want." Roger's eyes sparkled like he'd won the lottery as he dragged his feet out of the room.

"Who the hell is requesting you for a lap dance?" Maria asked.

Ladasha smiled brightly—a genuine smile. She was coming back around to her normal, cheerful self. "Cooper Davidson."

My eyes lit up at the idea of Coop being in the other room. Just hearing his name from my best friend's lips made me want to go deliver the best lap dance ever. "Well, who the hell is Cooper Davidson?" Shelly hissed as she overdosed on hairspray.

"HE'S MY HUSBAND and you're sleeping with him!" she hollered at me. My heart was in my throat and it seemed like all of the air had been sucked from the filthy VIP room. Sweat started spewing from my forehead as my knees began to shake. I opened my mouth to speak yet nothing came out. So she continued to talk. Something about me being a home-wrecking, smutty, vomit-worthy slut.

My eyes shifted to her stomach. Oh god…Cooper didn't tell me she was pregnant.

Wait.

Cooper didn't tell me anything about Iris. "I don't know what to say."

She laughed in a mocking tone. "Don't say a word. Just stay the hell away from my husband." I turned to leave and she glided herself in front of the door, blocking me in. "Seriously. I can ruin your pathetic life in an instant. You understand me? In. An. Instant. I can take whatever you have and destroy it. Don't test me."

"Go to hell!" I yelled. I hated her. I didn't have much knowledge of who she was, but what I'd discovered in the last five minutes was that she seriously lacked people skills. And I also hated that she was so damn gorgeous. More beautiful than anyone I'd ever seen. Her face was flawless, her stance was ballerina worthy. For a moment I paused to think why Cooper would come to me when he had her waiting for him at home.

Oh my god. I was a slut. A home-wrecking, smutty, vomit-worthy slut.

"Is there a problem?" Frank opened the door when he heard me holler, and his eyes narrowed in on me, checking if I was all right.

"Yes, there actually is a problem." Iris stood up tall in her high heels and held her Michael Kors purse close to her chest. "I want her fired."

My eyes bugged out as I looked at the crazy psycho. I searched for a glimpse of sarcasm, but it wasn't there. Whatever. There was no way I would be fired because of this woman. Roger just told me I was a money maker. Dollar bills flashed in his eyes back in the dressing room. It wouldn't be good business to get rid of me. Before I knew it, I was having a yelling contest with Iris as Frank tried to control the noise. But he should've known, once women attack each other, it's pretty much useless to do anything about it.

"What the hell is going on?!" Roger screamed,

storming into the heated fight, panting. He was out of breath from the short jog over to the VIP room.

Iris crossed her arms and looked to him. "Are you the owner of this place?" she asked.

He was. She continued. "I want her fired." She pointed at me as Ladasha walked up behind Roger to see what all the commotion was about.

Roger arched an eyebrow at Iris as if she were crazy. "There's no way in hell I'm firing my best employee. I'm sorry you two had a dilemma, but let me get you another girl..." He put on his charm to try to get Iris to calm down. I knew Roger wouldn't get rid of me. He may have been an asshole, but he wasn't a heartless asshole.

"I'll pay you ten thousand dollars," Iris insisted.

Oh no. This time Roger raised both eyebrows. Ladasha's mouth dropped as she jumped into the conversation. "Roger I swear if you get rid of Andrea, I will walk out with her." He lowered the brows. He couldn't lose us both. I could have kissed Ladasha for standing up for me the way she did.

"Twenty-five thousand to fire both," Iris sang.

She must have sung the right tune because the next thing I knew, Ladasha and I were walking home, jobless, boxes filled with bras and costumes, with no form of income to support us.

"So, we have a few choices for tonight," Ladasha said as we walked in the snow to our apartment. "We can track down Cooper and kick his ass, we can go cry in a corner and realize we won't have a place to live soon, or...we can watch *Pretty Woman* and get wasted."

I smirked at Ladasha. Her whole life was about taking

it one step at a time, never knowing where she would be the next day. I somewhat envied that. So the idea of finding a new place to live didn't come off as a life or death situation to her. At least she didn't show it as one. I linked my arm with hers, we walked in our ridiculous heels and rested my head on her shoulder.

Although the idea of kicking Cooper's ass did sound promising, I secretly knew if I were to see him again, a part of me would want to melt into his arms. And by this point, crying seemed to be useless. I'd cried so much these past few months that I wasn't certain I even knew what the point of it was anymore.

So that made the choice quite easy. We were getting wasted and watching the hell out of *Pretty Woman*.

WALKING TO OUR apartment, there appeared to be a strange man sleeping next to a suitcase. Ladasha's eyes shifted towards me. "Do you...?"

I shrugged. I couldn't tell who it was, so we approached with caution. The man's head was resting in his lap as Ladasha got closer and poked him with her heel. My heart got stuck in my throat, noticing the old, scuffed up brown shoes... I knew who it was.

"Hey, freak. This isn't a homeless shelter. Get the hell out of here before we call the cops, assho—" Ladasha's voice trailed off as she stared into eyes that were now slowly waking up.

Oh no. "What are you doing here?" I asked, watching him stand.

"Well, after going to the diners that didn't have any clue who the hell you were, and calling your cell phone one hundred times, I tracked down your apartment. And I've been waiting here since six in the afternoon to find you. And clearly now it's..." He brought his watch to his eyes and looked back to me. "It's two in the morning."

I choked back my words, shaking my head, "No. What are you doing in New York?"

"Looking for you, Anders! Mom is freaking out! You didn't come for Thanksgiving, she said you weren't coming for Christmas, and we haven't heard from you in weeks!" My older brother Eric was here, in New York City, in front of my apartment. And I was holding a box with bras, whips, and chains. This had the possibility of getting extremely awkward.

His eyes landed on the box, they traveled to my fake nails, heavy makeup, and then they shifted back to the box. "What the hell is going on, Andrea?!"

CHAPTER TWENTY

COOPER

HEY, WHAT'S UP? I typed into the message. *No.* Delete, delete, delete. **We should talk.** Talk? Talk about what? How my wife was blackmailing me to never talk to Andrea again? How her secret would be world news if I were seen with her in public? It was two in the damn morning and I couldn't stop pacing this hotel room. I really needed to get my own place as soon as possible.

I fell onto my bed, blankly staring at my cell phone. Son of a bitch. I needed to call.

"Hello?" the tired, but deep, voice said on the other line.

"Kyle. I need advice." I was desperate, so I reached out to the one person who I knew wouldn't hate me for calling at ridiculous times during the night.

"I fucking hate you," he whined. He didn't mean it.

"Seriously. I don't know what to do. Iris is blackmailing me. I can't see Andrea and she has no clue why. And I can't tell her because Iris is threatening to expose her darkest secrets. And I fucking miss her. And I don't just mean the sex. I mean *her*, Ky." I ran my fingers over my eyebrows, allowing realization to set in. I missed Andrea more than I have ever missed anything.

"You know what you need?"

My ears perked up, ready to hear his advice. The last time he gave me advice, I ran into Andrea. So I was anxious for some of his knowledge.

"You need to be single for awhile. Clearly you can't fuck and leave it at that. You get all twisted in emotions like a little bitch." He was extra harsh today; he must have been really tired. "You need to deal with your issues with Iris. Deal with your dad issues. And I mean really fucking deal. Stop burying that shit and stop thinking that finding a second choice will make it better. Listen, I was up late helping a friend out of a sticky situation. I'm tired, all right? I'm going to sleep, asshole."

I sat in my dark hotel room again. With my thoughts. Fuck my thoughts. I didn't want to be thinking about her, but she wouldn't get out of my head. I sure as hell didn't want to be thinking about him, but there he was, in my mind. I wanted everything about my past to disappear, but the memories started to resurface.

I'D STOOD BEFORE my father after he returned home from a heavy night of drinking. He stumbled into the living room, where Mom had fallen asleep waiting for his arrival.

He walked past me, shoving me in the shoulder. "Get the hell outta my way, kid."

I had enough; I couldn't stand the hollowness of his words. I shoved him back, telling him that I would be better than him. I would never lay my hands on a woman, never drink, and I'd be a better father than he could ever be.

His laughter was dark when he looked me in the eyes. I could smell the rum on his breath as he whistled a tune. Grabbing me by the chin, he pulled me close to his face, and his voice lowered. "You see what you're looking at right here, Cooper?"

My body tensed up and I narrowed my eyes, wanting to knock the jerk to the ground, but even as a drunk, he was ten times stronger than me. "Look real close, real fucking close into my eyes, son. You see what's there? That's your damn future."

"No it's not." He was wrong. He was wrong. He was...

He shoved me again, chuckling in a wicked tone. "Yup, it is. You're exactly your father's son. You can try your hardest to run from it, but the apple don't fall far from the damn tree, kid."

I SPENT YEARS proving him wrong, being a better person, giving back to the community, and loving my wife the best way I knew how. And when she became pregnant, I knew I would be better than him. I was ready to be a dad.

A damned good one at that. I just didn't plan for what happened next.

The first time she had a miscarriage, I wasn't there.

I'd been doing voiceovers for our reality show. Iris had finished her voiceover work earlier that day and headed to her doctor's appointment. She kept calling me on my cell phone, but I didn't answer. I had to get the work done so the editing process could begin. The world of television worked on a time schedule, and if you didn't show up and do your job, you could cost the network a shit-ton of money. My wife could wait, seeing as how she'd dragged me into this fucked up world of reality television.

The calls kept coming, and I kept ignoring. It wasn't until she texted me '911' that my eyes shot up and I removed the headphones from my ears. Everything slowed down. I was sure I was running, but it felt as if I were going nowhere. When I arrived at the doctor's office, Iris was sitting in the waiting room, drained, but not tearful. She must have cried before I arrived. The doctor told us a bunch of bullshit I didn't understand. I started hollering at him, tagging him as the cause of my newfound suffering. My eyes shifted to my silent wife. *Our suffering.*

I demanded a real reason. "Y'all better fix this! Do you know who we are!? Your ass better make this right!!" He'd fucked up and he should have been able to fix this. Fix him or her.

Fix our baby.

Iris stood up and started to walk away from me, nearing the exit. I narrowed my eyes at the doctor— eyes filled with unwarranted hate— and informed him that this wasn't the end of it. I rushed over to Iris and wrapped my arm around her. "We'll fix this, all right?" I whispered over and over again, stroking her hair.

By the time she fell asleep, I'd had a drink. Or three.

The second time it happened, I wasn't there.

I'd been out having a drink with my manager when I got the call. I looked at her in the hospital bed and her shoulders shrugged. She looked away from me. We didn't speak a word. When she was released from the hospital, I offered her my hand to hold, but she refused it. I was slapped with a feeling that things would never be the same. As we stepped into the apartment, Iris went to the living room couch and allowed the cushions to soak her in. I asked her what she needed. She whispered a harsh reality. "A husband."

I wanted to reach out to her and wrap her in my arms, but I couldn't.

"Can you change the bed sheets? I want to go to sleep." She rubbed her puffy eyes and rested her hands over her face. She must have cried in the hospital before I arrived. She'd never cried in front of me. Not even on our wedding day. I wandered to our bedroom, willing to at least fill one of her requests. If I couldn't be the husband she needed in that moment, I could change the sheets.

The red stains on the 800 thread count Egyptian cotton sheets reminded me of how I hadn't been there. A vexatious amount of guilt washed over me as my tongue tasted the whiskey still upon my lips. My wife had lain in bed by her lonesome, while our second unborn child cried out for her to notice. Cried out for Daddy to wake Mommy before it was too late.

But Daddy hadn't been there. And Mommy had to

wake to excruciating pain. Mommy probably reached out for Daddy but only found his pillow.

A week later, we were on a red carpet, showing up at a charity event for some celebrity 'friend' of ours. "Save the whales. Save the goldfish. Save the goddamn fruit flies." What a fucking joke. None of these people were our friends—they didn't know the shit we had been through. We hadn't even had time to mourn, but that evening on the red carpet, I wrapped my arm around Iris's waist and she smiled, my hand almost touching her stomach. I flinched at the thought and moved my hand closer to her side.

That was the closest connection we'd had in weeks, and it was all an act. An image for the paparazzi and media to relish in. Season three of our reality show was about to premiere in a few weeks, so of course we had to hold up our appearances.

No, we didn't find time to mourn, but I found a few moments to have a drink.

Or six.

After we'd gone through the two previous miscarriages, it had been really hard on the both of us. She never spoke of it, but I knew it ate at her spirit. It sure as hell ate at mine.

I couldn't think about it anymore. I forced myself to go to sleep, to shut my mind down from all the issues I refused to face.

CHAPTER TWENTY-ONE

Andrea

"YOU'RE A STRIPPER." A ghost-faced Eric sat across from me with his head resting in his hands. He couldn't look at me. But I couldn't blame him. His baby sister. A stripper? I could tell he was having a hard time connecting those dots. To be honest, I could hardly connect them myself. The room was filled with a dirty air neither of us was interested in breathing. The moment Ladasha realized it was a family affair, she and Freckles disappeared into her room. *Dang it.* I could have really used her help trying to explain.

I needed to say something. To somewhat give him some level of comfort that it wasn't as bad as it looked. I wasn't as bad as he was envisioning me. I bit the bullet and opened my mouth. "I know what it looks like."

He looked up at me as if I were a complete stranger and shook his head. "Mom and Dad are going to flip."

"No! You can't tell them. Daddy will die." I was pretty certain Dad would fall over and never get up again. I could almost feel my mother's pain from finding out about me. It would be even worse if the town got a hold of the story. They were still sizzling from Derrick's death, and this would be another dish to add to Mom's book club meetings.

This was my fault. I should have called my mom more. Checked in and pretended as if all were well. Made up fake stories about the diners. Told her lies about seeing Broadway shows. I'd slipped up. I hadn't thought. And now I was embarrassed—but mostly pissed—that I hadn't thought to cover my tracks better.

"How long have you been working there?"

My voice softened; I could already hear his reaction. "Since I moved here."

Eric shot up from the sofa. He didn't even have time to be angry with me. It was all so new to him. His fingers kept brushing across his forehead, trying to figure out where to start. Searching for answers. That was when he started scolding me with questions that could have come directly from our mother. It was a known fact that he was a mama's boy and I was a daddy's girl. So he came to me as a grounded spirit, a teacher, an educator. He didn't even leave time for me to answer all of his questions. He kept rambling off.

Did I not even stop to think about how dangerous the life I was living could be? Did I not stop to think how degrading it was for me to take off my clothing for money? How could I be so foolish? Many people have issues, but they don't fall apart over them. He couldn't understand. I didn't blame him. "I'm gonna need you to start from the beginning because I'm definitely missing something. How could you be so stupid, Andrea?"

"You won't understand."

"Try me."

Defeated, I tossed up my hands, "I lost my best friend. And I was stuck in a place where I couldn't breathe. Everything reminded me of him. Everything *was* him, Eric. I had to move away. I had to leave that place."

Sarcastically Eric rubbed his eyebrows. "So of course the next step is stripping. How easy is it? To take off your clothes each and every night?"

"I just recently started onstage, all right!? It's a form of dance..."

"It's a step away from being a hooker!" He didn't know how much his words stung. I was growing more and more disgusted with myself as the heaviness of his disappointment came into focus. That was the second time that night I'd been called a hooker. Once by my friend with benefits pregnant wife, and once again by my brother. Eric continued. "You should get tested."

"For what?" He lifted his eyebrows and I quickly realized what he was talking about. "I'm not a prostitute, Eric! Jesus Christ!"

Eric stood against the wall, pounding his fist against his mouth repeatedly, trying to get a glimpse of my mind. I could see he was beating himself up a bit for coming on so hard. Perhaps it was the tears forming in my eyes which made him ease up on me. His eyes softened as he began to realize the last thing I needed was to be disciplined. "Come home, Andrea."

"I can't."

"Why not? You said you got fired tonight anyway! What are you going to do? Get kicked out? Live on the streets? Start a crack addiction?" I hated how extreme he was. But he had a good point. *What am I going to do?*

"Listen, you can stay with Michelle and me at her parents' house for awhile. It's right outside of town, and no one would bother you there. Come home and pull yourself together for a little while."

All I could think about was texting Cooper. Escaping from the world for a bit. Losing myself in his arms and forgetting about all the troubles surrounding me. But Cooper was the main reason I was jobless. Cooper was the reason I'd walked home with that box in my arms. And Cooper was the reason my brother thought I was a whore. I had a growing level of hate filling my stomach for him. But at the same time I wanted to snuggle my head into his shoulder and hold on to him because he too, knew what it was like to be broken.

"Listen. I don't want to do this, but I will tell Mom and Dad." He was serious. It made me sick how much Eric was like our mom. He had her brown hair and her dramatic personality, always taking things to the extreme. And I hated him for it because he was always right.

Ladasha opened her door and walked into the living room with Freckles in her arms.

"You should go, Andrea." She looked at me and I was shocked she would even think any of this was all right. She went on to explain how Simba didn't want to go back to Pride Rock, but he had to—to take his place as king. Sometimes I wished her movie references didn't fit so perfectly into situations.

"You're not the same girl you were when you left Wisconsin, but maybe that's why it's better. Maybe you fit there now."

"I'm sorry, who are you?" Eric's eyes were locked with Ladasha's, and he seemed to be smitten by her. She was beautiful, so it wasn't a surprise; all guys looked at her as if she were a goddess. It was a bit weird seeing Eric fixated on someone who wasn't Michelle.

"Eric, this is my friend, Ladasha. We met in college."

Eric nodded. "Hi Ladisha."

"It's La*dash*a."

"Spell it."

Ladasha rolled her eyes, went to the couch, and made herself comfortable. "L. A. Dash symbol. A. La-dasha-ah."

Even I was taken aback. I raised an eyebrow. "Seriously? A dash symbol?"

"That's sexy." Both of our eyes shot to Eric who appeared to be infatuated with the extremely different creature before him. It didn't help that Ladasha had slipped into her booty shorts and a tight tank top for the night.

"What?" I asked.

"Huh? Nothing. Listen. I'm gonna book your flight back with me." Eric quickly changed the subject as he shifted his eyes from Ladasha. The sweat dripping down his eyebrows showed how guilty he felt for even laying eyes on someone who wasn't Michelle.

"If I come back with you, you won't tell Mom or Dad?"

"I won't. But you have to stay awhile, Anders."

"And you'll help with the apartment payments while I'm there? I want to come back to New York, Eric."

"Yeah yeah, whatever. We'll leave tomorrow night. But there's one more thing." Eric gave me hopeful eyes. I knew he was about to ask me something annoying; he always scrunched his nose when he was going to say annoying crap. "You have to come to the Christmas party."

"No." Eric pulled out his cell phone and started dialing, but I wasn't going to be pushed. Crossing my arms, I stood tall, unable to be moved. "I'm not going, Eric."

"No, that's fine. I'm just gonna leave a quick message for Dad."

"Screw you. Okay, okay. I'll go." All right. I'd been pushed, moved, and bullied.

Perking up with excitement, Ladasha joined in. "And I'll come too!" An air of silence filled the room. Ladasha could see the worry on our faces. Albany wasn't really a place where Ladasha's loud personality and sexy, flirty style belonged. But she began to beg.

"Andrea. Pleaseeeee!?" The puppy dog eyes appeared. But let's be honest, there was no way I was going to leave her here. She showed up when I'd needed her most, and I knew in her heart, after finding her mom, she was ready to relocate. It wasn't a want—it was an actual need. "And she comes too." Eric agreed to the idea of Ladasha coming with. I personally thought he'd secretly hoped for her to join us.

"I'm going to bed." I was drained and needed this night to end.

As I walked into my bedroom and slammed my door, I could hear Eric and Ladasha talking. The paper-thin walls were my enemies that night. I could hear the concern in my older brother's voice as he spoke to my best friend. "Ladasha, you seem like a nice girl. You really do. I don't understand why you two would do that to yourselves."

"Do what?"

"Strip."

There was a silence. I figured Ladasha was in search of the right words to come to her. The right film comparison. My heart was pounding; would she be able to make him understand? *Please make him understand, Dasha.*

"It's like a kite."

She didn't go for her normal movie explanation. I grew quite intrigued, not knowing where this was leading. I sat down against the door and listened to the exchange of dialogue between the two of them.

"What does that mean?"

"A kite. There are millions of kites in the world. Different shapes. Different sizes. Some kites are made for the crazy winds. Some get torn a little. And some plop! Instantly hitting the ground right out of the package. Andrea's kite can still be repaired. She'll be fine."

"What about your kite?" Eric's voice softened; he knew what Ladasha meant, even with her somewhat random comparison. But that was the thing about Ladasha; in her mind, everything was connected in some way. You just had to take the time to figure out how.

"My kite?" I could hear the self-doubt in her voice. It was the same sound I'd heard escape her voice in the dressing room at the club. She didn't think her kite was worth saving. My heart broke for her. She didn't dare answer the question. "Let me grab you some pillows and blankets. It can get chilly in here."

And that was the end of the discussion.

I went to bed, unable to sleep. The idea of returning home was filling my mind. I could hear the whispers now. I

could see the saddened eyes staring at me.
I didn't want to go home.
But where else did I belong?

CHAPTER TWENTY-TWO

COOPER

"GO TO HELL, asshole."

Welp. Didn't see that coming. After a night filled with memories, I had to get back to the real issue at hand—finding a way to keep Andrea's name out of the tabloids. I knew I hadn't responded to her text messages, but I didn't think it was *that* serious for name calling. I was, after all, trying to save her image. I held the cell phone to my ear as I listened to Andrea call me every negative name on the planet.

Pig. Vomit. Ass. Jerk. Liar. Idiot. Stupid-ass. Asshole. Freak. Twit.

As she continued, I slipped a few words into the conversation. "What's going on here?"

"I don't know, Cooper. How about you ask your pregnant wife who got Ladasha and me fired last night?"

Oh no... She didn't. She wouldn't. I paused and thought about Iris and her recent threats and hatred. She would. Son of a bitch.

"Where are you?" I asked. I needed to meet with her.

To try to explain myself. There was so much Andrea didn't know, and it was only fair I tell her myself. I would hate for her to hear it from anyone else.

"Ma'am, if you could please turn off your cell phone? We are about to take off."

I heard the stranger's voice in the background and felt chills run down my spine. She was leaving. "Andie, wait."

Click.

I ran my hands across my face and felt the prickly hairs against my palm; I hadn't shaved in a few days. My mind hadn't stopped racing. I needed to talk to Andrea. And she needed to hear me out. Iris kept crossing the line, and she was really in need of a fucking reality check soon enough.

"WE TRY TO *create the best weddings for the couples. It takes a lot, to be married. And it's important to have this special day to look back on." Iris smiled to the cameras and crossed her long, sexy legs.*

I completely agreed with my wife as we sat filming a confessional scene for our 'reality' show. "Yeah. It's a reminder of all the things you love about each other. But some don't need the big crazy wedding to remember those things."

"What's that suppose to mean?" *Iris looked to me with a confused look as I shrugged my shoulders.*

"I think that when people are lucky, they can look at

each other to remember why they made the promises that day." I took her hand into mine and kissed it gently, "I got lucky."

Iris smiled brightly and looked directly into the camera, pulling her hand away from me. "Yeah. But a big wedding wouldn't hurt."

"And, cut! Let's take a break, everyone." The director yelled, as the camera crew stopped rolling. Iris's makeup artist came over and started powdering her face.

"What the hell was that, Cooper?" Iris harshly whispered in my direction. Pushing her makeup artist away, she stood up, walking to her dressing room. "We have to reshoot that now because of you. Just stick to the damn script they gave us, all right? And next time I would rather you not make me look like a raging bitch, asshole."

I ran my fingers through my hair and sighed.

Well, if the shoe fits.

CHAPTER TWENTY-THREE

Andrea

AS WE PULLED up to Michelle's property, I slid my sunglasses down, taking notice of the other car in the driveway. "What are Mom and Dad doing here?" I hissed at my brother. He shrugged his shoulders.

"Did you really think Mom wouldn't want to see her daughter? Come on."

I mumbled to myself and sat back in my seat. "Overbearing much?"

Eric watched as I slid my headphones back into my ears, and I heard him as he whispered to Ladasha. "She's a lot ruder than I remember."

"Oh. That's because you're not holding up any money." Eric's face instantly lost color. I couldn't help but chuckle to myself as I watched my brother's face turn to horror, probably thinking of me collecting money from nasty men.

Ladasha stepped out of the car and gasped. Her brown eyes widened in amazement as she stared at the mansion in front of her. The property had everything she had seen in movies. There was an indoor swimming pool, a tennis court, fireplaces in bathrooms, a private coach house... Everything. The newly fallen snow added to the magical moment my friend was taking in. The home had over twenty-five rooms, holding within it over seven bedrooms, eight bathrooms, and a built-in home theater.

"Holy shit. People live like this?" Ladasha smiled widely, looking around in complete awe. I stepped out of the car, rolled my eyes, and joined my friend.

"No. They don't. Come on, let's get this over with."

Ladasha went to help Eric with the bags, but he assured her he could handle it. She smiled to him, and still picked up two pieces of luggage.

"You coming, Michelle?" he asked his girlfriend. Michelle was standing perfectly in her pair of heels. The sunlight kissed her blond locks, yet her blue eyes were hidden behind her large sunglasses. With her cell phone attached to one hand and her Michael Kors bag attached to the other, I was instantly reminded of Iris and her stupid Michael Kors bag. Did I mention I hated her?

Michelle's loud laugh echoed through the air as she held her gut from the conversation she was having on the phone.

"I see she still has that unique laugh." I smirked.

Eric shot me the dirtiest look. "Really? You really think you have the right to judge *anyone* right now? Don't start, Anders."

I shut up.

Before we even had a chance to enter the foyer, I was attacked by my mom, who wrapped her arms around me. The lack of air filling my lungs was uncomfortable, but I didn't push her away.

"Anders!"

"Hey, Mom."

Mom stood back and looked at me. I noticed a level of alarm form within her eyes. "You look skinny. You're so skinny." She was right.

"I'm not. This is my friend, Ladasha." Perfect. Change the subject away from me.

"Nice to meet you, honey. I always forget how huge this house is. I got lost trying to find your father earlier!" Mom squeaked as she poked me in the side, frowning at my recent weight lost.

"Where is Daddy?"

"In the study. Well, one of the studies. This place, I tell you!" As if cued, Dad entered the room, holding a glass bottle with a ship crafted inside it.

"It's a nice place." He stared at the ship through his thick glasses. "How does anyone do these? I might have to try it."

Seeing my dad made me sigh with a breath of relief. I was a lot of things, but first and foremost I was a daddy's girl. I loved the feeling of calmness he had with his personality. He balanced out my 'always on edge' mother so well. Dad walked over, and gave me a hug and kissed my forehead. His hug wasn't as tight as Mom's, yet it was the exact kind of hug I needed. Not too overbearing. Yet not nonexistent.

"Come on, let's all go into the family room to catch up." Mom ushered everyone into the other room. I could feel my mom's eyes on me as I tried my best to blend into the couch cushion. "Andrea. I really do hope you're hungry. They are preparing a big dinner for us tonight."

She was overly concerned with my weight. I was pretty damn happy actually that ever since I'd met up with Cooper I'd started to gain a few pounds back. But she didn't know that. She saw me as an extremely skinny girl who'd lost her fiancé. I bet she had nightmares at night about the life I'd been living in New York. I guessed she had good reason to have the nightmares; I wasn't exactly making Mama proud out there.

Michelle came bouncing inside and joined us with the biggest grin I'd ever seen in my life. Eric asked her what was up, and she smiled even wider. "I have a surprise for you all! But you'll have to wait until dinner tonight!"

"Perfect, maybe I'll go rest for a few hours." I faked a yawn to get out of there and headed to what was to be my bedroom for the next few weeks. This sucked.

"WHAT'S THE MATTER with you?" I asked to the distant Derrick. He shrugged his shoulders as he lay in my dorm bed.

"Just thinking."

"About?" I questioned. He ignored me, staring at the ceiling. Ever since he arrived that weekend, he was off. "Answer me."

He sat up on the bed, rolling his eyes. "Andrea, I'm just off, all right? You have your days, let me have mine."

"You don't have to be an ass, Derrick." I hissed. I hated when he closed himself off to me like this, and it seemed to be happening a lot more since the engagement. "Do you not want to marry me?" My eyes moved to the floor, not willing to meet his eyes. Fearful of his response.

I felt his arms wrap around me from behind. He buried himself into my shoulder and shook his head. "Of course I want to marry you. It's just..."

I turned to him, feeling ill. "It's just what?"

"You're doing something with your life. You're getting a college degree. You're preparing for your future. And I'm just here."

"You have your music, Derrick." He was amazing at his music, and I never looked down on him for not going to college. It wasn't for everyone.

"What if I'm not enough for you? What if I end up fucking all of this up? Screwing us up?"

I wrapped my legs around him and held on tight.

"Don't talk like that, all right? You'll always be good enough. We're in this together, okay? You and me."

"You and me," he sighed into my neck. "You and me."

THE MOMENT DINNER was being prepared I had my mom barging into my bedroom to wake me up. Personal space was not something she believed in. And there we were again, waiting in the living room. She could have let me sleep for a little while longer.

"I'm so happy you decided to come!" Perfect Michelle grinned as she walked into the house with a guest.

"Holy shit!" I screamed as my eyes connected with Cooper's.

"Language!" Mom scolded.

"Sorry Mom. Excuse me. I—I have to use the bathroom." I shot up from my seat and hurried away. *How dare he.*

How dare he come here. Hasn't he done enough already? It was because of him I was in this damn situation. I turned on the faucet in the bathroom and started splashing water against my ghost white face. Breathing was becoming a problem.

"We should talk."

The sound of his voice sent chills down my spine, and as I turned to look at him, my heart started pounding against my chest. He was unshaven, wearing a button-down shirt and a pair of dark blue jeans. *Dammit. He looks good.*

He closed the door behind him and stepped near me. I stepped back. This continued until I was up against a wall and he was staring me in the eyes.

"What are you doing here?" I hissed. I'd left him in New York. I'd called him a dirty, disgusting, vomit-worthy asshole and left him in New York.

"I can explain." He put his hands up as a sign of peace, but my body was still ready to defend myself from his smooth accent and strong arms.

"I hope you know what you're doing is a form of stalking, Cooper."

His green eyes smiled with his lips as he chuckled and

reached into his back pocket. "No. You don't understand, I was invited. I'm staying in the coach house here for a few days until the party." He pulled out the invitation to Michelle and Eric's Christmas party and I was sure smoke was coming from my ears. I was fuming.

"This is my life, Cooper. This is my life you are playing with. And I don't appreciate you taking it as a joke."

"You think I would screw with your head, Andrea?" He was sincere in his words, but that didn't change the fact that he'd lied to me.

"Your wife is pregnant."

"Yeah, I know. With another man's kid."

Oh no. His hand somehow found mine and I felt my warrior stance fading away. I spoke softly as I avoided eye contact. Those eyes would be the end of any form of dignity I was trying to hold on to. "You got me fired. And Ladasha."

"From a strip club. Not to be rude, but I think y'all can do better." I could feel him getting closer to me.

"Says the man who showed up to the strip club in the first place." I shut my eyes. I tried to fight away the feeling of wanting his lips connected to mine, but I kept hearing the words soda pop running through my head.

Fight it.

I began to nervously twiddle my fingers as Cooper spoke. "You want the truth? My manager said I would get over it. That I should have a lap dance. A one-night-stand to clear my mind of all of it. Probably not the best idea, six hundred dollars later."

"Well I'm sorry you wasted your money."

"I didn't mean it in a rude way. It's just, that's not who I am."

"And you think that it's who I am!?" I hissed.

"Of course not, Andrea. You know how I feel about you."

My breaths were heavy, I was ashamed of what had happened between the two of us the first night we met and the guilt of being home, in this town, was weighing heavy on my soul. I needed to make myself clear to Cooper that I had no plans to be with him. "Listen, shit happens. People go through things and people make mistakes. What happened between us these past few weeks was a mistake and it's probably best we never talk about it."

Cooper agreed with his words but his actions spoke differently. He lightly brushed the side of my face with his hand.

"Okay, so it never happened," I whispered. My eyes landed on Cooper's hands, which were holding mine. I would be lying if I said I didn't feel a glimpse of comfort.

He whispered back. "What never happened?"

My skin began to heat up as I continued trying to stay strong. I missed his lips. I wanted his lips to miss mine, too. I wanted them to first kiss my bottom lip, followed by my top. My knees were slowly going out on me. His face was hairy—out of his norm. I wondered what his unshaven face would feel like against my face. Against my chest. Against my stomach. Against my...

No. I had to focus. I looked into his eyes. "We were two people who were experiencing weakness at the same time."

Cooper closed his eyes and rested his forehead against

mine. "A stupid mistake."

"An accident," I agreed. My eyes closed again. This wasn't going well for me.

"But since we are both going to be here for a while, maybe we should at least keep one of our rules."

"Be friends?" My eyes opened as he stepped away from me and held his hand out for me to shake. I could be his friend. I could tame my hormones and be his friend. I shook his hand and it was done. We were officially friends. We didn't let go of the handshake. I could see it in his eyes that he wanted exactly what I was secretly longing for. I ran my tongue across my upper lip and pulled him closer to me. "Maybe one more soda pop. For the road?"

"Like a final hurrah?"

In an instant our lips connected. The heat running from my neck and down my spine ignited all of my senses. Everything was heightened. I tasted the peppermint flavors left on his lips. I smelt his shampoo—coconut. I could hear his breaths. I saw his passion, but what I loved the most was that I could *feel* him. I missed him more than I was ever willing to admit. A moan escaped me while he slid his tongue into my mouth. He lifted me up against the wall and next thing I knew, my fingers were unbuckling his jeans.

His strong body holding me up against the ice cold wall turned me on in an instant. His mouth began to nibble on my neck, where his tongue licked me up and down. Left and right. Figure eights. Oh, the things he could do with that mouth of his... My inner thighs were throbbing as he went examine my jeans...

"Anders? Are you okay?"

Ughhh. Nothing could kill a moment more than having

your mother knock on the bathroom door when your legs were wrapped around a Cooper Davidson. Cooper lowered me to the ground as I tried to hide my giggles in his shirt. Placing a finger across his lips to silence him, I grinned as I felt him kiss that finger.

"Get in the shower," I instructed. He obeyed, and I looked at myself in the mirror to fix myself up, buttoned my jeans, and opened the door to the bathroom to find my nosey mother standing there.

"Are you okay?" she repeated.

"Yeah, Mom. I'm fine. I think I had a bad bagel on the plane," I lied. I hadn't eaten a bagel, but I knew the idea that I was eating would make her calm down.

"Yeah, well, dinner's ready. Did you see where Cooper went?"

"Probably to one of the other millions of bathrooms in this place."

"He looks good. He grew up quite a bit. You remember him when he used to come visit here as a kid? You two were close."

I rolled my eyes, trying to play it cool. "No, I don't. Let's go eat." I bet Cooper was smirking at the compliment my mom had paid him. Mom's hand landed on my forehead as she looked at me concerned. I cocked an eyebrow at her. "What are you doing?"

"Your cheeks are as red as a tomato. You sure you're feeling all right?"

If only she knew.

CHAPTER TWENTY-FOUR

COOPER

AS I ENTERED the dining hall, the first thing I noticed was Andrea seated next to Ladasha, whispering something to her. Ladasha's eyes shifted to me and she gave me a halfway smile. I was sure she was being informed to act as if we'd never met.

"Cooper, you can sit here!" Michelle grinned and patted the seat next to her. My cousin was the same ol' happy-go-lucky girl she was when we were children. There are some people who are born to be cheerleaders. They have a joy that can sometimes be overbearing and to some appear pretty damn annoying, but Michelle was so damn small and adorable it was hard not to love her.

"Thanks." I took my chair at the overstocked table. It was filled with food, but nothing on the table would fill my appetite—only Andrea could at this point.

"Okay, really quick. Let me introduce you all to my one and only favorite cousin, Cooper Davidson. I know you probably remember him from when we were younger, but since then he went to become a successful photographer who I am so proud of." She beamed with pride. Instant guilt took over me as I realized I'd walked away from the family that took me in each summer when I was a child because I'd become famous. I'd turned my back on the people who took care of me because I'd made a few bucks. Sure, I sent them a Christmas gift every year, but it was nothing personal. I guess I forgot how nice it was to be around people who loved you without any judgments. But after Mom's accident, it was hard to look back. I guess I could understand that with Andrea.

"It's nice to meet you, Cooper. I'm Ladasha." Ladasha winked and I smiled widely, greeting her as if it were our first time crossing paths.

Andrea's mom, Betty, told me how handsome I'd grown up to be. I thanked her and informed her that Andrea was a spitting image of her. Her cheeks reddened up and she nodded. "Well, she was, until she got this horrid haircut. Really, Anders. Tomorrow I'll take you into town and we'll have Ms. Sally help you out."

"Mom, my hair is fine," Andrea argued. I quickly learned an argument with Betty would normally be pointless, because the woman may have been short and petite, but she had a big-ass personality with opinions she wasn't afraid to speak.

"It's so nice to have everyone here. Together." Michelle grinned as she patted my shoulder. I squeezed her hand as I agreed.

"I agree," Betty chimed in. "It's a shame Derrick isn't here..." Her head lowered and my eyes landed on Andrea. I could tell the words stung her as I saw Andrea's hand being held by Ladasha's.

Betty wasn't done. She looked at me with tears in her eyes. "Derrick was Anders fiancé. He passed away earlier this year, and this is the first Christmas without—"

"Mom, do we really have to talk about this?" Andrea barked at her mom. That stone wall I had spent the past few weeks breaking down with Andrea was slowly rebuilding itself.

"Andrea Mae, I am just saying. It's different, that's all." Betty truly appeared shocked by her daughter's sharp tongue. I felt sorry for the both of them; they dealt with their feelings differently. Betty spoke, and Andrea didn't.

"I'm so sorry." I made sure my eyes locked with Andrea's—to let her know she wasn't sitting at this table alone with her past. She had both Ladasha and me there now. "I'm so, so sorry."

Her eyes softened and she bit her bottom lip. "Thank you." If we were going to be friends, I planned to protect her as best I could.

Time for a change of subjects. "So this Christmas party, it's a big deal?"

My cousin's face lit up. "Huge! And this year's theme is *Pride and Prejudice* Christmas. So a group of my and Eric's friends are taking dance lessons. Oh my gosh." Her eyes lit up as she turned to me, Andrea and Ladasha. "You three have to do it!"

"Oh no. I'm not a dancer, but I'll take photos." I grinned but knew she wouldn't let me off the hook that easily.

"No! No you have to! We are having a rehearsal tomorrow afternoon. You have to come!"

Well, I guess I had to come.

"Andrea, eat something," Betty whispered. The whisper wasn't quiet enough to keep everyone from hearing.

"Mom, give her space," Eric requested. Watching him step up for his sister gave me a quick idea of the type of person he was. He was perfect for my cousin. A good guy.

"Well, I was speaking to Ms. Jacobson a few days ago as we were working on costumes for the party and she mentioned something that bothered me."

This couldn't be good.

"She said she read an article about how young people who lose someone feel as if they've lost themselves, too. And sometimes turn to alcohol or drugs or such things. Ms. Rivers also said life in New York City can been tough with its fast pace. And you show up here looking extremely skinny and…"

The sad thing was, she really meant well. Andrea slipped lower into her seat and her eyes narrowed as she studied her plate in front of her. "Are you asking me if I'm a drug addict?"

Betty's eyes widened as if her worst nightmare had come to life, "It's just that they said…"

"Betty." Walter, Andrea's dad, stepped in to ease the conversation. He was a quiet man, but only spoke up when truly needed. Yet I feared it was too late to put out this fire.

Andrea hissed at her mom. "Ms. Rivers and Ms. Jacobson spread rumors that I was drinking when the car accident happened. Ms. Rivers and Ms. Jacobson called you a bitch behind your back at last year's Christmas party. Ms. Rivers and Ms. Jacobson can kiss my skinny ass!"

"Andrea Mae!" her mother hollered.

Andrea stood from her chair and slammed it against the table. "Home, sweet home."

With that, she disappeared to her bedroom. Ladasha was quick to follow behind her. I wanted to run to her. I wanted to tell her it would all be all right, but I knew I couldn't. So I remained seated. I felt for her because it seemed to me Ms. Jacobson and Ms. Rivers were the paparazzi of the small town of Wisconsin, baking up lies to keep them busy.

Michelle tried her best to keep a smile on her face. Everyone was quite shaken by the events that had occurred, yet my cousin kept on with her happiness.

"Who wants dessert?"

CHAPTER TWENTY-FIVE

Andrea

LESS THAN TWO hours. I had been home less than two hours and I had already had enough family time. I sent Ladasha away, telling her I was fine and needed some rest. Before I could let out my first breath of relief, there was someone knocking at the door. I didn't feel like talking to anyone. What didn't they understand about that? "Come in."

When the door opened I released a sigh when I saw Daddy standing there. He was holding one of his craft airplanes in his hand and dangled it in the air as he made animated airplane noises. He walked over and landed the aircraft on the dresser before sitting next to me and patting my leg. "How you doing, kiddo?"

"I'm fine."

"Today was interesting, eh? She doesn't mean any harm." He was justifying Mom's actions. Of course he was; he always backed her up, even when she was outside her mind.

"I've only been here for a few hours and she's already

driving me up the wall, Daddy. I don't know how much I can take."

He chuckled. "She can be a handful at times."

Eyebrow raised, I smirked. "At times?"

Lifting the model airplane off the dresser, Daddy studied it and grinned. "I always get my hands in crazy projects."

"You're talented."

"I'm wacky. A few weeks ago, I built my own snow blower machine, and as I was using it on the sidewalk, the engine exploded, knocking over the neighbor's mailbox."

"Ms. Kathy's dog-shaped mailbox?"

He nodded. "A paw went flying down the street. Your mother told me to stop with my projects. That I was wasting time, and she hated how the town laughed at me. That same afternoon, she brought me a model airplane kit, saying she saw it and thought of me. Anders, she just wants to protect us from..."

"The world," I finished for him.

He placed the airplane into my hands and stood up to walk towards the door. Mom entered the doorframe with blankets in her arms. "I thought I would bring you extra blankets before we head home. This house seems a bit drafty."

My eyes locked with my dad's and my heart softened a bit. "Thank you, Mom."

Mom studied my face. She smiled and lightly brushed my hair with her fingers. "We'll get this mess fixed tomorrow. Ms. Rivers would have a field day talking about this in our book club. And you really do look skinny. You don't feel the need to be a certain size to make strides in your dance career, do you? You don't struggle with that?"

I saw Daddy cringe as he listened to Mom tear apart the precious moment he had previously built up with me. "Did you just ask if I have an eating disorder? First I'm a drug addict and now I'm anorexic?"

Clearing his throat, Dad wrapped his arm around Mom's waist and kissed her forehead. "It's late. I think we should get going. Have a good night sweetie," He kissed my forehead too and disappeared out of the room, dragging my mom with him.

I stood up to shut the door, and right after it closed there was yet another knock. *Leave me alone.* Seriously! What didn't these people understand about that? Swinging the door open, I waited to hear how my mom had planned to unknowingly offend me now.

"I think your hair looks sexy." Cooper smirked and leaned into the room, moving a piece of my hair behind my ear.

CHAPTER TWENTY-SIX

COOPER

THERE IT WAS! A smile. Well, a partial smile, but I would work with whatever I could get. She looked drained. I gave her a 'friendly' nudge on her shoulder. "Can I come in?" She opened the door wider, and that was enough of an invite. I took it.

I closed the door behind me and took a seat on the floor, legs crossed. She raised an eyebrow and sighed. "You know, there are chairs and beds to sit on." I patted the spot across from me, and even though she was reluctant, she joined me. "Why are you so nice to me?"

"Why wouldn't anyone be nice to you?" I asked.

"Come on, Cooper. One day I'm all over you, and the next I'm crying in your bedroom. Then I'm needy. Then I need my space. I'm angry. I'm dark at times. If bi-polar was a person, it would be me."

"I wish you could see yourself the way I see you."

She chuckled. I fucking loved that sound. "What is it you see?"

I rested the palm of my hand under my chin. I was

astonished that she didn't see herself at all. I wondered what she saw when she looked in the mirror. "I see a spirit that was broken the day her loved one died. I see someone who is waffling back and forth between being happy and feeling guilt for that happiness, trapped in the space between holding on and letting go. And I see someone I want to help put back together."

I meant it. I was dedicated to her. And whatever she needed, I wanted to be the one to provide it for her. Even if that meant we would only be friends.

Her head lowered to the wooden floor panels and she ran her fingers across the cracks. She began to shake a small amount and looked up to me with tears trying their best to stay hidden from the world. "What if I can't be fixed?"

I glanced to the floor panels and copied her finger movement along the cracks. "Then we'll be broken together."

PRIDE AND PREJUDICE. I'd never seen the movies. I'd never read the book. And it wasn't that I didn't dance, I *couldn't* dance. So the idea of walking into a dance studio tomorrow afternoon for my cousin's party terrified the fuck out of me. After leaving a tired Andrea's side, I headed through the house towards the backyard to get to the coach house.

After passing many different doors and many different hallways, I saw a bedroom door swung open and a cat sleeping on the ground. My skin started to feel like spiders were creeping across my whole body. I fucking hated cats. Not kidding. HATED them.

But I glanced up to the bed to see a lovely lady sitting up, with her eyes glued to the television screen. Her eyes sparkled as if she were waking up early on Christmas morning in time to catch Santa Claus. "What ya watching?" I asked outside Ladasha's bedroom. She grinned and waved me in. I glanced towards the sleeping cat and rubbed my earlobe. "I'm good here."

"*Sleepless In Seattle*," she responded as she walked over to greet me at the door.

"Never seen it."

"I'm not surprised, Mr. 'I've never seen any romance or romantic comedy movie ever.' What are you? A guy?" she sneered. Ladasha was one of the most charming people I'd ever come across in my life. Her ability to make people feel comfortable and safe around her was incredible. She was intelligent, highly educated in the world of film. She was a good friend; the way she'd squeezed Andrea's hand at the dining table showed me that. Let's be honest, she was sexy as hell and she was hilarious. For the life of me, I had no idea why this girl was single.

"Have you seen *Pride and Prejudice*?" I inquired. I required her help.

Snickering out loud, she placed her long brown hair up into a messy bun. Her hand found the perfect placement on her hip as she glared at me. "Psh. Have I ever seen *Pride and Prejudice*. Did you really just ask me that?"

Biting the tip of my thumb, I put on my best puppy dog eyes. "Can you do me a favor?"

"IT'S ALL RIGHT. Try again."

She remained calm as I stepped on her foot for the fifth time within the last thirty minutes. We stood in the emptied living room of the coach house as Ladasha tried to teach me a few dance moves of the English Country Dance. She told me the dances of the eighteenth century were simplistic moves with a few steps easy to follow. For some reason I thought it was rocket science.

"You're overthinking it. Stop thinking. Turn off the left side of your brain and allow your creativity to flow. Like with your photos. When you take the pictures your body isn't tight. It's not overthinking about what the photo may turn out to be. You're allowing the photo to flow to you."

She made sense. I tried to stop thinking about the movements and fell into the art of dance. "So, you like her a lot." She assumed I was learning the dance moves in order to impress Andrea. Ladasha wasn't a dummy.

"I do," I said as I glided myself around Ladasha. She informed me that tomorrow we would have to trade partners, which seemed much more complicated than I was ready for. So I pretended she never said that. One step at a time.

"I wish you could have known her before the accident."

"I'm hoping to know her after it." We kept dancing into the night. I wasn't good—let's not be crazy. But I wasn't horrible. My feet stepped on hers more than I wanted to admit, but she was a great teacher. She allowed me to make mistakes and cheered me on when I fixed them myself. A brilliant instructor she had turned out to be.

When we decided to call it a night, she stuck around to help me move the furniture we had previously pushed into the kitchen back into the living room. As we carried the sofa, she told me she was in need of a few questions to be answered from me. If I had plans to be around Andrea for the long run, I had to first pass the best friend questionnaire.

"Have you ever been hooked on drugs? Alcohol?"

"No."

She shifted the oversized blue chair into the far corner of the room. "STDs?"

"No."

"Are things really done and over with your wife?"

That was a very clear yes. Minus the messed up paparazzi threats.

"Any children you may or may not know about?"

I grew quiet. She must have seen the sadness in my eyes, so she was quick to tell me that everything spoken during the questionnaire was strictly confidential.

"Two miscarriages and one lie."

Her look of understanding was comforting. She didn't judge me; she just listened. Hell, it was good to just have someone listen for once. I could see why Andrea spoke so highly of this unique woman. She was somethin' else.

As she prepared to leave the room, she revealed a small fact about herself. "My mom cared more about her drugs, and my dad…God knows who he is. And as far as miscarriages are concerned…" Her voice trailed off and she lost herself in her memories, "Let's just say I know how you feel." I returned the same understanding look to her. She smirked and went back to her sassy self instantly. "But that's off the record."

"Of course."

I opened the front door for her and walked her back to the house. I watched as she wrapped her arms around herself to keep warm in the falling snow, and I placed my jacket around her shoulders. As we said goodnight, she smiled and said the kindest thing to me.

"Cooper, you would have made a great father."

I walked back towards the coach house that night with a few new dance moves and a brand new friend.

Ladasha's parents had no clue about the treasure they'd let go.

Dumbasses.

CHAPTER TWENTY-SEVEN

Andrea

I WAS HAVING a nightmare. I was smiling, I was dancing, and I was lying next to Derrick. We were laughing at the neighbors, drinking in the bars, and living happily ever after. I snuggled my head into the curve of his neck and we fit so perfectly together. Yet when I looked up, Derrick was gone. I was standing alone, lost, and confused, crying out. *Derrick!* Why would he leave me? My breaths were short and my screams were loud, but no one could hear me. I raced through the house, searching for an explanation, searching for clues of his escape, *searching for him*. But he was gone. And I was left crying.

How could he leave me? We were so happy. We had everything. We had each other. Wasn't I enough? How could he walk away and not look back? I continued searching the house— thinking I'd missed a spot. I had to have missed something, right? The tears kept falling, and I kept searching and praying for him to be there next to me. So I traveled to the front door and opened it to reveal the darkest truth.

Another man. He was handsome, charismatic, and mine for the taking. He looked at me and didn't just see me, but he *knew* me. He knew the curves of my body—he knew the whispers of my heart. And he was waiting. Waiting for me to step out of the house. Waiting for me to walk down the pebbled sidewalk with him. He didn't pressure me. He simply leaned against the porch railing and smiled.

He was handsome, charismatic, and mine for the taking.

And I closed the door in his face. I couldn't leave the house. It was my safe haven. It was my place to find peace. But somehow—before my eyes—it had become a prison. The walls were the chains holding me down, and the memories were the nourishment I was so desperate to have.

`And I woke up. I could tell by the swelling of my eyes that I'd not only been crying in my dreams, but also as I lay asleep in the bed. I glanced in the mirror at myself and studied my face. Patting my fingers lightly under the puffy, red eyes, I began to wipe away the lone tear that was left as evidence to my semi-sleepless night.

Nightmares were the worst.

"Anders, are you all right?" At the sound of the word Anders, I knew it was my mother. What was she doing here so early? Why could I not catch a freaking break? I breathed in the dry air of the room and turned to the bedroom doorway.

"I'm fine, Mom. What are you doing here so early?" I watched as her eyes widened with even more worry, and I shifted myself to the alarm clock on the nightstand. 1:04 pm. Crap. It wasn't early.

"I made an appointment with Ms. Sally for your hair,

it's in thirty minutes. I've been calling you all morning but there was no answer." I remained in my seat at the desk and watched through the mirror as my mom started straightening up the room around me. The suffocating feeling always seemed to arise whenever my mom came around; I didn't know how much more I could take. But I remained silent and went digging through my luggage to find something to wear.

I heard sniffles from behind me—oh no. Mom was crying. Again. She looked at me and pulled me into a hug. The type of hug I needed from my mom—not too overbearing, but not nonexistent. She must have taken notes from Daddy.

"I'm sorry Anders. I know this hasn't been easy for you. For any of us."

I agreed. "I'm sorry I missed Thanksgiving, Mom."

She pulled away from me and nudged my arm. "I saved you a plate in the freezer. After the dance tonight, you should stop by and eat."

She loved me. She was crazy, a worry-wart, and extremely dramatic, but she was my mom. And I was so happy to have her there with me.

"Now. Let's go do something about this hideous hair of yours."

MS. SALLY STOOD BEHIND me, clipping away at my

hair after it had been washed. The amount of hair falling to the ground was somewhat worrisome. I was almost positive I was going to be bald by the time she was done. But I didn't say anything. Questioning Ms. Sally's tactics was like questioning God. You just didn't do it.

Chop chop chop. Gossip gossip gossip. Within that hour, I found out that Rachel had officially moved back into town, Derrick's mom was on anti-depressants, Fred's Bakery made a new strawberry jam and...

"Wait. What!?" I looked up to Ms. Sally, who stood with an 'oh crap' look pasted on her face. Her eyes shifted towards my mom, who was holding a magazine. She, too, had the 'oh crap' look plastered across her face.

"Oh...I thought. I mean, I assumed you knew, honey." Ms. Sally slapped her chubby arm against her waist. "My gosh Betty, you could have told me Andrea didn't know! I hate spreading gossip."

"Is it true?" How could my mom keep this from me? How could she NOT tell me this big detail?

"Well...yes. It happened over Thanksgiving. We were hoping you would come but, well, what did you want Eric to do? Wait until you called? Because you never did." She huffed and puffed, making up excuses of why it had 'slipped' her mind to inform me that my brother and Michelle were now officially engaged.

I returned to my seat. I couldn't talk. I didn't want to talk. They were getting married. They were about to begin the journey of their happily ever after. And I was jealous, bitter, and saddened by the idea. What kind of monster had I become?

The outcome of the change in my hair was beautiful.

Ms. Sally did a fantastic job. I was now sporting a pixie cut, platinum blond hairdo which was much more me. It felt good to get back to the blondness, yet my blue eyes still stared back at me in the mirror like they didn't know who I was looking at.

"That's much better." My mom smiled at me through the mirror and squeezed my shoulders. The look of joy beaming from her was proof that she was satisfied with my new look. "Now, time to get you to your dance rehearsal."

Ugh. I shook my head, stood up, tossed on my coat and gloves, and informed her that I would walk. It wasn't that far, and the fresh air would be nice to knock the grumpy out of my system.

MY HEART SKIPPED a beat as I stood outside the dance studio and saw everyone laughing inside. There were quite a few people in the room, but my eyes landed on the most important people. I saw Eric's best friend, Bobby, talking with him and Michelle. I saw Ladasha smiling, chatting it up with Steve—Derrick's best friend. And I saw Cooper in a corner with Rachel, who was laughing hysterically. Surely nothing could have been *that* funny. Jealousy filled me up while watching Cooper lean in towards Rachel and her beautiful grin. I had no right to be jealous; he was a free man to do whatever the hell he wanted to do, and we were just friends.

It was clear Cooper was the man in my dream, waiting for me to step outside—or in this case, *inside*—with him and move on. What was I waiting for? And how long could I expect a guy to wait for me? His head rose towards the window and I stumbled back. His dimples appeared as he locked eyes with me. I didn't look away, but I didn't move closer. Cooper held up a finger to Rachel, excusing himself and it was less than five seconds before he was standing outside in the chilled winter's air next to me.

"Hey, you," he said as I watched his breath hit the cold air. He rubbed his hands together and wrapped his arms around himself. "You look amazing."

I gave him a half-smile and rubbed my mittens over my new hairdo. "Thank you."

"What are you doing? It's freakin' cold out here. Come on in. They were about to get started."

My foot shifted on the snow resting against the sidewalk. I pointed towards Ladasha. "That guy with Dasha? That's Derrick's best friend."

"Ahh, I see." He walked over next to me and stared into the dance room. He was wearing a short-sleeved black t-shirt and jeans, and I could see the hairs standing up on his arms. He was freezing. But he wouldn't show it because he didn't want to leave my side. "So here's what I have learned about *Pride and Prejudice* dances. They move quickly. You change partners fast. And you hardly have enough time to chat with anyone. So I doubt Steve will even have enough time to notice you. But it's completely up to you what you want to do. In or out?" he asked. No pressure, just a question.

I let out a breath.

THE SPACE IN BETWEEN

In.

As I opened the door, the room filled with laughter came to a screeching halt. It wasn't long until the heartrending, poignant glances towards me arrived. They saw me as a sad, abandoned puppy. The air was filled with an overwhelming amount of whispering. At least in my mind that is what I heard. They were questioning how I looked, how skinny I was, how alone and depressed I must have been. They were judging me. They didn't say it, and I doubt they meant to, but I could feel it.

I took off my coat and tossed it on a chair in a corner. Cooper was wrong—the dancing didn't start soon enough. As I turned from dropping off my coat, I stood before Steve. Not only was he Derrick's best friend, but he was a best friend of mine too. I hadn't spoken to him since the accident, and I'm not sure if I'd even glanced his way at the funeral, yet there we were. Face to face.

Don't cry.

I opened my mouth to speak but choked on the air. What did you say to your dead fiancé's best friend? He gave me his gracious smile and ran his hands through his sandy brown hair. I smirked back towards him and tilted my head. He lowered his eyebrows and held a hand out to me. "Wanna dance?"

I grabbed his hand and moved to the dance floor. The lightness of the room returned as everyone realized I wasn't dead. I was just going through the motions of dealing with death. The laughter came back, which was so much more pleasant than the utter silence. Before I knew it, the dance lessons had began and everything wasn't as bad as my mind was making it up to be.

So what did you say to your dead fiancé's best friend? Absolutely Nothing.

You just looked at each other and came to the realization that words couldn't bring much comfort, but the touch from an old friend could.

As the night continued, I grew comfortable. These people were still my friends, and it felt good to be around them. During a break, I slid down the wall and sat on the floor. Rachel walked up to me and handed me a water bottle. Cooper was standing across the room, laughing with Eric and Steve. I thanked her for the water and she sat down next to me. Her eyes wandered over to Cooper. "He's pretty sexy, eh? Do you know if he's single? I heard rumors about him and his wife, but that's all I know…"

I rolled my eyes. Rachel thought everyone was sexy. I wanted to tell her he was off limits, but I couldn't.

Her head lowered and she took a long gulp from her water. "I never got to talk to you at the funeral and…" She grew serious. Much more serious than I was interested in her being. I glanced around the room for an escape, but everyone else was enwrapped in mindless conversations. Crap. She continued, "I mean, I know we were never really close but I wanted to say, I mean. I just wanted to…" She started to stutter. It was as if she were searching for the right words.

"What is it, Rachel?" Something was bothering her—no,—something was eating away at her mind.

"I just. I mean. You're a good person." She became teary-eyed. I remained silent. "And what happened to Derrick…"

"What are you two ladies chatting about?" Steve

appeared seemingly out of nowhere and joined us on the floor.

Rachel's eyes locked with his. "Andrea and I were having a talk." She narrowed her eyes towards him and gave him the 'get the hell out of here' look. He returned a stern look and I was confused out of my mind.

"What's going on?"

Their look broke and they both smiled at me. Before Rachel could speak, Steve opened his mouth. "Nothing. Rachel, that Cooper guy over there was asking about you. Maybe you should go say hi."

That perked her right up. And pissed me right off. She excused herself to go chat with him and my eyes followed her the whole way.

"What's her deal? She was acting all weird," I asked Steve. Steve smiled and stood up.

"You know Rachel." He tapped the side of his head. "She's not all there at times."

I chuckled, took the hand he extended to me, and stood up, ready to continue dance rehearsal.

CHAPTER TWENTY-EIGHT

COOPER

THE MOMENT I stepped onto the dance floor, I forgot everything Ladasha had taught me the night prior. I tried my best not to gawk, but Andrea looked so stunning that I couldn't help it. Her blue eyes really pierced me with her latest hairdo. My eyes traveled down her body, studying every inch of her being. She had a loose cream sweater hanging over her black dress. The dress hugged her in every place I have embraced before. It was a perfect fit. She appeared taller today—she was wearing heels. Nothing too high, but she was almost my height, so I noticed.

"Ouch!" I broke from my trance as I turned towards my cousin and apologized for stepping on her toes. My mind was clearly somewhere else.

"It's fine. Perhaps we should call it a night, everyone. I have waters and some snacks in the back room if anyone wants to grab some before we head out." Michelle skipped over to the stereo system and turned off the music.

"You weren't half bad for a beginner." I turned to be greeted by a cheerful girl who was nudging me in the side.

Rachel was quite a sight to look at. Her long brown locks of hair had been curled prior to her arrival, and they bounced against her shoulders.

I smirked. "I was terrible."

She stepped closer to me and leaned against the bar attached to the wall full of mirrors. She informed me that the 'bar' was actually called a barre and she had taken ballet since the age of three. I guess she wanted me to be aware of how flexible she was. Hell, I really didn't care. I glanced through the mirror and saw Andrea in the back corner. She was sipping on a water bottle and staring at me and Rachel. If I didn't know any better...

She looked jealous. Holy shit, she *was* jealous. The flaring of her nostrils and the narrowing of her eyes were all the conformation I needed. I couldn't help but feel a little excited by that fact. That meant that somewhere, deep down inside, she had some type of feelings for me. Before I could express that there was nothing to be jealous about, Rachel placed her hand against my chest and said something. I'm not sure what it was, but it was enough to make Andrea roll her eyes and walk away

"I'm sorry, what?" I asked Rachel, who was extra friendly.

"I said we were all planning on going out for a few beers tonight. You should join us." Her sexy grin almost pulled me in, but my mind was imagining how this must have looked to Andrea. My eyes took a trip around the room—where did she go?

"Yeah. Yeah, that could be fun..." There she was. She was putting on her coat, ready to make her departure. I took the hand Rachel still had placed upon my chest and removed it. I didn't want to offend or embarrass the poor girl, so I gave her my largest smile. "I'm so sorry. If you can excuse me again." That was the second time I had excused myself from Rachel's presence to go chase after Andrea, but hell, I had priorities. Well, I had one priority. And her name was Andrea. I grabbed my jacket, tossed it on, and headed out of the building.

"You have a way of disappearing," I somewhat shouted to her as she was walking down the street. Andrea turned and stared at me. The snow had started up again and was falling against my eyelashes, forcing me to blink nonstop.

"Coop, aren't you sick of chasing me?"

"Never."

She ran her hands through her short hair and wiggled her nose as she met me halfway. The streetlights had turned on; each one dressed with wreaths and white Christmas lights. Down the way, I could see a large tree in the center of the park dressed up with a large star placed on the top.

I could tell they took their holidays seriously in this town, and I would be lying if I said it wasn't a nice treat. I couldn't remember the last time I had a Christmas tree—or a holiday at that. Iris and I were always working, making money instead of making memories.

"Where are you heading?" I wondered out loud. She couldn't have been on her way back to my cousin's place. That was way too far to walk. Especially in this weather.

"I told my mom I would stop by for dinner."

"You two doing all right?"

She delivered a short smile and ran her hand over her eyebrow. "Better than yesterday. Did you know Eric and

Michelle are engaged?"

I nodded. I'd congratulated them yesterday. "Yeah, I saw the ring right away."

She grumbled to herself and cussed out loud. "How did I miss that?"

"To be fair, you were getting your ass chewed out by your mother."

"True fact." She shifted her body and removed her eyes from me. "It looked like Rachel and you were getting along great."

"Jealous, are we?" I joked. She looked to me and raised an eyebrow.

"Rachel McLean has slept with every guy on the high school football team at least four times around. And I'm sure she did the same when she went to college. So if that's what you're into, go for it."

Her cheeks were turning red, and I doubted it was due to the chill. "Do you have her number?" I laughed as I saw her mouth drop open from shock, and she punched me in the arm. Not a light little tap. No, she fucking slugged me.

"Cooper Michael, I swear if you—" she started to scold me and I gracefully changed the subject.

"Let me give you a ride," I offered. I had the rental car from the airport and didn't feel comfortable with her walking alone at night. Sure, this place wasn't New York City, but who knew what kind of small town creeps there were around?

"It's right down the way."

"Andie, come on. Don't let our friendship suffer like this," I whimpered. She giggled and nodded as she joined me on the walk to the car. "You really look amazing," I kept telling her.

Rolling her eyes, she bit her lip. "I'm not going to sleep with you again, so you can stop trying so hard."

"I'm not looking for sex."

She paused from walking and faced me. Her petite body was being sprinkled with snowflakes. I took her hand in mine and spun her around in the winter wonderland. It was a gorgeous night and I was pretty damn lucky to be spending this moment with her. After I spun her around, I took her in my arms and dipped her before pulling her in close to me. So close our lips were almost touching. I could see her breath as she tried to control her nerves. She didn't dare look away, and we held onto the connection for as long as we could. And she spoke softly. "If you're not looking for sex, what are you looking for?"

I ran my finger across her cheek and let go of her, allowing her to move back if she wished, but she remained close to me. I leaned in closer and whispered into her ear. "You."

I stepped away from her and continued on to the car. For a moment, I wasn't sure she was going to follow me. The sounds of her high heels were not heard, but I had to trust my gut. I had to trust Andrea that she would join me in my offer to drive her to her parents.

It took her awhile—her steps were so soft I hardly heard her approaching—but when I opened the passenger's door and turned around, she was patiently waiting to enter the vehicle.

THE SPACE IN BETWEEN

"DO YOU WANT some more stuffing?" Betty asked as she picked up my plate that had been cleared after round two and headed to the kitchen. I watched Andrea pick around at her food—she was still on her first plate. I could see Betty wanting to say something, but she kept it to herself. A big improvement from the previous night, but I assume she didn't want her daughter to storm off again. You live and you learn.

I patted my stomach and sat back in my chair. Even if I wanted more stuffing, there was no way it would be able to fit in my gut. Mrs. Evans knew how to cook. I hadn't had such a wonderful tasting Thanksgiving meal since my mom...

"No, thank you. I am stuffed with stuffing."

Betty reentered the dining room with a huff and puff holding a chocolate cake. No, not just a chocolate cake. A triple layer, chocolate chip, dark fudge chocolate cake.

I couldn't be positive, but I was pretty damn sure I drooled.

"Are you sure, honey? There's cake! I made it this afternoon."

I rubbed my hand across my face, narrowed my eyes, and poked my bottom lip out, making it look as if I were really thinking of not having the delicious dessert. Hell, I didn't even have to taste the cake to know it was outstanding. There was no way I wasn't going to have any of it. But I smirked and nodded. "You know what, Betty? I think I'll have a small slice."

She smiled, quite pleased with my reply, and went to get plates. I looked over to the stunning girl sitting across from me and winked at her. Her rosy cheeks which followed my wink made my night.

I looked over to Andrea's dad, who was reading a car manual. During dinner he told me how he had planned to learn how to fix cars. Andrea informed me that he was Mr. Fix-It. Walter only grinned and informed me that he was Mr. Try-It-Break-It-Throw-It-And-Then-Sometimes-Fix-It.

She loved her dad.

He loved her just as much.

Nothing wrong with a good father figure.

As Betty reentered with the plates and sliced us each a piece I began to devour the hell out of dessert.

I smiled as I watched Andrea ever so nonchalantly rub her finger against her plate pick up the remains of cake crumbs, and eat them. Betty's eyes sparkled with excitement when she saw this, and she watched as Andrea reached for another piece. In that moment, Andrea made her mama really happy. After they finished, Andrea helped her mom clean off the table and they left us two men to ourselves.

"Walter, your wife really has a way with cooking. This was probably the best meal I've had in a long time," I praised.

Walter sat back in his chair and removed his glasses, placing them on the table. "I lucked out. A perfect wife." Walter wiggled his nose towards Betty, who was smiling towards him from the kitchen.

"How long have you two been married now?"

"Thirty-six years." He grinned. He was proud to call her his. And she was equally proud to call him hers. I couldn't imagine. Iris and I were only married for four years and damaged to the core.

"What are your secrets?"

He thought for a moment. He rubbed the bridge of his nose and narrowed his eyes. His voice lowered to a whisper and I waited for the wisdom. "Whiskey."

I laughed out loud as he smirked and continued. "But really. The secret is to listen to what she doesn't say, see what she doesn't do, and hold her when she doesn't cry."

Solid advice.

"And, each night, two shots of whiskey." I chuckled again at his joke. But I was quick to notice his stern look and I knew the shots of whiskey truly were the key to his successful marriage. If I were to ever get married again, I would need to discover my own secrets to success that didn't involve drinking.

I saw Betty head back into the room and Andrea walk off down the hallway with her cell phone glued to her ear. Walter raised a brow, nonverbally asking where his daughter was going.

"She's on her phone, talking to her friend Ladasha." Her lips frowned when she said Dasha's name and Walter shook his head.

"Betty, don't start."

"What is it?" I asked. I couldn't stop wondering what it was they were exactly saying without saying. That must be exactly what Walter had been talking about for a successful relationship—listen to what she's not saying. But I wasn't trained that well. I needed it to be spelled out for me.

"I don't feel comfortable with Anders being out in New York with this friend we've never actually met until yesterday. And she seems like a nice girl but..." Betty paused and placed her hands in her lap. "I'm not racist."

"Of course not," I said.

"And Ladasha seems like a fine girl. But it appears like she has a dark past."

"Don't we all?"

"Yes. It's true. But some people don't come out of it. And I want Andrea to be able to come out of the dark past and have a future. And I wish I could feel as if Ladasha was a good influence."

I lowered my brows and rested the tip of my thumb between my teeth. "With all due respect, Mrs. Evans, I had the opportunity to sit down and speak with Ladasha. And her path was carved into shape before she had a chance to inhale her first breath. The odds were stacked against her, but she keeps smiling. She doesn't live in self-pity and she doesn't blame the world. She strives to be her best. She keeps pushing to be better, and if I had to choose a best friend for my daughter, if I had one, there would be no doubt in my mind that I would choose Ladasha."

She rubbed her bottom lip and bit it. I saw where Andrea picked up a few of her traits. "I've embarrassed myself," she said. She had, it was bullshit the way she judged Ladasha. But, I told her she shouldn't feel that way. Her cheeks became red and she picked up a glass of water to sip. "It's just, I worry, that's all."

"I would, too. About a lot of things. But if I could go ahead and ease some of your worries right now...Ladasha is not something you should worry about." I grinned and watched her sigh with relief.

"Okay."

"Okay." I stood up to step away for a moment. "Now, if you would excuse me please. I must use your bathroom."

Or, well, go find Andrea.

Same difference.

CHAPTER TWENTY-NINE

Andrea

I'D NEVER BEEN so frozen in place. It was all the same. I didn't know why I'd thought my mom would had changed anything around, or taken anything away. She didn't handle change well—I guess it ran in the family.

The photos were still taped to my mirror and the walls. And looking at Derrick and me smiling made me realize that the photos were still, attached to my heart. But that wasn't what made me freeze.

My eyes shifted to my open closet. There it was—my wedding dress hanging in the closet, zipped up and sealed in the plastic bag for protection from any harm. I aggressively cleared my throat and murmured to myself. "Don't be stupid."

I wanted Order, and I knew if I kept letting myself feel weak and falling into these moments of weakness I would never get to it. I had to face my demons instead of letting them trample over me. It was time to face it.

One step closer.

My heart started to pound in my chest. The blood flow

to my brain must have slowed down because a dizzy spell took me over.

Two steps closer.

My tongue pressed against the roof of my mouth as I wrapped my arms around my body. It felt as if the windows were opened. My eyes shifted towards the window frame, but I was shocked to find it sealed shut. How could that be? I was freezing.

Three steps.

There was no going back. The closet was before me and the white bag was peacefully resting on the hanger. It hadn't been bothered in months. Did I truly have the right to open it? What if it didn't give me any comfort by looking at it? It would only remind me of him. It would only push me back into the house and away from the porch I was desperate to step off in order to follow Cooper to a new beginning.

One step back.

"Don't you dare."

My head swirled around and landed on Cooper leaning against the doorframe. He was calm, and I wondered how long he had been there. I nervously patted my fingers against my lips and glanced back towards the white bag.

"But what if..." I whispered turning back to the handsome man who had found it his job to make sure I was all right.

"No what ifs. Keep moving forward." He nodded at the dress and I let out a short sigh. A few more steps I took. The sound of the zipper lowering was the only noise heard, but I was almost certain Coop could hear the beating of my heart.

And there it was. Still perfect. Still white. Pure. Everything I wasn't anymore.

And I laughed.

I cracked up. It was so beautiful and I was so not the person who would have worn that dress. I laughed so hard my stomach started to cramp up. This was such a funny situation I had found myself in and I couldn't control myself. I looked to Cooper to join in with my laughter and was surprised when he didn't.

He slipped his hands into his pockets, stern look on his face, and he continued leaning. "Look again, Andrea."

My chuckles vanished as my eyes traveled over the satin dress. I allowed myself to run my fingers across the beaded waistline. I caressed the sweetheart neckline. And I allowed myself to remember.

The tears followed. I turned to Cooper and wondered why he had asked me to face the truth, the loss the dress stood for. He walked over to me and wiped my tears as I shook my head back and forth. "I feel like such a baby."

"There's nothing wrong with that," he promised.

"What do you mean? Coop, since we met up you have seen me cry more than anyone. There is something wrong with that."

"Why do babies cry?" I didn't say anything. I stood there as he placed his hands on my shoulders. His green eyes stared into my blues. "Babies come out crying for a reason. It's not a sign of weakness— it's a sign of strength. It's a battle cry, saying to the universe, 'I am here and I am fucking alive.' So if you were quiet and empty after the horrific accident you experienced, I would be terrified. But tears...tears mean you can feel. Tears are a sign of life.

And I'm so happy you are alive, Andrea. Because I'm almost certain for most of the past six months you have been dead."

He was right.

After awhile of talking, I informed him that Ladasha said we should meet her and the others at the bar. He agreed, saying it sounded like a decent plan and it would be good to get me around some of my past so I could start moving towards my future. If I didn't face the people, the places, and the feelings Derrick's and my hometown, I would never be able to move on.

A FRIDAY NIGHT in a small town bar was always like a high school party. You knew everyone, and they were all drunk, loud, and dancing. When Cooper and I walked in, I smirked at seeing Michelle dancing on top of the bar with Ladasha. Michelle kept dancing closer and closer to Ladasha, and Dasha giggled. They were both wasted out of their minds and looked to be having a grand time. I needed a drink.

Walking to the bar with Cooper, I smiled to the familiar face behind the counter. "Well, well, well. Look what the cat dragged in! Andrea Evans, as I live and breathe!" Colin Gates hollered over the loud music as he leaned forward and kissed my forehead. Out of the corner of my eye I saw Cooper's eyes narrow and watched as his jaw tightened up.

Oh...look who was jealous now.

"Colin! I thought you moved down to Florida!" I yelled.

"Yeah, well, I came back to help my dad out with the bar. You know this town— it has a way of pulling you back in." I knew exactly what he meant. Colin and I went to school together, and he was the sweetest guy next to Derrick. He moved to Florida right after high school and I hadn't seen him since.

Colin lowered his eyebrows and leaned in even closer, taking my hands in his. "Hey, I'm sorry about..."

I grinned and nodded. "I know." Colin pulled my hand up to his lips and placed another kiss on them. Cooper cleared his throat loudly and I spun around to glance in his direction. "Colin, this is my..." I paused and bit my lip. "This is Cooper. He's Michelle's cousin."

Cooper gave Colin the manly nod and held his hand out for a shake. I laughed lightly as I watched the lion try to mark his territory. "Hey man, nice to meet you." His southern accent was thick—thicker than normal. So sexy.

Colin grinned and accepted Cooper's handshake. Cooper's tight handshake. "Nice to meet you. I've seen you all over television. My girlfriend loves your show. Not to sound gay, but you're a bad-ass photographer, man, and I would love for you to photograph my wedding. So! I'm guessing you two aren't here to talk but to join your friends in their drunkenness. What can I get you?"

Cooper eased up; I guessed the mention of a girlfriend brought him comfort. "I'll have a cola."

Pointing towards Michelle and Ladasha, who were

sitting on the bar counter giggling into each other's shoulders, I said, "I'll have what they're having."

Five tequila shots later, I was hammered. I hadn't been drunk since...crap. I didn't even know. But I did know it was time to dance. I tried to pull Cooper out onto the dance floor with me, but he refused, saying he would join me soon enough. I didn't have time to care; I dashed to the dance floor with Ladasha and Michelle.

These girls were a freaking good time. The fact that my best friend and soon-to-be sister-in-law got along together was excellent. Eric joined the dance floor with his socially awkward dancing and we all couldn't stop laughing. My eyes shifted to Cooper, who was talking to Steve. It looked like they were in a deep conversation, but I couldn't tell what about.

Oh well.

Time to dance.

CHAPTER THIRTY

COOPER

STEVE WAS HAMMERED. My mind slipped into parental mode as I thought about who was going to drive all these drunk-ass people home. Clearly Andrea and Ladasha were driving home with me. And Michelle was too, if Eric didn't sober up any time soon.

Steve stared out towards the dance floor with me and shook his head in Andrea's direction. "It's fucking sad, man. Derrick, he was my best friend, ya know?" He sipped on his drink as some spilled down his shirt. He didn't even notice. "And Andie was a best friend to me, too. So how do you allow yourself to hold on to a secret for so long?"

I had no clue what Mr. Drunk was talking about, but when I heard the word secret and knew Andrea was involved, I piped up.

"What do you mean by secret?"

Steve's eyes wandered across the room and landed on Rachel. Rachel waved towards me and winked. Steve made a gagging face towards her. "Fucking slut. You know, when two people love each other, fuck other people. Right?

I mean, shit. Yeah he made a mistake but as his best friend I was suppose to overlook that shit. Andie deserved better though."

Better? Better than what?

"And now she's sitting here mourning over someone who didn't even love her enough to be faithful." Steve's eyes shifted to the ground as he sipped on his drink. "But man... he was my best fucking friend."

Holy shit.

Derrick had cheated on Andrea. And from the way Steve hissed towards Rachel, I was pretty sure it was with her.

Andrea, the drunken beauty that she was, stumbled over to me and patted the sides of my face. After me, she moved on to Steve's face. I could smell the alcohol on her breath as she puckered up her lips and hissed at us in her best Joker voice. "Whyyyyyy sooooo serious?!" She giggled. I offered her my seat, knowing she couldn't stand much longer.

Colin walked over to us, looking towards Andrea, "Hey hun, what can I get you?"

Andrea stared at me; her eyes looked as if she were undressing me from my head to my toes. If I wasn't still trying to process the information just presented to me, I would have fucking loved for her to undress me with more than those eyes. She turned to Colin, bent forward, and whispered loud enough for me to hear her. "I'll have a soda pop, Colin. I really, really want a soda pop." As she swiveled around in her seat, she stared into my eyes. Her hyper, drunk self seemed to disappear as she stared at me. Her look was stern and hopeful.

"Cooper. Would you like a soda pop?" Her long eyelashes blinked once and her beautiful blues resurfaced. I was still in a stage of shock from what Steve had told me. Andrea had spent the past few months mourning over someone who had cheated on her repeatedly. She'd spent the past few months living in her mind about how she and Derrick were destined to be together. And he'd spent the last few days of his life sleeping with Rachel.

I didn't understand. Cheating. If you are so unhappy with someone, why not just leave? Why make a situation so messy? Iris could have told me she wasn't happy. She could have come to me and expressed herself in another way instead of screwing a groom in a broom closet.

Giving her a short smile, I shook my head. "I'm not too thirsty right now. But I'm going to run to the restroom and after that maybe we should all head out." I turned away from her before I could watch her face drop. I was certain there was a look of disappointment because as I walked away I heard Andrea say to Colin, "Screw the soda pop. Two more shots of tequila."

After I went to the bathroom I knew I had to get drunk girl out of the bar. My eyes shifted to the dance floor where Ladasha and Eric were dancing *very* close to each other. I couldn't even see a gap between the two of their bodies. Their eyes were locked together as if they were in some kind of deep connection. Zombie-fucking-dancing. Damn alcohol.

Where was Michelle?

"Bobby, stop it..." I heard hissed from a young girl's mouth. The voice sounded afraid of the situation before her, and as I turned towards the bathrooms, I saw Michelle pinned against the bathroom wall with Eric's best friend standing over her.

It looked like he was begging her for something. Asking her for something. It looked shady as hell and I forcefully ripped him away from her.

"Is everything okay, Chelle?" I looked at my cousin, who was so wasted with her mascara smeared under her bloodshot eyes. I wasn't sure if that was due to the tears, the alcohol, or a mix of both.

She nodded towards me as I watched Bobby run his hands through his hair. "Hey, man, I'm not sure if we actually met during dance rehearsal. I'm Bobby." He held his hand out towards me. I denied it.

"Yeah, Eric's best friend, right?" I pulled Michelle towards me and whispered, "You're drunk. Go sit next to Andie at the bar and get some water. I'll be right over and then we are going home, all right?" Her doe eyes stared at me, but she nodded in understanding and wandered over towards Andrea with the best drunk-zombie walk I'd ever witnessed. I gave Bobby a short look before heading towards the restroom.

This was one fucked up town.

CHAPTER THIRTY-ONE

Andrea

MY EYES WERE trying their best to stay open as a hot mess Michelle was sitting next to me. She stared into my eyes and for a while there appeared to be two of her...then three...okay, back to two. I apologized to her for not noticing she was engaged, and she informed me that she didn't want to throw it into my face after the accident. I shrugged and told her I was happy for her and Eric. It was about time, actually. They had been dating since middle school like Derrick and me.

They were meant for each other—everyone knew it. So there wasn't much of a different road they could have traveled down.

Or so I thought.

"How did you know, Andrea?" she whispered as she laid her head against the nasty, sticky bar countertop. She didn't care. I didn't try to stop her. Her eyes were looking at me with real concern and I smirked towards her.

"Know what?"

"That he was the one. That you were ready to spend

the rest of your life with him? I mean heck. Am I really ready to settle down for the rest of my life?" She was looking at me, but she wasn't talking to me anymore. It was as if she were looking through me. Her eyes were heavy with sadness and I couldn't help but sober up a bit. Tears started falling from her eyes and she was quick to wipe them.

"Michelle... Are you okay?" I was concerned. I'd never seen her in such a state of un-perkiness. Something was seriously wrong.

She blinked and came back to me. She shook her head, put on her bright smile, and laughed loudly. Her typical Michelle laugh. Tossing her hands up in the air she looked towards Colin and yelled, "Two more shots!"

"No more shots. Time to go." I turned in my chair and stared at Cooper standing over me. He tossed Michelle's coat to her and held mine up to help me into it. I was still so embarrassed—drunk, but embarrassed nonetheless—by how he had rejected my soda pop offer. I snatched my coat from him and rolled my eyes.

"I can do it myself."

I watched him frown as Eric stumbled over to us with his arm wrapped around a drunken Ladasha. It appeared he had sobered up quite a bit, but Cooper still said he should drive us all home.

Piling us three girls into the backseat of the car, Cooper and Eric sat in the front. I was lucky enough to ride bitch, also known as sitting in the most uncomfortable seat positioned between Michelle and Ladasha.

"Questions!" Michelle drunkenly screamed. I knew exactly what she was referring to when she said it. I remembered taking many drunken walks, drives, and runs with Michelle where we would always play the game of Questions on our way home. I explained to Cooper and Ladasha that Questions involved asking any question you would probably not ask if you were sober.

"I don't think it's a good idea," Cooper murmured from the driver's seat. He was really determined to be a party pooper.

"It's a great idea!" I yelled. "You go first, Michelle."

"Okay. Question. Is it normal to smell your breath in the palm of your hand and then lick the air to taste it?"

I burst out laughing at the random, stupid question from Michelle. And, all of us except Cooper, cupped our hands, blew into them, and licked the air. Gross.

"My turn." I smiled and shifted over as Michelle rearranged her body in the car. "Would you rather have a soda pop or a sour lemon?"

Eric smirked. "Who the hell calls it soda pop?"

I glanced at Cooper through the rearview mirror and knew he was looking towards me. He was giving me a stern look—warning me to not push the subject. My heart skipped a beat as I broke eye contact. "I don't know. Some people."

Michelle giggled, yawned into my shoulder, and closed her eyes. "That's the stupidest question ever." She was fading to sleep—probably the best idea.

"I think this is the stupidest game ever," Cooper huffed. I'd never seen him in such a bad mood. I wondered what the hell was wrong with him.

"Okay, my turn." Ladasha turned towards me, smiling as I kissed her nose.

"Could a stripper who was a bit wacky and a teacher who was handsome and smart and charming ever have a shot with one another?"

My heart sank into my stomach as I placed my hand on my chest. "Oh Dasha..." I felt so awful for her, and I looked as Eric turned to stare at her from his seat. Luckily Michelle had fallen asleep. Otherwise this had the possibility to be an extremely awkward situation.

Eric cleared his throat and turned back forward. Ladasha rolled her eyes and spoke softly. Tears formed in her eyes. "I'm so stupid..."

"You're not," I promised. Even Cooper's look showed sadness. Ladasha had lived a tough enough life, and the last thing she needed was to set herself up for another heartbreak by going for an engaged man. My brother.

The silence filling the space was heavy, somewhat tainted. Eric cleared his throat again stared straight out into the darkness. "It depends," he said. Ladasha sat up and looked at him, waiting for him to explain.

"On what?" she asked.

Eric turned as far back to face us as he could, ready to enlighten us. "It's like a kite. There are millions of kites in the world. Different shapes. Different sizes. Some kites are made for the crazy winds. Some get torn a little. And some plop! Instantly hitting the ground right out of the package." He locked eyes with Ladasha as he continued.

"And then there are the kites that are breathtakingly beautiful. The kites that have never even tried to fly because other bad kites told them they weren't good enough to soar. So that breathtakingly beautiful kite believed them. It wasn't her fault. She did what she was taught. She lived in self-doubt. She stayed grounded. That kite was stripped of a chance to ascend from the ground and rocket past the trees, into the blue sky."

Oh crap. Ladasha wasn't the only one who was tearing up now. Eric continued.

"So your question was, could a stripper who was a bit wacky—in the best possible way—and a teacher who was…" he said, smirking and winking towards Ladasha, "handsome, smart, charming, dapper, strong…"

"Yeah yeah, we get it." Ladasha laughed.

"Right. Could they ever have a shot with one another? Well, for starters, I think the girl isn't a stripper. She just stripped. There's a big difference. But if the timing was different, and the teacher wasn't already engulfed in a different lesson plan, there would be no way in hell he could let her beautiful kite pass his way without entangling their strings together forever. And ever."

And that was the end of it. He turned back forward and everyone went silent. Cooper pulled up to the house and Ladasha quickly shot out of the car, running for the house. Cooper chuckled to himself as he helped Michelle out of the car. I followed after her. Cooper laid the passed out Michelle in Eric's arms. He continued to chuckle as I turned away from him to get rid of the idea of how much I was falling for his laugh. Eric turned towards him. "What is it?"

"That was a good speech you gave."

Eric laughed and shrugged as he opened his door. "I majored in English."

CHAPTER THIRTY-TWO

COOPER

I SHUT THE car door, watching Eric carry Michelle towards the house. What a fucking night. Andrea looked at me and I gave her a half smile. She still looked pretty drunk, and cold. "Let's get inside."

"Wait," she said as she walked closer to me. I took her cold hands and rubbed them together between my hands to warm them up.

"What is it?"

"I'm sorry," she whispered. "I know from day one my signals towards you have been confusing and all over the place. And I make rules. And I change them. I cry and say panda. But next I'm begging for soda pop. Then I want you to go away. And I change the rules again. And now we are friends, with no benefits, and I don't know how I messed this up so much."

"It's all right, Andie."

She chuckled. "It's not. I just wish..." She wandered off with her sentence, shifting her feet on the ground. I kissed the top of her head and rubbed her arms.

"You're drunk."

"No," she shook her head. "I'm wide awake. And I know deep down in my heart that if today were opposite day and you had told me you hated me…I want you to know that I would say I hate you, too."

Her eyes glimmered like the white snow as she poured her heart out to me. *She loves me.* I went to open my mouth to speak, but before I could, she was bending over, violently vomiting on my shoes.

How fucking romantic.

"THIS SUCKS," ANDREA moaned into the toilet as I sat on the edge of the tub.

"At least with your new haircut you don't have to worry about holding your hair back." I chuckled towards the tequila-suffering beauty. Tequila was never a good choice. It had a way of making you feel like its best friend and suddenly, without any warning, it stabs you in the back and mocks you.

"I'm never drinking again…" she whispered. I laughed, secretly hoping she would remember her confession to me. My smile faded a bit as I thought of the other confession I'd heard today from Steve. I was beating myself up for knowing the lies Derrick had kept from her. But Derrick was gone, so what good would it be to tell her about Rachel and him? I wondered if she would still be mourning over a cheater...

I should tell her. If it came out I'd known and hadn't told her, she would kill me. Even worse, she would hate me. And I didn't mean the 'opposite day' kind of hate. And there were all the things I already wasn't telling her—all the information about Iris, my past, and the paparazzi that she deserved to know.

I'd tell her when the time was right—and when her head wasn't in the toilet.

CHAPTER THIRTY-THREE

Andrea

I WOKE UP with the need for a garbage can next to my bed. I felt awful. *Dammit Jose.* No more tequila. Ever. Pushing myself up on my elbows, I was pleased to see Cooper walking in with a tray of all types of liquids and foods on it.

"You're up."

"I'm up." And I remembered everything I'd said the night before. And I still meant it.

He placed the tray on my bed and gestured towards it. "A hangover kit. I dropped two off to Michelle and Ladasha, who both look worse off than you, may I add." He pointed towards the tray and explained what was included in this magical hangover kit.

"We have water. Coffee. Bloody Mary." I wiggled my nose as he said Bloody Mary and he removed it from the tray. "Okay, no Bloody Mary. We got toast, crackers, some weird baked bread type crap the chef made and two Tylenol."

That I could do. I opened my mouth for the Tylenol,

and he dropped them in and gave me a sip of water.

"Do you have any flaws?" I wondered out loud.

He studied me with a serious look. "I have many flaws, Andie."

I removed the tray from between the two of us and placed it on the ground. I pulled him closer to me. Stroking the side of his face, I leaned in and gave him a soft kiss on the lips. We rested our foreheads against one another and sat in silence. My head was still spinning and I wanted nothing more than to fall back to sleep in his arms.

"Speaking of flaws..." His brows lowered as he spoke.

"No." I didn't want to speak of flaws. I wanted him to lie next to me. The sun was peeking through the window shades as I lay down and patted the spot next to me. He listened to my wordless request and joined me. My body slid into the curves of his body and he held me as if it were the last thing he ever wished to do on this planet. I'd *never* felt so safe and protected in my life—and that's saying a lot.

"The costume designers are coming tomorrow for the party. We have to try things on...but until then, can we stay here?" He kissed my earlobe. I assumed that was him agreeing, and we both fell asleep. A lazy Saturday was very much needed after last night's crazy events. Plus, my head hadn't stopped pounding and I was almost certain if I got up out of bed I would pass out.

"IT'S A LITTLE tight." Ladasha sucked in her stomach as Ms. Jacobson tightened her corset.

"Suck it in!" Ms. Jacobson hollered. "I swear, Rose, these dresses weren't made for people like this," Ms. Jacobson whispered to Mrs. Rivers, who was working on Cooper's costume. Ladasha quickly placed her hand on her hip and looked to Ms. Jacobson.

"What's that suppose to mean? People like what?"

"Nothing. Nothing. Don't get your panties in a bunch. You're just a very curvy girl," Ms. Jacobson hissed. Ms. Rivers, her gossiping, rude, sidekick joined in.

"It's true, honey. And back in the time period of *Pride and Prejudice,* I'm sure there weren't any people of color involved in the balls. You should be thankful to be able to wear these pieces of clothing. Let alone take part in the dance."

I watched as Eric's fists tightened at the way the two older women were being so blatantly disrespectful towards Ladasha. Ladasha's eyes met with mine and I mouthed an apology. Michelle bounced over to Ladasha in her costume and smiled brightly. "I don't know what they are talking about. You look fabulous!" She placed her hands on Ladasha's waist and smiled. "I would kill for your curves." She winked at my best friend and walked away to help Cooper locate some of his costume pieces.

"Ouch!" I whined as my mom stood behind me and poked me with a pin.

"Hold still!"

I looked towards Ladasha and could tell the women's comments were truly bothering her. "Mom, why do you hang out with those ladies? They aren't nice people."

My mom glanced at the two women and shook her head. "I've been friends with those two for years. Besides, they weren't exactly wrong," she murmured.

I was shocked. I had heard my mom say some terrible things to me, but saying them about Ladasha pissed me off. I was embarrassed by how closed-minded this town could be sometimes. I was sure Dasha already felt a bit out of place being one of the only black people in the town, but for them to speak to her in a way to draw attention to it was too much.

"IT'S FINE," SHE told me after we finished trying on costumes. We walked around the backyard, Freckles meowing in Ladasha's arms, and sat at a bench after brushing off the snow covering it.

"It's not," I insisted.

"I ran into Eric last night." When she said that, I raised an eyebrow. I wasn't sure if they had spoken since the drunken car ride home on Friday. Whenever I mentioned it to either of them, they shrugged it off as if it had never happened.

"What happened?"

"It's embarrassing," she said. I asked her once again. It appeared Ladasha had been standing in the bathroom, door closed, giving herself one of her pep talks. "I realized I hadn't felt comfortable or had confidence in myself in a long time…and after Eric mentioned it in the car that night, I knew I had to find it. So I stood in front of the mirror and said it over and over again. 'I'm good enough.'

"And I kept saying it until I somewhat felt it. And when I opened the bathroom door, there he was. And he took my hands and said it back to me. Over and over again." Her voice sang as she remembered her moment with Eric. She started to frown. "And then his fiancée had to go and be one of the nicest people ever. I've never met a person who hugs so much and is so touchy-feely. And I'm falling for her soon-to-be husband. I'm a terrible person." She sighed, sticking out her bottom lip.

"It could be worse." I smirked.

"How so?"

I opened my mouth to speak and closed it. My shoulders shrugged. "No. You're right. You're a terrible person." Ladasha laughed and nudged me in the arm. She rested her head on my shoulder.

"What are we going to do with our lives?"

I had been wondering the same thing. There was one thing I knew—I didn't want to stay in this small town anymore. I had outgrown it. And I didn't want to be far from Ladasha. We needed each other. "Let's go back to New York."

Her eyes lit up and she grinned ear to ear. "I'm so glad you said that because I kind of sort of applied to a summer program at New York Film Academy." I was ecstatic for her! Film was the right road for her to take. It was her everything and I knew she would shine at it. "Eric pushed me to do it last night."

"Dasha, that's amazing!"

"That's not all. I kind of sort of applied for a job at a dance studio in New York. Under your name." She closed her eyes to avoid seeing my reaction, "I would need a roommate and I couldn't think of anyone else I would want to live with. Please don't kill me."

I didn't kill her. I hugged her.

THE WEEK FLEW by, and it was two days before the big Christmas party. I was actually pretty excited for it all, surprisingly; it seemed to be shaping up to be a good time. I sat in the coach house with Cooper as he stared at his laptop, going over emails. "Have you seen my cell phone?" he asked. "I swear I hate those damn things. If it's not physically attached to my body, I lose it."

"I haven't seen it."

His hands ran across his face. I watched him murmur something under his breath before he spoke loud enough for me to hear him. "Shit. My manager said he has been calling me all week. He said it's urgent. I need to go back to New York for a day to meet with him."

"Why?" I wondered. It seemed like he was holding back from telling me something, fighting the urge to let me into his head completely.

"I have to take care of some work. Figure out a few issues."

The sound of his voice was filled with worry, which in

turn made me feel extremely troubled. "Coop, is everything all right?"

He bit the tip of his thumb and smiled. "Yeah. I'm sure it's fine. He didn't say what the problem was. Kyle overreacts. I'm sure it's nothing." He closed his laptop, leaned over, and kissed my nose.

I felt a vibration under me and pulled his cell phone out from the couch cushion before handing it to him. My heart raced as I looked at him with hopeful eyes. "Let me come with you."

CHAPTER THIRTY-FOUR

COOPER

WE SAT ON the airplane, and I was freaking the hell out as I thought of landing in New York City. I didn't let Andrea know how worried Kyle actually was in his letters. Something was definitely not right, and I needed to find out what was going on as soon as possible.

"Did you bring sunglasses?"

"No, why?" she asked.

Damn. I knew the paparazzi would be waiting at the airport for photos. Kyle had already set it up for them to get their shots of me returning to the city. He said it may be needed down the line.

As we got off of the plane, I slid on my sunglasses. Andrea looked at me with questioning eyes. I took her hand into mine and rushed her out of the airport. There were a ton of people flashing their cameras in our faces. The look of horror on Andrea's face made me cringe. I felt awful. I quickly pulled her into a taxi and slammed the door behind us.

"What the hell was that?!" she hollered, looking at me,

shocked. My head hung low in embarrassment. I felt terrible.

"Welcome to my life."

We arrived to the hotel, just to be tackled by more paparazzi there, and I raced her inside before any questions could be asked. As we finally made it to the room, I sighed heavily and fell onto the bed. Andrea stood with her hands on her hips and raised an eyebrow.

"Cooper. What's going on? Why are they following you?"

"Iris and I are filing for divorce. Ya know, they love their drama."

Her hand flew to her mouth, "Oh my gosh. They are going to think I'm the other woman!" She paused before continuing, "How do you get used to that?"

I took off my shoes as she joined me on the bed. "You don't." I needed to warn her if she came across the paparazzi when I wasn't around. "Andie...those people. They have a way of knowing things about us. Things we don't know about ourselves. And they lie. It's their fucking jobs to lie. Just...don't feed into any of it if you cross paths with them." She nodded with understanding, but I knew it wasn't something she could understand without experiencing it firsthand.

"When do you meet with your manager?"

"Tomorrow morning."

She removed her shoes, and climbed behind me, and started giving me a back massage. My eyes closed with satisfaction as her fingers rubbed me down.

"We should go to a world where there is no drama. No death. No cheating. No divorce. No one else but us. Back to where we started," she said as she lightly kissed my earlobe. A slight moan escaped my mouth.

"Back to our space in between," I agreed.

"Back to us."

I turned towards her and rotated her body on top of mine. I brought her face close to mine and studied her beauty. She wasn't the same girl I'd met that one Friday night. That girl was hardly there. But today, Andrea was staring back at me, her eyes sparkling. Her light had been found. My lips ran across hers and she slightly parted her mouth, before pulling back. Raising an eyebrow, I asked her what was wrong.

Her blue eyes blinked and I watched them reappear. "I know people have told me that I need time. Time to heal. I need space to find my way. But what they don't know is I have found my way. I was led to you during my lowest form of Chaos. I found my Order. I found you. Cooper, I love you."

Our next kiss was the best kiss we had ever shared. It was as if our lips were destined to be together forever and always. I pulled back and smiled towards her. "I love you, too."

I laid her on the bed and stood over her. She was wearing a light blue button-down shirt and tight blue jeans, fucking stunning. I started with the top button and worked my way down. She was patiently waiting with her arms to her sides, and I took my time. We weren't in any hurry. We were going to enjoy this moment together, making love for the first time with one another.

Before when we had sex, it was a way of forgetting. Of getting lost, of letting go of reality, and finding a single moment when we could shut off our brains from overthinking. But now... now we did it for us. Just the two of us. No one else.

    I bent down and kissed her stomach with gentle pecks. She lifted my arms and pulled my shirt over my head. Her fingertips ran across my chest as she pulled me closer to her. I began kissing her neck, running my tongue across the same spot, massaging her skin with my mouth, sucking lightly, moving down to her collarbones. I continued to explore her body. She moaned my name, begging for me, but I was the one addicted.

    "Cooper..." she sighed as I curved my tongue to outline her bra. Sliding my hand behind her back, I unhooked the bra and slid it off her body. Her breasts were so perfect, and I was happy to glide my mouth over her hardened nipples. Her whimpers pleading for more of me turned me on so fucking much. She unzipped my jeans and slid them off, allowing her hands to travel into my boxers before she slid them to the ground. For a moment I just lay there.

    "Mmm...Andie..." I whispered as my lips explored her breasts a moment longer before I covered her mouth with mine. I kissed her hard, and she kissed back harder. Deeper. She parted my lips and allowed our tongues to get to know one another on a deeper level. I loved her kisses. I loved her so fucking much.

    We didn't leave the hotel room. We stayed wrapped in each other's arms. I never could have dreamt of the beautiful moment we had shared with one another. That night, we stayed up, learning more about one another. Finding out more details about our drives in life. Our passions. I asked her everything I could think to ask about her life. And she asked me the same. Her mind brought out the best memories, and she would start laughing as she shared them with me. I wanted to know everything about Andrea Mae Evans, and I was so thankful she took me there.

She didn't put her clothes back on. Instead she wore one of my white t-shirts that swallowed up her small frame, yet somehow it appeared to be a damned perfect fit in my mind. She picked up my camera and started taking pictures of me. I felt uncomfortable because being behind the camera was where I belonged.

"Tell me what you like about me," she grinned, holding the camera up and snapping away. I hesitated, rolling my eyes, knowing how this game ended the last time. "Don't worry. I'm not freaking out this time." Her smile pulled me in, she looked so sexy in my t-shirt.

My hands wrapped around her waist and I lowered her down to the bed. Straddling her, I smiled, allowing her to keep taking photos of me. Then I took the camera away, sitting it next to us, and stared at her. "Alright...but I'm warning you, if you panic, I'll hold you down forever." I cautioned. She smirked wider, wiggling her nose.

"And that's supposed to be punishment? Come on, we don't have all night."

I brushed my fingers up and down her neck, watching her relax into the bed. "I can't say what I like about you, but I'll tell you a few things. When you were seven, Eric broke a lamp, but you took the blame for it—afraid that he wouldn't get to go to his baseball game, where you cheered the loudest. When you were eight, you lost a tooth and buried it in the backyard so a weird creep wouldn't walk in on you at night.

"When you were thirteen, you cried because you thought someone kidnapped Oscar the cat...Sorry about that one." Her lips curved up even more, and I felt everything inside of me fall even deeper for her. "And today you're twenty-two, wearing my t-shirt, your body under mine, looking up at me. And your eyes lock with mine in such a sexy way that it makes me want to rip off your shirt and just lay with you naked. It's not even that I want to have sex with you. I just want to fucking lay with you."

Her eyes started to glass over with water and I shook my head. "So I'm sorry, I can't say what I like about you. Because it stopped being 'like' a long time ago for me. I stopped liking you at age nine and fell in love with you at nine-in-a-half."

I watched as a small gasp released from her lips. She wrapped her hands around my torso, pulling me down to rest my mouth against hers. "Thank you," she murmured.

Picking up the camera, I started taking her photos. The light in her eyes right then and there had to be captured. It was the most beautiful thing I'd even witnessed. It was the best feeling, taking her picture; at least I thought that until she started taking photos of the both of us together.

Best fucking night of my life.

CHAPTER THIRTY-FIVE

Andrea

I OPENED MY eyes to the sunlight shining. It was the first good night sleep I'd had in quite some time. Turning to my left, I noticed a body was missing and had been replaced with a note:

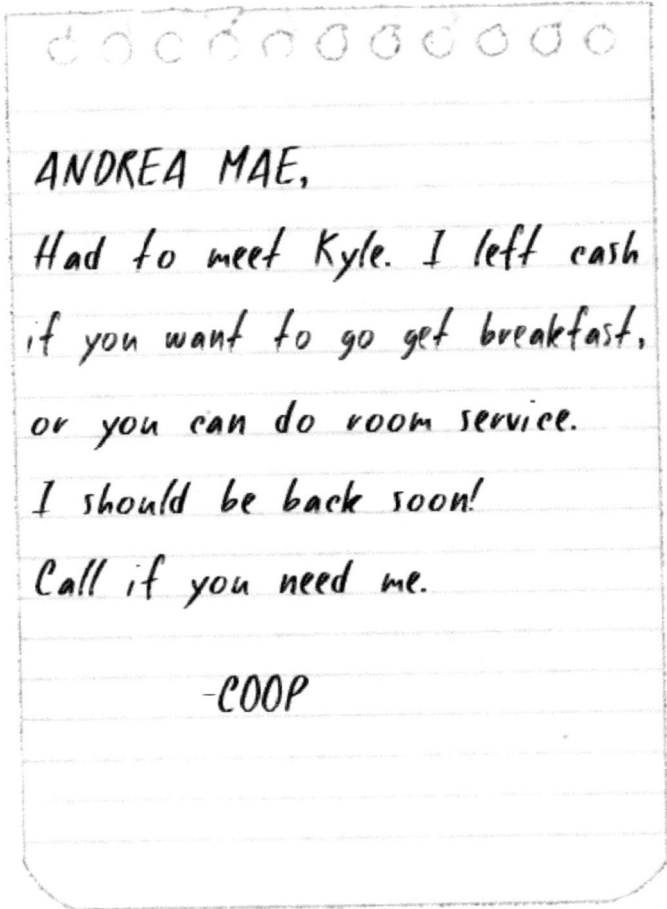

ANDREA MAE,
Had to meet Kyle. I left cash if you want to go get breakfast, or you can do room service. I should be back soon! Call if you need me.

-COOP

I looked down at the cash left on the bed—a one hundred dollar bill. Yeah, because everyone spends that kind of money on breakfast, Cooper. Next to the money was a pair of sunglasses—in case I needed to go undercover? As I went to get out of the bed, I paused. A wave of sickness washed over me. I rushed to the bathroom, throwing up.

Something was wrong. I'd never had a hangover that lasted this long. Splashing water across my face, I stared into the bathroom mirror and a level of concern grew in me. My mind mentally started to check the invisible calendar in my head. Crap. No...

I splashed my face again. All color was drained from my body. I couldn't be. Grabbing the money off of the bed, I tossed on the sunglasses and headed out of the hotel. I needed to find the closest corner store. When I dashed into one, my mind was working faster than my feet could travel. Where was it? I glanced around the space and found the pregnancy tests. I got three—couldn't hurt.

What if I were pregnant? Crap...I drank so much the other night. I hoped...Stop. I had to slow down my mind. Too much was going on and I wasn't even sure if I was...

I paid for the tests, and as I walked out, I was shocked to see the paparazzi standing around me. How did they track me down? "Where are you heading? Where's Cooper?" they hollered. I remembered what Cooper had told me and kept walking with my head down. "Rumor has it Cooper is with Iris right as we speak. How does that make you feel?" one of the paparazzi guys yelled. I paused when I heard it and shook my head. He was meeting with his manager.

The next person's question freaked me out a bit more. "Is your name Andrea Evans?" They could probably see how stunned I looked through my sunglasses. I turned to go the other way as they began to feed on my sudden nervousness. "How does it feel to be a home wrecker? They are still married, you know."

"Is it true you are a prostitute?"

What? That's ridic—I took off my sunglasses as I saw the photo the fat paparazzi man was holding in his hand. It was a photo of me almost taking taxi money from Cooper the first night at his hotel, but for some reason, that photo made the exchange look a lot shadier than it was.

My heart started to race. I couldn't go back to the hotel. Instead, I broke into a run. As fast as I could. My eyes filled with tears as I found my way back to my apartment building.

Opening my apartment door, I rushed in, slammed the door, and approached the couch. Next to it was Derrick's cologne, and I sobbed as I sprayed it into the air. The smell of Derrick filled my body, and I slipped a few inches closer to Chaos. How could this be happening? Where did those pictures come from? Why was Cooper with Iris?

My mind was flashing recent memories of Cooper and me. Within an instant, flashes of Derrick and I appeared. My past was once again controlling my present, with its hands wrapped brutally around my heart. *Squeezing it* with so many doubts. *Filling it* with so much sadness that I was almost certain I was dead. There was no way my heart was strong enough to deal with the memories and questions that my brain was dishing out.

My teeth bit down on my tongue as I dumped out the contents of my purse onto the ground. Shifting through it, I allowed the tears to fall, not taking time to breathe, not taking time to feel. I saw it glimmering under a pen and picked it up. My engagement ring was staring me down and I sobbed into my hands, knowing I didn't deserve the right to ever wear it again.

Everything hurt, nothing made sense. Just last night

everything seemed so perfect. Last night everything was right. And this morning...this morning I couldn't breathe.

CHAPTER THIRTY-SIX

COOPER

I DIDN'T KNOW why, but Kyle had made it completely clear I had to meet with Iris. He said I needed to clear some things up before he and I could start handling the big issues.

I sat in the chair across from her in the apartment. As far away as possible. The last time I saw her, she was blackmailing me to stay married to her, so I had enough reasons to doubt this was going to be a pleasant visit. "What's going on?" I said with a dark tone. I didn't have any need to be polite to her.

"I need you..." she said, looking down towards her hands resting on her ever-growing belly.

"Iris, seriously."

"You never asked me," she whispered as she looked up at me. "You never asked me how it was after the miscarriages."

I hadn't. But I hadn't been able to bring myself to talk about it. It hurt too fucking much. We dived into work, wrapped our worlds around material things, and forgot—

together. Iris never showed any signs of breaking. She kept going strong. Doing her job. Holding up her appearance.

"How was I supposed to know? You never cried, you never talked, you never said..."

"I'm your wife!" she bellowed. "Did it really need to be stated that I was broken? That the one thing I knew you wanted more than anything in this world, I couldn't give to you?"

I thought of what Walter had told me during 'Thanksgiving' dinner—what it took to make a marriage work. *The secret is to listen to what she doesn't say.* Iris had been crying out to be heard. She'd been screaming, and I hadn't noticed. She buried herself into the reality show, never talking about our loss.

See what she doesn't do. I hadn't seen her. I had been so wrapped up in my own grief that I didn't think I could have seen her. How did I not see she was *not* falling apart? That should have been the first warning sign. No one that went through having two children in their body and having them ripped away could be all right.

And hold her when she doesn't cry. I couldn't even think of the last time we'd held hands, unless it was being filmed and the producers had told us to or if the paparazzi were around and we had an image to uphold. Otherwise we'd walked past each other.

"I'm sorry," I said. I meant it.

"I wasn't going to tell the tabloids about your dad," she whispered. "I would never...Cooper. I'm so sorry. I was afraid you would never come back to me after..." She glanced down to her stomach.

I didn't think she was that evil. She informed me she'd

told Kyle that just to make me meet with her. She knew it was low, but she was in a low place. How far would I go to keep the woman I loved around?

Andie...

Hell, I had flown to a different state to keep Andrea. I felt terrible for Iris, but I knew our relationship was over. It had been over for years now; we just never spoke of it. The comforting look she gave me informed me that she, too, knew it was over. She reached into her coat pocket and pulled out an envelope. "Don't worry. I haven't been following you." She smiled as I moved over to the couch and took it from her. Divorce papers. "No sense in dragging it out." A short laugh escaped her lips.

I took her hands and pulled her into a tight hug. It'd been so long since I'd held her. "Thank you, Iris," I said as she pulled away and wiped her eyes. I made her promise me she would take care of herself and her baby girl. And if she ever needed anything, money included, she should contact me. She refused. Said she didn't deserve it.

"You really like this girl?"

A heavy sigh escaped my lips as I nodded, "I really do." Iris burst out into more tears, sobbing uncontrollably. "Iris. Shit, please don't cry. I wish things were different...but..." I tried to get my words together. *Dammit.* I wish English teacher Eric were here to speak on behalf of me.

"No, it's not that. It's just...I did something wrong. And you are going to hate me," she said. Her eyes fell to the ground and she cussed under her breath. When she looked up to me, I saw the way her lips turned down. There was a tiny twitch in the lower corner of her mouth and she said, "I'm so sorry." I knew *exactly* what it was she'd done by the sound of her voice.

And I was fucked.

"When does it come out?" I asked. If it came out later, I could somehow do some damage control. I could talk to the right people, and move things around a bit. Not to save my ass, but to save...

She shifted on the couch, uncomfortable, but she knew she had to answer. "They came out this morning."

They?

"Us Weekly. Star Magazine. And People. I didn't know what to do! The night we talked and you stormed out, I was still so angry with you and I wasn't thinking straight," she said, ashamed.

My mind was on the fast track. I didn't need Andrea to find out like this. I needed to tell her what was happening before someone else did. I needed her to know the truth behind the magazine articles, not just glimpses of truth she might read in those bullshit tabloids.

I knew there would be some terrible things said in those magazines about me, and I was prepared for that. Hell, I was used to that. If I looked at a person wrong, the magazines tagged me as the next Hitler. But Andrea...

Andrea's name was about to be pulled through the mud because of something I did.

She was about to be exposed.

SHE WAS GONE when I got back to the hotel room. I wasn't surprised. I was sure she'd found out by now. I went to her apartment and banged on the door, praying she would open it, but she didn't. I could hear her sobbing on the other side. *Fuck!* My forehead fell to the door and I closed my eyes. Praying for her to let me in.
"Andrea...Please..." I whispered into the crease of the door. When it opened, my eyes washed over her. First I saw her bloodshot, puffy eyes. My heart was ripping into pieces...I did that to her. Then I smelt *his* cologne. No words could form in my mouth. This ever-growing feeling that I was losing the one damn thing that made sense in my world took over me. My palms became clammy as I saw the last thing—I saw her wearing his sweatshirt and pants again. "Andie...no..."

She was closing herself off. She was retreating back to the land of Chaos all because of my fucked up issues. She didn't say a word, but her lips parted. I watched as her bottom lip began to quiver and her knees began to shake. She moved her lips again but choked on the air as a wave of fresh tears started to pour out. My arm reached for her, but she shook her head back and forth.

I couldn't be the wall that needed to hold her up that night. Because I was the one who pushed her off of the ledge, she was falling because of me.

She looked to the ground and wrapped her arms around herself tight. Her voice was soft, drenched in sadness. "Go away, Cooper."

I returned to the hotel, and kept trying to call and text her. As I picked up my phone and dialed again, I sighed, listening to it go straight to voicemail. I listened to

Derrick's voice on her voicemail and felt a twinge of jealousy, but I instantly felt like a dumbass and left my pathetic message. "Hey—it's me again. We need to talk...all right? Well, otherwise the plane leaves tomorrow at 10:15 a.m." My head dropped to the ground as I continued my message. "Andie...please call. I just want to know you're okay."

CHAPTER THIRTY-SEVEN

Andrea

I MET HIM at the airport. He rushed over to me to make sure I was all right. I wasn't. I felt used, foolish. But I wouldn't let him know that. After he saw me broken last night, I promised myself not to let him see me in that light ever again. I would stand strong. After a delayed flight, we finally boarded the plane, with not much time to spare. I ignored him the whole flight back to Wisconsin. Even he couldn't be dumb enough to try to talk to me. I noticed his eyebrows frowning, and his hollow cheeks, but didn't care one bit.

When we got back to Michelle's family's mansion, the house was already being set up for the party. Red and green decorations were draped throughout the house. The caterers were preparing the food, and the party planners were rushing around like madmen, finishing up the last details. I only had about fifteen minutes to get ready before our main dance, and I was a hot mess.

Walking into the living room, I saw Ms. Jacobson, Mrs. Rivers, and Eric comforting my mother, who was in hysterics. Daddy was sitting on the couch and looked shell-shocked.

"Mom, what's the matter?" When she looked up at me, I knew what she had learned. My eyes shot over to Eric. "You told her."

"No," he assured me. "You just did."

My mom was holding magazines in her hands and threw them at my feet. I bent down and saw the other magazines. My heart was breaking all over again. "I sure hope you know who this Cooper Davidson really is!"

She ran off crying, and Daddy and Eric raced after her. The two gossip queens followed after them, but I was pretty sure it was only to collect more details to share at their book club.

I STOOD SMOOTHING out my Victorian dress in the mirror when I heard his southern voice behind me. "We should talk," he said.

"I'm busy."

"I can explain."

Turning towards him, I locked into his green eyes. I was stern with my next words, because the answer to them would determine every action I made after. "Did you know? About the pictures? About the magazines?"

Silence.

My heart sank.

He knew.

I turned away from him, unable to look at the person who I had given so much of myself to over the past weeks. I gave him *everything*.

"Andie..." he whispered. I could hear him coming closer and I sharply turned around.

"Don't call me that! What the hell do you want, Cooper? You want me to act like we are now some couple falling deeply in love?" I shouted. I couldn't believe he even had the nerve to walk into my room right now. My hands formed fists, with my nails digging deep into my flesh.

He lowered his eyebrows. "What are you talking about?"

I rolled my eyes, tossing my hands up in frustration. "Let's stop acting like we are normal. Like *this* is normal. The first night we met, we fucked. The first few weeks all we did was have sex with each other."

Shaking his head, he stepped closer. I stepped back. "You're going backwards."

"I'm telling you the facts." I bent down to start putting on my shoes and cringed when I heard him use my nickname again.

"Andie, please."

"DO NOT CALL ME THAT!" I screamed. Every ounce of me was boiling. I could feel my insides twisting, my stomach feeling sick.

He looked at me as if I were a stranger, and let's face it, I pretty much was. His voice lowered in tone. "You need to get a clue. Figure something out because you are acting crazy."

I couldn't believe him. He was really trying to push me to the edge. My mother was sitting in the other room crying her eyes out because of him, thinking I was a whore of a child. Daddy was probably having a mini-heart attack thinking about his baby girl and what she'd done in New York City. And then he had the nerve to call *me* crazy? "You think I'm crazy?" I picked up my shoe and threw it at him as hard as I could. I cringed, watching him dodge it. So of course I threw my other shoe, harder. "You think I'm a lunatic? You were the one in the fucking mental hospital, not me!" I turned away from him before I saw his reaction. I knew it probably stung him, because after it came out of my mouth, it stung me.

"Who told you?"

Walking over to my desk, I tossed the magazines my mom gave me onto the floor in front of Cooper. As he bent down and picked them up, he shook his head back and forth.

The title on one read, *"Iris Davidson speaks out: Cooper abandoned his family and takes trip to loony bin."*

Another title read, *"Cooper Davidson addicted to prostitution, three different women tell their sides of the story."*

And another: *"Cooper Davidson violent anger rages on as Iris shares her side."*

He tossed the magazines on the bed and turned towards me. A firm look took over his eyes—a look I had never witnessed before on him. "Yeah. I'm sure you learned a lot about me from those tabloids. I bet you feel like you know who I am now."

"No. I don't. I don't know anything about you. Let's

face it though. You don't know anything about yourself either. You don't talk about Iris because it makes it real. Reality check, Cooper—it's real. And the kid you abandoned is real too. I can't believe I believed you when you said it wasn't your kid. Deal with your fucking issues."

"You want me to deal with *my* issues? God forbid something reminds you of your dead fiancé!"

I was beyond pissed now. How dare he bring Derrick into this. "Fuck you!" I screamed.

"You already did!"

I couldn't believe he'd said that. And from the look in his eyes, he could hardly believe it either. "I hate you," I whispered as I shoved him hard in his shoulder. I shoved him again, and again..."I hate you! I HATE YOU!" I felt his hands wrap around my wrists as I kept pushing him. "Let me go, *let me go!*" I screamed, fighting the tears that were begging to fall. I wouldn't let them. I couldn't let them.

His eyes moved to his hands around my wrists and he instantly dropped them and turned away from me, running his hands over his face. "God dammit, Iris! Will you listen for one fucking second?!"

I paused as he turned back to me and I stared into his eyes. "My name is Andrea."

His body shifted as his eyebrows frowned, recognizing his mistake. "I know that."

My body began to tremble. I could hardly hold myself up, but I did my best not to show it. "You just called me Iris. See? This isn't real. You and me. We are two screwed up people trying to get over those who screwed up our minds."

"Stop," he begged. I wouldn't. I couldn't.

"Your mom tried to fix your dad and look how that worked out for her. Stop following in her footsteps. Stop trying to fix other people…"

"What are you talking about?"

"Your plan, Cooper. To try to fix people who are terribly broken. Iris messed up your first plan. She was too damaged for you to fix. So I'm your second choice."

"That's not it."

"Then what is it, Cooper? What happens when I mess up your plans? Do you run off and get a third?" He didn't answer right away. His face fell to the ground and he rubbed his hands across his mouth, annoyed by my questions.

"Andrea."

"But the truth is, you're my second choice. If Derrick were here…"

"He's not. He's dead Andrea. Derrick is gone." He looked at me in the most sincere fashion, but his words bit me. His words slapped me. His words almost fucking slaughtered me.

"Stop it." I softly spoke. The trembling was getting worse. Crap.

"You're living in a lonely place. And it's dark and scary. And whenever you get *close* to moving on you panic and run back into your shell. And the truth of the matter is you don't even know who Derrick really was."

"Don't you dare talk about him!" How could he say that? How could he speak about the one person who loved me?

"He cheated on you, Andrea," he said quietly. So quiet

that I almost missed the words.

What a sick bastard. I couldn't believe he would stoop that low. "Get out!"

His face dropped and he realized what he'd said. "I'm sorry..."

"You're disgusting. You were so desperate that you actually paid someone to spend fifteen minutes with you in a dirty club." I wanted to make him hurt the way he'd attacked me with his words.

"Don't do this," he begged, his concentrated eyes glossing over with water.

I had to. "You are so pathetic that you found the need to sleep with someone from the strip club. You're a fucking creep."

He tossed his hands up in defeat. "What do you want from me? You want me to yell at you? Is that what you want?" He raised his voice to a level that was somewhat frightening. "You want me to *fucking yell*?! You want me to tell you that you were, in fact, the whore I paid to spend fifteen minutes with?"

"You should leave. Really. Whatever this was was fun. But it's over."

"So that's it?" I remained silent when he asked. "What's going on in your head, Andrea?"

"I took a pregnancy test in New York." His eyes widened and pure shock washed over him. My insides twisted tighter. I knew what I was about to say would make him leave forever. "It was negative. And you know how I felt? Happy. Because I would never want someone to have such an asshole as their father. You would make a terrible parent. And you would walk out on us just like you did Iris and your daughter."

All color was drained from him. He was silent for a moment before he nodded his head in understanding. Sliding his hands into his pockets, he rocked back and forth. The same way he rocked the first night I met him in the club... "Maybe you're right. Maybe we are two people trying to make something work when, in all honesty, it just isn't there. "

He turned to leave and looked towards the magazine covers one last time. "And for the record, I would never abandon my child. It's kind of hard to abandon something that was never yours. Tell your tabloids to get their shitty facts straight."

And with that, he was gone. My body continued to shake, but I turned to face the mirror, ran my hands across the back of my neck, and went back to smoothing out my dress.

I had a party to get to.

THE MOMENT I walked into the ballroom, I knew it was going to be a long night. But first, I had to dance. Thank God for dance. The group lined up. I avoided eye contact with Cooper and followed the steps. When I passed Ladasha, she whispered, "Are you all right?" I shook my head and kept moving. I switched to Cooper as my partner and looked away from him, our fingers hardly touching.

I overheard Bobby, Eric's best friend, telling Michelle tonight was the night. I had no clue what they were talking about. But I didn't care. I didn't have room for more drama. I kept moving. Eric looked at me with worried eyes as I curtseyed towards him and moved to Steve.

"You all right, Andrea?" he whispered.

My eyes started to tear up when I heard him ask. I was breaking. We switched partners. I glided by Rachel and she looked at me with concern. She turned towards me. "You found out?"

Wow, the gossip queens got around fast. I nodded to her as we moved around the group again. Once again, I was the main talk of the town. As I danced past Rachel again, she said, "It only happened a few times after you went to college."

My eyes froze on her as she flowed around again. I curtseyed towards Bobby, and kept moving with my eyes on Rachel. When she came back around I had a knot in my stomach and listened to her say, "And after you two got engaged it only happened once after that. We felt it was wrong."

No. I couldn't dance anymore. I couldn't move any longer. The shocked look on my face made Rachel realize I hadn't had any idea about her and Derrick. I thought Cooper had been lying, being spiteful in the moment of our argument. *No way...*

I looked to Steve for conformation. His eyes told me Rachel wasn't lying. I needed air. No. Not my Derrick. Derrick never would have done something like that. We were committed to one another. We had our promises we made to each other. *Til death do us part...*

I couldn't dance anymore. I stopped moving and the whole room began to spin. My eyes locked with Cooper's. He stepped towards me and I put up my hand to stop him. I couldn't do this. I was breaking. I was shattering. Memories started flooding back into my mind as the dreadful truth settled in.

My eyes widened with excitement. I loved when he wrote songs about me. I bit my bottom lip and looked up to my baby. "He loves me, huh?"

Steve cleared his throat and nodded, chugging his drink. "The best way he knows how."

The best way he knows how? *Stop*...I was going to be sick. Everything was hitting me at full speed and I couldn't bring it to a standstill. My heart was trying to escape from my chest, pounding for a way out, begging for an escape route to make the hurt stop. I could hear Derrick's voice echoing through my head.

"What if I'm not enough for you? What if I end up fucking all of this up? Screwing us up?"

Sweat was painting my face; I could feel everyone's eyes. I could *hear* their thoughts. Poor lonely Andrea. Her dead fiancé cheated on her. How could she be so blind? What did it even mean?

How was I supposed to process this? I had to leave. Forcing my feet to relocate, I rushed out of the room, trying to get away. Ladasha began to follow after me and I shouted for her to leave me alone. I wanted everyone to leave me alone.

CHAPTER THIRTY-EIGHT

COOPER

I WATCHED HER storm out. When Ladasha came back from chasing her, my heart cringed as I heard Mrs. Rivers mumble that if it weren't for that black girl, Andrea wouldn't be such a mess. Ms. Jacobson joined in. "I bet she's a stripper and prostitute, too. I'm sure she dragged Andrea into it."

"What did you say?" Eric's eyes widened as he walked over to the women. Ladasha looked worried.

"Eric, don't," she said softly, not wanting to start trouble.

"No, what did you two just say?" He was angry. With good reason. What those two were saying was out of line.

"So she *is* a stripper, isn't she?" Betty asked her son. She looked so disappointed. Crushed.

"Yeah, Okay, Mom? She's a stripper. But so what? Big deal. She's also a brilliant classical dancer. She has an insane knowledge of movies and she also has feelings. Okay? Is everyone happy?" No one said a word. Michelle looked towards Eric with confusion in her eyes, but he didn't notice. He kept talking. "And so what if Ladasha does something a little different for her night job? I mean, haven't we all made mistakes in our lives? Haven't our kites all been torn before?

"The truth is, Ladasha can do anything she sets her mind to. She's a beautiful woman who I am falling in love with." As those words came out, the whole room gasped. Even Eric gasped after he said them, as if it were the first time he'd realized his feelings. He turned towards Michelle, who had tears in her eyes as Bobby wrapped an arm around her. "Michelle, I'm so sorry. It's just…"

I had a feeling Michelle was going to be okay with what happened. I was almost positive that if she was ever going to announce the secret relationship that I was pretty sure was happening with Bobby, right now would be the best time. Hell, everyone else was telling their secrets tonight. She might as well join in. "I'm a lesbian."

Oh. I hadn't seen that coming.

"I'm sorry, what?" A shocked Eric swallowed hard as he looked at not-so-much-his-fiancée.

"Bobby has been trying to get me to talk to you and tell you…and I was going to before Thanksgiving but you proposed and…" She looked over to her parents and Eric's parents. "Everyone was there and happy, and after what happened with Derrick…it seemed like everyone could use some good news."

Eric laughed. "You're a lesbian?"

Ladasha giggled out loud. "Oh my gosh! That explains all of the touchy-feely hugging!" Her hands covered her mouth. "Oh wait. So when you said you would kill for my curves…you actually meant you wanted *my* curves…?"

Michelle blushed. "I'm sorry. It's just that... You're so sexy and funny and..."

"...Off the market." Eric chuckled defensively.

It was clear the night was over. I walked towards the back of the house to head to the coach house and pack my stuff. There was nothing left for me in good ol' Wisconsin and it was time for me to get back to my world.

"Are you leaving, Cooper?" I followed the sound of the voice as I walked past a study. Looking inside, I saw Walter sitting there, working on building a ship in a bottle. I paused, turned towards him, and stood in the doorway.

"Mr. Evans. Yeah, I'm on my way out."

"Have a seat, son."

I obeyed.

"As a father, you worry. You start to wonder what's going on when you call to the restaurants your daughter says she's working at out in New York, and they say they never heard of her. But you patiently wait, hoping she will come to you when she sees fit. And then..." He leaned forward against the desk, and clasped his hands together. "And then you show up, Mr. Davidson. And I see a light in her I hadn't seen in a long time. You're making her better."

I shook my head. "She won't let me in."

"Anders will never say it...but she's like her mom in so many ways. She's not as dramatic as Betty, but she is as passionate. Stubborn like no other. And I'm sure she said some awful things to you."

"I deserved it," I promised. I couldn't imagine what was going through Andrea's head with not only a pregnancy scare, but also dealing with the paparazzi, the tabloids, Derrick. I was surprised she wasn't completely insane yet.

"If she's as much like her mother as I believe, you didn't."

Biting the tip of my thumb, I sat back in the chair, wondering what to do next. "I've never dealt with something like this. Someone like her."

Walter nodded in understanding and sat back in his chair. Picking up his ship in the bottle, he held it out to me. I took it, studying it as he spoke to me. "The time and commitment it took to make this was excruciating. I'd almost completed the ship. Then with one mistake, one quick movement, the sail fell over. But I didn't give up—I tried again. And now we have a complete ship that is ready to sail. I'm so glad I took the time to fix it."

"How do I fix something that doesn't want to be anywhere near me?" I asked.

His crooked smile and kind eyes paired well with his soft tone. "I'm not saying it will be easy, and I'm not saying it will happen overnight. Whatever demons eating at her have to be dealt with. But if you care for her as much as I think you do...you'll do anything. Even if that means loving her from a distance."

Another secret from Walter Evans. Not a secret to a successful marriage—yet more of a secret to holding on to an Evans female.

"WHY WON'T YOU stop? Can't you tell it's over?" she hissed as she turned to see me standing in her doorway. She was packing her bags to escape again. I stepped into the room and approached her. "Cooper, I'm serious," she warned, dropping a few t-shirts into her luggage.

I didn't say a word. The closer I stepped, the more she tensed up. I reached out for her and she shoved me away. *Hard.* I stepped closer. "Panda!" she hollered, pushing me again. Her face was angry, but her eyes were dry. There were no tears to be found. She started swatting at me, kicking, screaming for me to go away. She screamed panda over and over. I didn't leave.

I pulled her into a tight hug and held her close to me. I could feel her body trying to revolt. Trying to yank itself away from me and her hands slapping me hard against my chest, but I didn't care. The hits became fewer in frequency, and the screams got quieter. She began to sob. Her body trembled in my arms as her legs gave out and she slid to the floor. I glided her down, not letting her go.

"Panda..." she whispered, tears unable to stop themselves from falling. I held on tighter as she wrapped her arms and legs around me.

"I know...Panda, I know..." I spoke softly against her ear as I felt her pulling on my shirt, holding me even closer as she cried.

It wasn't long before I noticed Ladasha and Eric standing in the doorway, watching their loved one fall apart. I nodded them in, and they slowly entered. I released my grip from Andrea and replaced it with the arms of her best friend and brother. They covered her with their love as I stood up and walked towards the doorframe. Andrea's eyes looked up, blue as ever, and locked with mine. We both knew it would be a long while before we saw each other again.

I understood what Walter was telling me. Knowing when to step away, and knowing how to say goodbye. I had to trust my gut. And right now, my gut was telling me Andrea didn't need me around her to bring more confusion into her life. My heart was breaking as I tore away my eye contact with her and left to the sounds of her tears. But I didn't care about my heart. I cared about hers having the time to heal.

And to tell the truth, I hadn't given myself the time to let my heart heal—from my parents, the miscarriages, from the cheating, the failed marriage.

We could both take the time to heal our bodies, minds, and spirits.

Together.

From a distance.

CHAPTER THIRTY-NINE

Andrea

HE WAS GONE. Waking up the next morning and knowing he wouldn't be there stung me. Waking up the next week and Cooper still not being there was almost unbearable. Christmas came. New Years went. And I kept myself busy. Eric kept up his word that he would help with paying for our apartment in New York while I pulled myself together in Wisconsin.

I told him that he didn't have to, but he informed me that Michelle had insisted. She went out of her way to allow Eric, Ladasha, and I to stay at the mansion while I collected myself. I secretly thought it was because she still had a semi-crush on Ladasha. Who could blame her? My best friend was beautiful. Smart. Funny.

After I scolded my mom for the way she treated Ladasha, she realized how much of a disappointment she had been.

"Andrea Mae...I..." Her head lowered as I sat on my parents' living room couch, Ladasha next to me. My mom turned to my friend, "Ladasha Marie. I am so sorry for the way I have treated you."

Ladasha smiled, revealing her dimples and shrugged her shoulders. "It's all right, Mrs. Evans. I've come to learn that people treat you the way you allow yourself to be treated. I should have stood up for myself."

Mom placed her hand on Dasha's knee and shook her head. "You should have never had to. And Anders has told me how good you have been to her. Watching after her. I want you to know, if you ever need anything…know that my family welcomes you with open arms."

That was true. Ladasha was my sister. If anything showed that, it was how harsh Mom was towards her—the same way Mom was harsh towards me. After Mom welcomed her as part of our family, she began to scold her about how dangerous stripping was and said Ladasha should have thought more of herself to stoop to that level. She turned to me, pointing her finger, and sassed me on the same topic. She informed Ladasha that she would, indeed, finish her college degree. She followed all the sassiness up with hugs.

It was kind of what my mom did—worried, judged, worried some more, and then hugged. I told Dasha that she would get used to it. She smiled and told me it was the most mothering she had ever received in all of her life.

Daddy walked into the room smiling at me with what looked like a toy robot in his hands. It was made of metal and stood about five feet tall with a weird looking tail. "Look at this." His eyes glimmered through his thick-glasses that sat across his gray sideburns. All of us raised an eyebrow to Daddy's newest creation.

"What is it?" Ladasha asked.

"It's my automatic snow blower! I fixed it!" he squeaked with excitement. Mom's eyebrows lowered.

"That's nice, dear. Maybe we should wait until after lunch to test it out..." I giggled to myself when I heard the hesitant sound in my mom's voice.

Daddy pouted when she said that. "But the snow just fell to the perfect levels." He sounded like a whiny five year old who wanted his mom to allow him to go play in the snow. Walking over to Mom, Daddy pushed out his bottom lip and gave her the biggest puppy dog eyes I had ever seen in my life. He began to give her puppy dog kisses all over her face until she reluctantly agreed.

"For Christ's sake, Walter! Fine. Let's get this over with!"

Daddy jumped up with excitement and told us all to go get our winter coats on. I was pretty excited. I hadn't seen one of Daddy's creations in quite some time and I was ready to be impressed. As he sat it in the driveway, Mom made Ladasha and me stay behind the porch, in case something went wrong. Daddy made sure to hush my mom as he turned on the snow blower, but he too, stepped behind the porch with his remote to control the robot.

"This is going to be amazing," he promised as he pushed the on button. Nothing happened at first. "Just give it time. It has to warm up." We waited. The weird robot started to shake. Daddy insisted it was normal. The robot started to walk down the driveway, Daddy guiding it with his remote. It was working! It was a three foot, mini TinMan, shoving our snow. We all cheered for him as the robot finished clearing most of the snow. It approached the end of the driveway. Daddy shut off the robot and tossed his hands up in celebration.

"You did it!" Mom hollered as she kissed Daddy's cheek. She was so proud of him in that moment.

"Um...Daddy..." I stuttered. I nodded in the direction of the robot, now heading out into the street.

"Oh no," Mom murmured.

The robot started to smoke. Daddy flicked on his remote again and started trying to control the robot to come back to us. His remote started to spark flames. "Holy shit!" Ladasha and I hollered as Daddy tossed the remote into the snow. Mom pinched both of our arms for our foul language as we mumbled an apology.

The robot was still on the move. "Go get it, Walter! Before the neighbors see!" My mom warned him. He went heading to the robot but stopped right as he saw it blow up across the street.

Ms. Kathy came out yelling as she watched her newly replaced dog-shaped mailbox go up in flames with the robot explosion. I saw the doggie's tail land on her roof. She started hollering and shaking her fist at us, saying words that would have made Mom pinch me to the point of drawing blood. Mom's eyes widened as she looked at us girls and Daddy. "Run! Come on! Inside, go!"

As we entered the house, the four of us busted out into laughter, replaying the horrified look on Ms. Kathy's face. It felt good to be back with my parents and able to laugh. It felt better than I could have imagined.

CHAPTER FORTY

COOPER

AFTER I LEFT Wisconsin, I headed back to New York. It was time to get back together with Kyle and get my career going again. It seemed like a whole life had been lived since I'd last sat across from him at his desk. He was scrolling through his emails while checking messages on his cell phone, and for the first time in awhile, it felt like things were slowly getting back to normal.

"What do we have?" I asked him, wondering what offers were being shot my way to clean up this mess I had made for Ky.

He started sifting through the papers stacked on his desk. "The norm for magazines. Us Weekly, People, Star. Television offers started flying in after those magazines came out. They want you to host shows—Wedding Disasters, Couple's Therapy, Dr. Drew's Rehab." His voice started off excited and he glanced up at me. He must have seen how uninterested I was in all of it, but I knew it had to be done.

"You know what, fuck them." Kyle picked up all of

the papers and ripped them in half.

"What the hell are you doing?"

He loosened his tie, shut down his computer, and turned off his phone. "Screw them, Coop. They don't deserve to hear your story. You know what you need to do?"

I looked to him, knowing I was talking to my best friend and not my manager. "What you need to do is go to South Carolina and be with your mom. Fuck all this other bullshit. You're a freakin' amazing photographer, not a cheap reality star. You go be with your mom, you decide exactly what it is *you* want, and you come back here. And I will make it work."

"Are you sure?" I asked. It would be a dream come true to go down to South Carolina and take care of my mom for a while.

"Get the fuck out of my office before I change my damn mind." Kyle threw the papers at me. I stood up, pulled him into a hug, and thanked him.

I VISITED MY mom every day and every night when I got back to South Carolina. Some days she thought I was her brother. Other days, a complete stranger. On the worst days, she saw me as my father. And on the best days, she called me Cooper.

Today I was Cooper, and she actually knew where she

was. The nurses told me it had happened before, but by the next day, she would fade back to the late 1990's. But I held on to it. We talked about life. How Iris and I had gone our own separate ways. I thought it would be best to plant a few new memories into her mind to try to help her remember. To unscramble the fog. I told her about Iris and the divorce. I told her about the paparazzi. I told her about Andrea.

She cried when she realized what had happened to her, and I sat there with her until she fell asleep. I went home, rested, and came back the next day.

"Cooper, she's asking for you," Ms. Wells informed me. Her soft smile gave me hope that Mom was having a good day.

When I entered the room, I heard soft sniffles. Mom was facing the window, staring out. I walked over to her and placed my hands on her shoulders.

"Mom, what's wrong?" I asked. As she turned around, I wiped the tears falling from her eyes. In her hands, she was holding a photo album, one of the many I had left with her in hopes that it would spark some memory.

Her small hands caressed my cheek and she gave me a short grin. "I've missed so much."

"It's all right."

She looked away, almost ashamed she'd let herself get so lost. How could she be ashamed? It wasn't her fault. I kept telling her it was all right. But I wasn't sure she believed me.

Walking over to her bed, she pulled out an old, broken down book. It must have been in the box of photo albums I dropped off. I saw the ribbon hanging from it and knew exactly what it was. It was the book I made for Andrea years ago when I was eleven. I sat down on her bed, flipping through it. Looking at how happy Andrea and I looked together. Mom sat next to me, resting her head on my shoulder and said, "Don't make the mistake I made, Cooper. Don't waste your life."

CHAPTER FORTY-ONE

Andrea

SPRING HAD COME, and I still missed him. Ladasha came and sat on the front porch with me.

"Why don't you call him?"

"It's not that easy, Ladasha." I thought about some of the horrifying things I'd said to Cooper. They replayed in my head over and over again. I didn't know how to face him. I wanted nothing more than to call him and tell him what was going on in my mind—that the idea of going on another day without him was unbearable. But I couldn't. I didn't deserve the right to talk to him.

"Why not?" she asked.

"You don't understand, Ladasha. I said some terrible things."

"Yeah I know. You told him he would be a bad father. You believed the lies those magazines made up. You turned on him in a second because his crazy ex-wife had him followed." Reminding me of all the terrible things I did made me feel even worse.

Her voice softened. "You spent the past few months

mourning over someone who cheated and lied to you. You listened to his songs and your voicemail over and over again. You sprayed his cologne just to hold on."

"Are you trying to make me feel worse? Because it's working."

"The truth is you're afraid of losing someone again so you pushed him away before you could be hurt. You're afraid that he too, might lie to you and hurt you. He never judged you for your past, and the fact that you threw his in his face, the shit that wasn't even true, is wrong. The way I see it, y'all are both fucked up. Might as well be fucked up together."

"Why do you even care? You got your happy ending. You have your future, so stay the hell out of my business."

Ladasha moved in closer and grabbed me by the chin, "You're acting like a bitch."

"Don't talk to me like that."

"I'm your best friend. I can talk to you however the hell I want. Wake up, Andrea. And don't try to push me away because I'm like cockroaches in the ghetto. I'll keep popping up, unwelcome."

I let out a small chuckle as she wrapped her arms around me. "I got a call from a few dance studios…which is weird because I don't remember applying to any, and you only told me about one." Ladasha's grin informed me that she had been going behind my back, pretending to be me. "They want me to come in and audition, dance for them."

Her face lit up with joy as she heard the news. "Does that mean we can go home now?"

"I CANNOT BELIEVE this is happening again. Walter, say something!" Ladasha and I sat in my bedroom as we listened to my dad, once again, try to convince my mom to let me, once again, go back to New York City. I stood up, walked over to my bedroom walls, and began to remove the photos of Derrick and me from the space. I was ready to move on. I was ready to let go. And I was ready to retry New York City.

This time was different though. This time I wasn't looking to go and become lost. No, I was going to find myself. I was going to make something of myself. Well, at least I was planning on it, if my mom would stop tearing up.

"Mom..." I looked at her as I entered the living room.

Her hands flew to her hips and she shook her head at me. "Don't you even say it, Andrea! Look what happened last time you went there! And this time you two girls don't even have jobs set up! What are you planning to do?!"

"Michelle is giving us a loan until we are able to pay her back. Also, I have auditions for dance jobs."

Mom huffed and whined. "If I had a dollar for every time I heard that this past year." I couldn't help but smile at her comment.

Ladasha entered the room grinning ear to ear. Mom's eyes narrowed in on her. "And what about you, missy? What are your plans?"

"Well, I can always go back to the strip club," she

smirked. She dodged the pillow flying at her head. "Okay okay. A friend of mine offered me a job at an art gallery as a receptionist. I'm going to work there through the summer and I'm enrolled in a summer film program."

Mom waved Ladasha over to us on the couch and she hugged her too.

"Let me and Dad send you girls money each month."

"Mom—no," I said.

"Okay," answered Ladasha. I hit her in the arm. "What!? She offered. And we'll need to eat."

Mom's worried eyes looked at my body. I had gained at least ten pounds since I came home, but you know Mom, the worry wart.

"Don't even start, Mom."

She smiled. "Okay. But if you two need anything, you'll come back. All right?"

I grinned and looked to Daddy who was smiling down at us three girls. Mr. Quiet, but always happy. He nodded at me in approval. I turned to Mom and shook her hand.

Deal.

ON THE NIGHT we got back into New York, we waited at the airport to try to get a ride out to our apartment. Every time we reached for a taxi, another person had already hopped in. "Hey, one sec..." I went digging into my purse and pulled out the card I had received from the old taxi driver who gave me a few free rides way back when. I dialed him up, and he was there in less than fifteen minutes.

"How was your trip?" Joe asked as he drove us to our apartment. I noticed he didn't have his payment clock on, and I couldn't help but smile.

"Ya know, same ol' same ol'. Stressful. Dramatic. Sad."

He nodded, keeping his eyes on the road. "Yeah. Sometimes trips can be more stressful than anything. Yet other times, they can be exactly what you need to realize what you're missing."

Ladasha raised her eyebrow at the interaction between me and Joe, and I could tell she felt out of the loop. Moving closer to me, she began to whisper. "What is this? You have your own personal Yoda or something?"

A personal Yoda? I wish. But as it turned out, I just had a Joe, which was good enough for me.

I LANDED A job at a small, but awesome dance studio. It wasn't completely paying the bills, but I was happy to have Michelle helping us out for a while. I was slowly getting into the groove of the city. And teaching dance to individuals who were new to the art form was the best thing I could have done.

Of course, I looked for any and every other dance opportunity that came up. Part of being a New Yorker was understanding the hustle of it all. Nothing was going to be handed to you; you had to make a name for yourself. And I was determined to make it. I owed it to myself. Everything was falling into place. I was doing what I loved, living with my best friend, and learning to stand on my own. But I still missed him.

I still longed for him.

He was a dial away on my cell phone, but I knew he had probably already found his Order. And I wasn't going to get in his way. Ladasha kept begging me to at least call him to see how he was, but I refused.

One Saturday morning during the beginning of June, there were terrible thunderstorms. I had no plans of going out any time soon except to go to the art auction Ladasha hadn't stopped talking about since she'd started her job. There was a knock at our door and I looked up from the couch to my best friend. "You expecting someone?" She shook her head, wondering who it could be. Dragging myself away from the couch, I walked over, opened the door, and was surprised to see Mom, Daddy, and Eric standing there.

"What are you guys doing here?!" I asked as they entered the apartment. Mom looked around and smiling, nodding in approval of our small space.

"We were just in the neighborhood and thought we would stop by."

"No, really..."

They all ignored me and made themselves comfortable. Eric's eyes lit up when he saw Ladasha, and I knew she had something to do with them coming here.

"Andrea Mae, must you be so dramatic? Just be happy

we stopped by!" I laughed hearing this from my mom, also known as the most dramatic person on this planet.

My heart skipped a beat as I watched Eric and Ladasha embrace. I felt a wave of a jealousy mixed with happiness for them.

"This is great! You all can come to the art gallery tonight! We are having a big auction party," Ladasha exclaimed as she held onto Eric as if he might disappear if she let him go. I was pretty sure Eric had no plans of leaving her side any time soon. That was until he came to a realization. "Oh crap! Andrea, I forgot!" Eric jumped up from his chair and raced over to his luggage, unzipping it. He brought out a package and handed it to me.

"What is it?" I questioned.

He shrugged. "Cooper sent it to Michelle and told me to give it to you."

...*Cooper*...

Just hearing his name made my heart skip as I opened the package. My eyes filled with tears as I opened the package to see a broken down book, with photos of us as children together. We both looked so happy...

"What..." I couldn't speak. I turned to my brother, looking for more of an explanation.

"He said to tell you that you were never his second choice. Something like you were his only choice. Michelle said he is in the city actually. Meeting with his manager at the Williams Management building."

The air grew thick. I wasn't sure what I was supposed to do with the information presented to me. I looked around the room for someone to tell me what to do. *Tell me what to do!* I felt faintish. Yup, I was about to pass out, and my legs were almost about to give up on me. That was until I turned to see Daddy's hand on my shoulder. I felt his love and support running through his fingers.

"Go, Andie."

I couldn't. What would I say? What would I do?

"*Notting Hill.*" I turned to see my best friend smiling towards me. A Ladasha pep talk was definitely needed. She always knew. "You don't have to prove yourself to him. Do what the girl in *Notting Hill* did."

Eric kissed her cheek and wrapped his arms around her waist. "You mean in the movie when she said, 'I'm just a girl standing in front of a boy, asking him to love me.'" It was Ladasha's knees that almost gave out now. She'd met the one person who understood her wackiness and saw her and loved her for exactly who she was.

I turned towards my mom, who rolled her eyes. "Oh for Christ's sake Anders. Go!" She handed me my purse, tossed me a pair of shoes, and pushed me out of the door before slamming it in my face. The door reopened and my mom held out an umbrella and jacket. "Make sure to use these. It's wet out there and I don't want you to get a cold. You know me, I worry." She winked as I leaned in and kissed her cheek.

And I took off running.

CHAPTER FORTY-TWO

COOPER

I SAT IN front of Kyle wondering what he was thinking. I'd just presented him with my idea, and he hadn't spoken a word.

"Are you sure this is what you want?"

I nodded.

"And you want me to actually call these people? Listen, like I said before—screw them, they don't deserve to hear your story."

"Yeah, they do," I said.

"All right." He shook his head as he went to his computer and started to type away. "I must say though, I'm surprised. You really pulled your shit together, my friend."

I watched as the rain danced against the window, and I bit my thumb. I felt a bit drained after spending the past few months with my mom, but she was doing much better and told me to get back to my life. So I did. Back in the public eye. Back to my so-called-life.

I stood up and stretched a bit. "I'm going to go get some air, maybe grab some lunch. You want anything?"

"Nah, I'm good. But Cooper, this stuff right here." Ky tapped the packets in front of him. "This is good stuff. If there was anything that could paint you in a good light, this would be it, buddy."

As I stepped outside of the building, I allowed the water to slap against my face. My hands slid into my pockets, and as my foot stepped off the sidewalk, I heard the tires of a taxi come to a screeching stop seconds before it hit me. Annoyed, I slammed the hood of the yellow vehicle and yelled at the stupid-ass driver. "Jesus Christ! Watch where you're going!!"

The driver rolled down his window and apologized. I didn't care; I began to continue walking until I heard the driver holler at me. "Coop? Cooper, is that you?"

Turning back to look at him, I couldn't believe my eyes. "Jesus!"

He laughed and waved me over to the taxi. "Yeah, well, they call me Joe on the streets. Get in." I sat in the back of the taxi, amazed I had just run into the one man who'd pretty much saved my life in the mental hospital.

"So how you been doin'? I didn't think I would see you again after we left the clinic," he said. Surprisingly enough, he didn't seem as shocked to see me.

"I've been all right. What about you? You still saving lives?"

"Nah, they put me on these meds that make me actually think I'm human. The man's always trying to hold us down. Or I should say woman—my wife puts the pills in my oatmeal."

"Yeah. Well, I'm sure you make a great human."I smirked.

"Did you ever find that girl?" he asked. He was the one who told me I would meet someone other than Iris, and he was far from wrong.

"I did."

"Yeah? And how did that work out?"

My head dropped to the ground. He noticed my look through the rearview mirror and changed the subject.

"Where do you need to go?" he asked as he rounded the corner.

I bit my lip. "I don't know. You got a minute maybe? We could get some lunch."

CHAPTER FORTY-THREE

Andrea

I RUSHED DOWN the streets of Manhattan, getting splashed by puddles, dodging cars, and trying to deal with an umbrella that didn't want to cooperate with me. Becoming frustrated, I tossed the umbrella to the side and became drenched in the rain.

The moment I made it to the Williams Management building I paused and took a deep breath. It was now or never, and I was ready.

As I busted into Kyle's office, my heart dropped.

"How can I help—" Kyle looked up at me with confused eyes.

"Is Cooper Davidson here?"

"He just left... Wait a minute. You're the girl. Holy shit," he whispered.

"Language," I murmured, taking after my mom.

"No! You're the girl! You're the one from the magazines! The strip club!" My cheeks flushed as I was reminded of the magazines. It wasn't the highlight of my life, and I was trying to forget it.

"Yes," I said with a soft voice. "Where did he go?" I asked, changing the subject.

"Lunch. You want me to call him?"

Please. I nodded and took a seat in the chair across from him. As he dialed, I felt sick. I knew calling wouldn't do any good because I felt the vibration of Cooper's cell phone under my butt.

When Kyle saw it, he gave me the saddest look. Before he could apologize and comfort me for the tears falling from my eyes, I shook my head. "It's fine." As I turned to walk away, wiping my face, I looked back at Kyle one last time, "And would it kill you to take Jasmine out on a date!"

He looked shocked. "What? Jasmine?" He looked down, and when his eyes reappeared, he had a slick smile on his lips. "Do you think she would be interested in me? I mean. Other than when we did…well…ya know." He raised his eyebrows and stuttered like a little boy who had his first crush.

A small grin slipped from my mouth as I told him to call her.

AFTER RETURNING HOME, wet and depressed, I let my family comfort me. "Did you try to call him?" Daddy asked. I nodded and told them that he left his phone at the building.

"Well maybe…" Mom tried to give a bit of hope, but I

wasn't interested. Maybe it was a sign we weren't meant to be. Maybe it was too late for the both of us.

Maybe it was time to move on.

I begged for everyone to stop talking about it and let it go. They finally agreed.

We all got ready to head to the art gallery, and again Ladasha told me how excited she was for it all. When we got there, I was shocked to see the crowd around the building, including the paparazzi flashing away outside. Ladasha told me it was a big deal, but I didn't think the paparazzi would be involved—and I was really hoping I would never see those people again.

As we stepped inside to see a ton of fancy people in fancy clothing, a loud cry escaped my lips as I looked around and saw large photos of myself throughout the room. There were photos of me dancing down in South Carolina on the tennis court. Pictures of me holding Freckles. Pictures of me crying.

Some were in black and white, others with faded colors.

I was overwhelmed when I felt a tap on my shoulder and turned to see Cooper standing before me. No words came to mind so I stood there like an idiot.

"Has anyone showed you around?" he asked. I shook my head. "May I?" He took my hand and walked me around. Feeling him touch me awakened my soul; his touch alone gave my heart the jumpstart that I had been looking for. His hair was longer, and he'd let his beard grow in a bit—he looked perfect. My eyes started to fill with water as I kept looking to him. *My gosh, so perfect.* He told me he was most attracted to the model in his photos because she was flawed. She had emotion in everything she did. She danced when she walked and sang when she talked.

He brought me over to the photo from South Carolina. He leaned in closer to me, his lips touching the rim of my ear. His hot, sweet breaths hit me as he spoke, "This is actually my favorite. See, during the weekend of this shoot, unlike ever before, the dancer showed up. Not just physically, but emotionally she was there. She was invested in this project. She laughed, she welcomed me into her mind. She allowed me to see her. Of course after that she tightened up a bit more and tried to run away, but that's another photo." He snickered.

I turned to him and realized how much I had missed his smile. His dimples. His laugh.

I found the strength to speak. "I'm so sorry. I just. I am still messed up from Derrick and I really am trying my best to put myself back together. I know I said some terrible things to you, and I started thinking...What if something happened to you? What if you cheated on me? What if you died? How could I handle that? But that was just me being..."

"Shut up."

I was a bit taken back by him telling me to shut up, but I had to make him understand where I was coming from. "I know you're probably still upset..."

"I said shut up." His southern accent was thick, and I knew it was time for me to close my mouth. "I'm crazy about you, Andie. I've been crazy about you since I was nine-years-old. I'll be crazy about you when I'm ninety. I'm crazy about everything I know about you. I'm crazy about everything I plan to know."

"Coop..." I whispered.

He shook his head at me and held up one of his index fingers. "Over here is Chaos." He held up his other index finger far apart from the other. "And over here is Order. I'm not asking you to leap from one to the other for me. I'm just asking that we meet somewhere around the space in between the two. We never have to get married. We never have to say I do or slow dance to a stupid first dance song. But I want you to know that *I do*." He took my hands into his and pulled me close to him as he continued.

"I do promise to give you all of me each and every day. I can't promise you it won't be hard, and I can't promise you bad things won't happen, but I do promise it will be worth it. I will give you all of me, the good, the bad, and the broken parts because I know you make me better. You make me whole again."

I smiled as he wiped the falling tears from my eyes and I bit my bottom lip. "I'm scared."

He nodded in understanding. "Yeah. Me too."

"But I would rather be scared with you than terrified by myself."

"We'll go slow. Maybe a coffee date."

I smiled at his offer and added to it. "Maybe breakfast."

"Maybe a soda pop or two," he chimed in. As my face dropped and I rolled my eyes, he quickly retracted his statement. "That was a joke. A bad one, bad moment, bad timing. All right, erase it from your mind." He ran his hand across my cheek. "You're so beautiful."

I laughed. "I'm not going to sleep with you, so you can stop trying so hard."

He grew serious in his demeanor. "I'm not looking for sex."

"Yeah? And what are you looking for?"

He smiled and winked at me.

I looked near the art gallery window and noticed all of the paparazzi cameras flashing away at the two of us. I said, "I really want to kiss you, but it appears we have an audience."

He smirked, placed his hand on my lower back, and pulled me closer to him. I could feel his breath against my skin as he whispered, "Let's give them their damn picture and they'll leave us alone."

"Promise?"

"Nope." He smiled as he pulled me into a deep, passionate kiss. Everyone disappeared the instant his lips met mine. It was just me and him in the moment, and no one, not even the paparazzi, could take that away from us.

EPILOGUE

COOPER

Six Months Later

"'WE'LL JUST GET coffee,' he said. 'We'll go out for breakfast,' he said." Andrea rolled her eyes, mocking me as we sat in the back of the black car. I laughed as I looked down to her growing stomach and kissed it.

"I can't help it that you're addicted to sex. We'll look into getting you help."

"We have arrived," the driver said.

I turned to him and smirked. "Thanks, Jesu—Joe. Thank you, Joe." I handed him a few bills and he shook his head.

"You don't have to keep paying me. If I'm going to be your driver, you gotta understand that I get a check every two weeks." He pushed the money back at me, and being unwilling to give up on the issue—I slid it into his pocket.

"I'm just paying you back for all of your sound advice. We'll be done around ten."

"I'll be here."

Suddenly, Andrea reached forward and placed her hand on Joe's shoulder. "Joe...Awhile back, you helped me through some of the hardest times. And it sounds like you helped Cooper, too. So, I still don't know if there's something bigger out there...Something helping guide us around this crazy world. But I just wanted to say thank you. Thank you for the ride, Joe." Her soft smile met with his as he nodded.

As Andrea and I got out of the car, we saw Eric and Ladasha stepping out of their ride. Eric had flown in to see the show with us, and the way he looked at Ladasha made me damned happy for them both. They were still trying to learn what their story was. They were learning how to make their relationship work with the distance and the different lifestyles between the two, but I could tell they both were willing to do the best they could. Ladasha had a few things from her past that she had to face, and Eric was there to help her through it all. I watched Eric whisper into Ladasha's ear and she turned to him, pressing her lips against his. They deserved each other.

I guided Andrea into the theater, where her dance company was performing that evening. When we reached our seats, I looked to her and saw the pride in her eyes.

As I took her hand into mine, we grew comfortable in our seats and prepared for a wonderful show. We took it one step at a time. One adventure. One event. One memory.

There was no hurry to plan our futures—other than which crib to buy for the nursery.

We didn't follow society's rules and walk down the aisle before having children. We made our own rules. We promised to give ourselves to one another completely—

mind, body, and spirit.

I leaned in towards Andrea, kissed her earlobe, and whispered to her. "Marry me."

She turned to me and huffed as she narrowed her eyes. She gave me a quick kiss on the lips, turned back to the stage, and said, "Okay."

One step.

One adventure.

One love.

We made the rules.

And we promised to always, *always,* live happily in the moment.

ACKNOWLEDGMENTS

FIRST AND FOREMOST I need to say thank you to the amazing world of authors, beta readers, bloggers, fans, friends, and family that have helped make this novel what it is today.

Special thanks to bloggers Can't Read Just One, For The Love Of Books, Crazies R Us Book Blog, One More Chapter, The World of Pinkishues and Midnightblues, 2 Chicks and a Blog, Books, Coffee, and Wine, and Nerd Girl for all your loving support and open arms to this new author.

A BIG thanks to the amazing cover artist, Kevin Kimmons: For making my cover 'dreams come true.' Your skills, eye for details, and talents are beyond outstanding. Thank you.

To Mickey, the BEST EDITOR EVER: For being simply that—the best editor ever. Thanks for not freaking out over MY freak outs.

And the list goes on: Amber, Kyle, Vickie, Melissa, and Jim. Samantha, Lazandria, Zonzerrias, Lauren, and Mary. Rayen, Sam, and Erinn. Love all around.

To my five brothers and two sisters: Bryon, Tiffani, Brandon, Candace, Isaiah, Ben, Will—So much love, respect, and pride to be able to call you all family. Love you!

To my papa: Thanks for the love and support! *And buying me the laptop that THIS novel was written on!* Love you, dad!

Lastly, this one is for you, mom: The one who believed in my dreams when I didn't know how to. Thank you for standing me in front of the mirror at a young age and having me say over and over again, "I am somebody. And I have a voice." You're the Sherlock to my Watson. Love you to the moon and back!

ABOUT THE AUTHOR

If you would like information about Brittainy
and her books, visit:

Facebook
https://www.facebook.com/BrittainyCherryAuthor

Twitter
https://twitter.com/BrittainyCherry